PENGUIN CANADA

ESTHER

Sharon E. McKay is an award-winning author of many books for parents and children. Her most recent books include *Charlie Wilcox, Charlie Wilcox's Great War* and, from the Our Canadian Girl series, *Terror in the Harbour, The Glass Castle, An Irish Penny,* and *Christmas Reunion.*

Also by Sharon E. McKay

Charlie Wilcox

Charlie Wilcox's Great War

From the Our Canadian Girl series

Terror in the Harbour

The Glass Castle

An Irish Penny

Christmas Reunion

Esther

Sharon E.
McKay

PENGUIN CANADA

Published by the Penguin Group

Penguin Group (Canada), 90 Eglinton Avenue East, Suite 700, Toronto, Ontario, Canada
M4P 2Y3 (a division of Pearson Penguin Canada Inc.)

Penguin Group (USA) Inc., 375 Hudson Street, New York, New York 10014, U.S.A.
Penguin Books Ltd, 80 Strand, London WC2R 0RL, England
Penguin Ireland, 25 St Stephen's Green, Dublin 2, Ireland (a division of Penguin Books Ltd)
Penguin Group (Australia), 250 Camberwell Road, Camberwell, Victoria 3124, Australia
(a division of Pearson Australia Group Pty Ltd)
Penguin Books India Pvt Ltd, 11 Community Centre, Panchsheel Park, New Delhi – 110 017, India
Penguin Group (NZ), cnr Airborne and Rosedale Roads, Albany, Auckland 1310, New Zealand
(a division of Pearson New Zealand Ltd)
Penguin Books (South Africa) (Pty) Ltd, 24 Sturdee Avenue, Rosebank, Johannesburg 2196, South Africa

Penguin Books Ltd, Registered Offices: 80 Strand, London WC2R 0RL, England

First published 2004

2 3 4 5 6 7 8 9 10 (RRD)

Canada Council   Conseil des Arts
for the Arts   du Canada

*We acknowledge the support of the Canada Council for the Arts which last
year invested $21.7 million in writing and publishing throughout Canada.*

*Nous remercions de son soutien le Conseil des Arts du Canada, qui a investi
21,7 millions de dollars l'an dernier dans les lettres et l'édition à travers le Canada.*

Manufactured in the U.S.A.

LIBRARY AND ARCHIVES CANADA CATALOGUING IN PUBLICATION

McKay, Sharon E
Esther / Sharon E. McKay.

ISBN 0-14-331204-9

1. Brandeau, Esther—Juvenile fiction. 2. Jewish girls—Canada—History—18th century—Juvenile
fiction. 3. Canada—History—To 1763 (New France)—Juvenile fiction. I. Title.

PS8575.K2898E87 2004   jC813'.6   C2004-902151-6

Visit the Penguin Group (Canada) website at **www.penguin.ca**

Dedicated to

Robert (Robby) Engel (1923–1999)
Boy Scout leader, chair of the Holocaust Remembrance Committee,
husband, grandfather, friend,
Holocaust survivor (Westerbork)
and
Barbara Berson, friend first

I call heaven and earth to witness that I have set before you life and death, the blessing and the curse; therefore choose life.
—Deuteronomy 30:19

Esther

Part 1

Chapter 1

❧

*I*ntendant Gilles Hocquart sat behind his great desk and held the likeness of King Louis XV up to the light. The king, dressed in silks and velvet, with cascades of silver curls rippling down his chest, gazed out from the miniature portrait. Once again it was confirmed in Hocquart's mind that his cousin, the beloved king of France, was the handsomest man in Europe.

Hocquart turned the palm-sized cameo over in his hand, then tapped it against his teeth. Yes, yes, the frame was made of solid gold. How might such an item have fallen into the hands of a young boy who could barely afford passage to New France?

A door opened and Hocquart's secretary skimmed over the flagstone floor, like a bird skipping over water. The secretary was an exceedingly tall man who preferred simple, dark robes to pantaloons, vests and jackets, and who had dispensed with wigs altogether. He gave a slight bow in deference to Intendant Hocquart, commissary of Marine, cousin of the king, and as such one of the most powerful men in New France.

"Is he here?"

The secretary nodded.

"Bring him in."

The man bowed once again and backed out of the room just as two guards moved forward, stopping on the threshold. Between them stood a smooth-faced youth whose thick hair, the colour of pitch streaked red with the sun, was tied into a small bundle at the back of his head and encased in a rough black bag. Hair that had escaped capture hung over his downcast face. His hands were clasped behind his back.

"Untie him."

The shorter guard hastily removed the rope that bound the boy's hands. A soft moan escaped the boy as his arms fell to his sides. Red and flaming-orange rope burns encircled one wrist. The other wrist had been protected with a bandage that covered his hand as well. The boy rubbed his wrist tenderly.

"Leave us." Intendant Hocquart waved away the guards and his secretary. Within a moment, Hocquart and the boy were alone.

"You are Jacques La Fargue, from the ship *Saint-Michel*?"

The boy nodded without lifting his head.

"You boarded the ship in La Rochelle, France, as a passenger. Is this true?"

Again, the boy nodded.

Hocquart's brow furrowed. "I have been told that you are a capable seaman."

"I am a sailor, Monsieur."

"Does this belong to you?" Hocquart held up the gold-rimmed likeness of the king. The boy's eyes darted up. A flicker

of recognition registered in them before he nodded and lowered
his head again.

"How did you come by this?"

"It was a gift, Monsieur."

"From whom, may I ask? King Louis himself?"

Hocquart was making mock, of course. This pathetic boy
would never have had cause to make the acquaintance of the king
of France. It was true that even commoners, so long as they dressed
in a way that pleased the court, had the run of Versailles, the king's
own palace and retreat. Even so, it was unfathomable that such a
coarse boy could have gained access to the royal inner sanctum. It
was far more likely that the portrait had fallen to the boy through
happenstance or ill-gotten gain. After all, the lad stood accused of
cheating, and by the look of him he was hiding something.

Hocquart walked around the boy. Instinct told him to go
slowly. Lies came easily, but truth took time.

The boy tucked his chin into his shirt, making it difficult to
get a good view. He seemed like a reasonably good-looking lad,
not pretty, and yet his bearing had a proud dignity, unusual in a
boy his age. His hands were rough, callused and scarred. He was
a bit on the slim side, fragile even, but after a long sea voyage
that, too, was to be expected. There was a dark, exotic quality
about him. Hocquart sniffed. The boy had no odour. Why on
earth would he have bathed?

"Look up," the intendant commanded.

The boy tilted his head and for a moment their eyes locked.
Hocquart drew in a breath. The eyes of the boy were as sharp as
flint. Their colour was of a deep, beguiling chestnut brown, shot
through with lightning bolts of gold. How extraordinary! His
features were strong, his nose almost aquiline. And his skin was
smooth, no bristles or blemishes, with a touch of rose colouring

on the cheeks. What ancestry might he have sprung from? Gypsy, perhaps? No, no, that wasn't it. He was a Spaniard, no doubt, but … something tugged at him.

"Are you a Jew?" Hocquart's words exploded, the question spoken before the thought was fully realized.

The boy staggered back, his startled eyes narrowed in fear.

Now it was Hocquart's turn to react. He fought to regain his composure.

"I asked you a question. Are you a Jew? Jews are not allowed in New France by order of the king. This is a Catholic colony." The government of France had gone to great lengths to prevent the contamination of New France by Jews, or followers of any religion other than the true Catholic faith.

The boy held his stare. It was Hocquart who looked away first. This was ridiculous. His time was being wasted.

"There is one way to find out." Hocquart pursed his pale lips and jutted out his chin. "Lower your trousers. We'll see if you are circumcised," he shouted. His patience was now stretched past its limit.

The boy's look turned into one of panic. His eyes flickered around the room, desperately seeking an escape.

Hocquart took note of his curious behaviour. Did the boy question his intentions? Surely not. At the age of forty-four, Gilles Hocquart was a man of the highest moral standards, with no motive beyond ascertaining the truth. What, then? The boy's status was barely above that of a servant. Such a boy would have no more modesty or shame than he would dignity. And yet he was clearly humiliated and seemingly in distress. This, too, was odd.

"Do you need assistance? Guards!" Hocquart roared. His voice echoed off the stone walls and funnelled down the chamber. The massive oak doors were flung open. Two guards stood at the ready.

"No," whispered the boy. "No. Please." The voice was filled with anguish. Indeed, his lips quivered.

Hocquart stopped. He raised a flat palm in the direction of the guards. There was a pause and then the doors closed with a thud. They were alone again.

"I'll say it for the last time, lower your trousers."

Slowly the boy's hands went to the rope around his waist. He fumbled at first, then undid the knot. The trousers slid to the floor.

Hocquart gasped. He stumbled backwards. A small, inaudible prayer escaped his lips. His hand made a frantic cross over his chest as he fell into his chair.

"Cover yourself," he hissed as he shielded his eyes.

The boy was a girl.

⟡

The corridor was dim, and keeping pace with the long strides of the silent man ahead of her was difficult. The secretary held a torch aloft but it cast a poor light. She groped her way along the passage. Her body shook with fright and cold. Could it be that she had come this far and sacrificed so much, only to find herself a prisoner in this remote land? She had survived a shipwreck, illness, imprisonment and grief beyond measure. She had lost family, friends, religion, statehood and her very sex. And now this. Shame followed humiliation sure as night followed day. But if she had learned nothing else, still she knew that shame, like humiliation, could be eaten and eventually digested.

The hall gave way to a staircase. The stairs were broad, even majestic, but still dim by torchlight. Her attempts to grasp the rope-railing anchored to the wall failed. She stumbled in the dark.

A rock, as sharp as a blade, jutted out from the wall and sliced into her leg. The pain was sudden and biting. A small cry rose up in her throat as she fell.

The secretary turned and gazed down at her from his lofty height. He offered neither a hand nor a word of comfort. It was understood that she would receive no compassion from this man.

She reached out to the craggy wall and grasped the rope-railing, pulling herself up onto her knees, then onto her feet. How could it have come to this? But, how could it not?

At the bottom of the staircase the secretary threw open a door, revealing a well-appointed salon. A woman, modestly dressed, rose from a chair. A maid stood behind her.

The secretary bowed. "Intendant Hocquart sends his greetings and gratitude."

The woman nodded but said nothing. She stared intently at the downcast lad who stood beside the secretary. The woman's confusion was apparent. She had been requested to bring garments suitable for a young maid, not a boy.

"Intendant Hocquart will commence his interview with the girl as soon as she is appropriately attired."

The woman drew in a breath. Could this male in fact be a female? How extraordinary!

The girl raised her head. Interview? Was she to be tortured? She searched the secretary's face. No, she need not fear for her mortal life—not yet, anyway.

The secretary bowed and backed out of the room. The woman snapped her fingers, and the process of returning the creature to her female state began.

Chapter 2

Hocquart lifted a bronze spyglass to his eye. From his vantage inside a massive stone building at the top of the hill, he looked through a leaden window down to the Lower Town of Quebec. He could see Place Royale, the marketplace and heart of the city, and the steeple of the much-loved chapel Notre-Dame-des-Victoires. Tall, stately stone buildings surrounded the rest of the square.

In the descending orange light of sunset he spotted a slave driver, trailing a cast of motley Negroes awaiting auction.

Hocquart cast his eyes to the far side of the square and noticed a small group of *les Sauvages* also awaiting auction. He scowled. These Indians, *panis,* had been captured from far afield. No good came from the sale of savages. Few lived beyond the age of eighteen years in captivity, most were untrainable, and they continually attempted escape with no God-given fear for their lives. It seemed that they would rather die in the wilds than face a life of free food, honest work and the opportunity to have their souls saved.

In Hocquart's opinion, Negroes were better slaves. Negroes lived to twenty-four years, and were suitable for both the farm and the house. Furthermore, for the Negroes, escape was impossible. While Indians might find refuge with the local natives, Negroes would most certainly perish in the wilds. No ship would take them back to their place of birth. Better a cow make a bargain with a butcher than a slave make an offer to a seafaring, Africa-bound captain.

Hocquart rocked back and forth in his heeled *souliers français* (Hocquart was fond of finely crafted French shoes). He wrinkled his nose. The whole issue of slaves was unsavoury.

He again lifted the spyglass and cast his eyes farther afield to the mighty St. Lawrence River. Small fishing shallops and ships of all sizes were anchored in the harbour. He spied the *Saint-Charles,* a ship that had just arrived. Opposite, on the far side of the harbour, was the *Saint-Michel,* the ship that had brought the girl to the shores of New France. It was the girl, and what was to become of her, that he must now consider.

He lowered the spyglass, stood back from the window and caught his own reflection in the glass. On this fall afternoon he wore a tall, powdered grey wig, a brocade jacket of the finest Persian silk and a rose-coloured cravat at his neck. According to custom, he was clean-shaven. In his own mind, at least, he was a fine-looking man. And while some found his sleepy-eyed look unattractive, no one could dispute his air of authority.

While replacing the glass in its wooden cradle he gazed over at the likeness of the king that lay upon his desk. "What have you to do with this, my king?" Hocquart whispered.

"My pardon, I did not hear you." The secretary stood at a distance holding out a small silver tray with a goblet of brandy.

"I said nothing." Hocquart cursed this new inclination to speak to himself, then turned to face the secretary. "Is the girl here?"

"She awaits under guard at your leisure."

"Is she suitably attired?"

"*Oui,* Monseigneur."

Hocquart took the goblet and sipped the brandy, allowing it to settle on his tongue, slide down his throat and ultimately mellow his mood. "Bring her to me."

As the secretary padded away, Hocquart continued to sample his brandy while gazing out at the darkening outline of his vibrant town. It had taken him many years to come to terms with life in a small outpost of the greatest empire the civilized world had ever known. To be away from court, with all of its beauty and intrigues, had been difficult at first. But now New France, under his tenure, was coming into its own power, a shining star. He had such hopes for this new country. The stone buildings, shops, elegant homes, convents, seminaries and the cathedral were a tribute to the power and glory of France. With continued hard work and economic development, Louis XV would soon reap the benefit of his wise investment.

It was then, in that moment of quiet reflection, that the brandy caught and burned in his throat. In the darkened window he saw the reflection of the figure behind. He turned.

The girl stood before him in modest dress. Her look was by turns defiant and arresting, contemplative and shy. How could this be so? Her hair was too short to achieve great height, yet it gave her an elegance rarely seen in the underclass. Her face was a pale mask, her neck an ivory column, and her lips were dark, crimson buds. But it was those dark eyes that one could scarcely turn away from. Only a bandaged hand gave a hint of the trials she had experienced. Hocquart took in a deep breath. As a boy she had been handsome; as a woman she was mesmerizing.

She made a deep curtsy, treating her limp, linen chemise as though it were a gown of the finest brocade. Her movements, her grace, left him momentarily speechless. Where might she have learned such deportment, such courtly grace? The king's portrait belonged to her, of that he was now sure. He must hear her story—only then would he know how to proceed. Intimidation, threats, coercion—such tactics would yield results, but it was the truth he was after. To obtain the truth he needed her trust.

Hocquart cleared his throat. "I ask you for a second time, are you of the Jewish faith?" Despite his best effort, his voice quavered.

"I am."

She looked directly into his eyes. Was she challenging him? No, he was sure not. Perhaps she was baiting him—women were prone to be coy. But no.

Hocquart remained silent for a very long time. How should he proceed? If the king was involved, this situation would have to be undertaken with great tact. To handle it badly would reflect on him, his career and his plans for New France. Instinct told him to go slowly. Time was on his side.

He placed his brandy upon his desk and crossed the room. "Do you know that it is illegal for a Jew to be in New France?" His eyes narrowed.

"Yes."

"And so you place yourself above the law?" Hocquart watched the muscles around her mouth tighten. But she did nothing to expose herself—no wringing of hands, no shedding of tears, nothing one might expect of a girl in distress. "How long have you used this male disguise?" He asked the question simply. He was not particularly interested and so was unprepared for her answer.

"Three years."

Hocquart's mouth dropped open. Three years? Was it possible for a girl to disguise herself as a boy for three years?

"How old are you?" was all he could think to ask.

"I am in my seventeenth year."

"And your parents?"

"They know nothing."

"What is your family name?"

"Brandeau." Her voice was unwavering and yet her dress swayed as though she stood in a faint breeze.

"What is your given name?"

"My name is Esther."

"Where are you from?"

"My family is from St. Esprit, diocese of Daxe, near Bayonne, on the west coast of France. My father, David Brandeau, is a cloth merchant."

"And how was it that you were able to carry out this disguise?"

"In the beginning, I had a friend."

"Ah, a friend. What name did this friend go by?" Hocquart was pleased at this revelation. She had a fellow conspirator.

The girl paused, as if considering. "His name was Philippe."

"Ha, a lover!"

"No ... Philippe is, was, a friend. I have not seen him in a very long time, nor do I expect to see him ever again."

"This Philippe, is he also one of *God's Chosen People*?" He spat out the words.

"No, he is a Christian." Esther spoke to the floor. Was she always to meet those who held her people in such disregard?

A door opened. The secretary entered, bowed and crossed the room in long, even strides. He leaned forward and spoke softly into the intendant's ear. Hocquart listened, nodded and paused.

He looked at the girl. His hand went to his chin, then flew up into the air as if to wave away an annoyance.

"You shall wait for me in the far chamber."

Thus dismissed, Esther rose, curtsied in a manner that again piqued Hocquart's curiosity and followed the secretary to an antechamber. The room was damp, the fire unlit. She gave no sign of being uncomfortable or cold. She sat on a hard bench and said nothing.

The secretary left her there under guard and returned to the intendant's office.

"Show the captain in." Hocquart spoke to the secretary while taking a seat behind his long, highly polished rosewood desk. He stood his quill up in a silver holder, placed inks, scalpels, blotting paper and penknife to one side and pressed his finger to his lips in thoughtful repose.

"Captain de Salaberry, Monseigneur." The secretary made the announcement then stepped aside.

Captain Michel de Salaberry, a descendant from the noble house of Irumberry and captain and owner of the ship *Saint-Michel,* entered and gave Hocquart a casual nod. He too was dressed in the finest silks and bows, including white hose revealing shapely legs that had been known to send a woman's fan fluttering.

Hocquart dispensed with pleasantries. "I trust that you have been informed that the person I have in custody is a girl and not, as presumed, a boy."

"Yes, I received a message penned by your assistant." De Salaberry made no attempt to hide a smirk. To think that the boy he had entreated to climb the ship's ratlines, who had faced down death as bravely as any sailor under his command, was a girl amused the captain no end. The small embarrassment he would suffer for not having found the secret out was well worth the tale he could tell at court. As for the pompous Hocquart, no great harm had been done. After all, young, fertile females were in great demand in New France. She could be married off by week's end—by day's end, for that matter.

"Are you telling me that a girl could disguise herself as a boy on a seafaring ship for weeks?" Hocquart stared at the captain in disbelief.

De Salaberry shrugged. Intendant Hocquart, for all his power on land, had no jurisdiction over him.

"Tell me, Captain de Salaberry, what do you know of this girl?"

"Nothing at all. It would appear that she was involved in a card game and refused to pay her losses." Captain de Salaberry looked about the room, noting the austerity of it. A cup of cider would have been welcome.

"Captain de Salaberry, I trust you are aware that, as ship's captain, you are responsible for all cargo and passengers that you deliver to this Catholic colony."

"I am."

"And that you are familiar with both the Black Code and the restraints placed on this great company of New France?"

"I am." What was Hocquart going on about? For the first time, de Salaberry felt slightly uncomfortable.

Hocquart turned. "So you are aware of the order decreeing that all Jews are to be driven out of New France as enemies of Christianity, *oui*? And yet the girl you brought to this great land is a Jew!" The word was hurled out of Hocquart's mouth with the force of a cannonball.

De Salaberry pulled back as if punched. *"Mon Dieu! Non, non."* De Salaberry grabbed hold of the back of a chair. "I shall take the girl back with me to France at once!" he sputtered.

Hocquart gazed at the cameo on his desk. Something irked him, but while thoughts may be slow to develop, decisions often arrive in a flash. His mind was made up. "The girl will stay, at the king's pleasure. I declare this the king's business."

"But the river will soon freeze over. We must leave soon or she will be in your care for the winter. And why would the king care about such a girl?" De Salaberry's lips were moist with his sputtering. He pressed a hand over his pounding heart and felt the rise of sweat around his neck. *Mon Dieu,* he had been taken for a fool by a Jew. He would be the laughingstock of court.

"You yourself made her my responsibility! As captain you could have handled the trifling matter of a disputed card game between boys on board your ship. You chose to relinquish that responsibility. What happens to this girl now is for me to decide!" Intendant Hocquart slammed his fist down on his desk and glared at the captain. His voice dripped with disdain. "You have conveyed an illegal person to these shores and stand in some disregard. This affair will remain in my hands."

Defeated, Captain de Salaberry's face took on a rosy, flushed hue. He lowered his head, stepped back and bowed deeply. "As you wish."

❧

Waiting in the damp antechamber, with only the dubious company of the guards, Esther writhed in anguish as she ran the conversation with the intendant through her mind. Not since she had cut off her hair and donned boys' clothes had she been so full of self-doubt.

She had made the decision to tell the truth as her boys' garments had been peeled off her and she had been returned to her female state.

Esther … Esther—how good it felt to say her own name.

She had spoken out loud. A guard turned and gave her a hard stare. Embarrassed, Esther looked down at her hands. But what did it matter? Few things mattered at this moment.

Esther sat back. Slowly, slowly the fear subsided. If there was to be no freedom in truth, then perhaps there would at least be relief.

Chapter 3

❧

Hocquart laid a two-pronged fork and bone-handled knife across his plate and addressed his secretary. "Send a letter to the mayor of Bayonne, France. Ask him to confirm the birth of the Jewess Esther Brandeau, daughter of David Brandeau, cloth merchant." He dabbed his lips with a heavy linen cloth then added, "Has the girl's wounded hand been attended to?"

"*Oui,* Monseigneur."

"Has she been fed?"

The secretary refilled the intendant's goblet with a heavy wine. "She has been given food, but I do not think she has eaten." He removed the dinner plate.

"Bring in bread and cheese, and more wine as well. What plans have you made for her confinement?"

"The jail is not suitable. For the moment I have arranged that she stay with a local woman. A guard may be posted at the door—as you wish, Monseigneur."

"That will do for now. I shall decide what to do with her after I have heard her story. I will have no interruptions during the interview. Record all that you hear."

"But Monseigneur, it is already late. Perhaps tomorrow …"

"Bank the fire and send her in." As always, the commands from the intendant were short and to the point.

Hocquart gazed into the flames. He knew well enough that if the girl had been spirited away to save embarrassment to someone in the royal household, returning her to France would put him in disfavour. Careers such as his had been destroyed for lesser crimes. Still, females were in short supply in New France. Should it prove that the girl was not involved with the king, or anyone within the royal household, a simple conversion followed by a marriage would solve all his problems. Regardless, the sooner he knew her story the better.

He wiggled his toes. While convention would not permit him to remove his jacket or vest, he had nevertheless replaced his French shoes with more comfortable *souliers sauvages*. (Many times he had lamented that the French had not invented moccasins.)

Again the doors opened. Hocquart looked up. Esther Brandeau stood on the threshold, then glided across the room with the grace of a princess at her coronation. He made an involuntary, almost instinctual movement to rise and greet her as a person of his own social rank. But that was ridiculous. He took hold of himself, then thrust out his hand in a brusque manner and pointed to the chair opposite. Wordlessly the girl sat.

The secretary placed a goblet of wine and plate of bread and cheese at her elbow before shrinking back to his post behind a thin curtain. He sat at a small wooden table, picked up a sharpened quill and dipped it into ink.

A heavy silence settled over the room. And when Hocquart finally spoke, his voice was so low that Esther had to strain to hear.

"I shall make you a bargain. You will tell all of how you came to these shores. You will tell the truth, for I shall know the truth when I hear it. *Falsus in uno, falsus in omnibus.* Do you know what that means?"

"Untrue in one thing, untrue in everything," whispered Esther.

"Ah, so you speak Latin?" Hocquart could not keep the sound of surprise out of his voice. But no doubt this girl had many such surprises in store. "Tell but one lie and I shall declare you a liar and be done with you. Your freedom, if not your very life, hangs in the balance. Do you understand?"

In the deepest recesses of his soul he prayed that he might know the truth when he heard it.

Esther looked into the fire. Her decision had already been made. As darkness fell over the St. Lawrence River, the story of Esther Brandeau rolled out like a ball of wool.

꧁

St. Esprit, France, April 1735 (three years earlier)

Esther sat by the dark window. Her sister Sarah's snoring had woken her up, again. Sarah's snores could wake the dead. Complaining did not work. Maman sympathized, of course, but with Papa, baby Samuel, five-year-old Joseph, fifteen-year-old Abraham, plus Grand-mère, the house was full. It was a good thing that her oldest brother, Benjamin, had moved to Amsterdam.

All the houses in the Jewish Quarter of this little bit of France were small. Papa said it was the same all over: Jews were almost always tucked up into little corners and crowded into small spaces. All the houses in the Jewish Quarter of St. Esprit were tall and skinny, some three, four, even five storeys high. It was hard to see the stars at night, harder still to feel the sun in the day. Sometimes Esther felt so crowded, so squished, that it was hard to breathe.

She bent down over her sewing. The candle offered just enough light to ply her needle over her brother's trousers. Benjamin (he didn't expect her to call him *Rabbi* Benjamin, did he?) was fussy about his clothes. He was fussy about everything, even his food. No, *especially* his food. He was old, so old that he didn't seem like a brother at all—more like an uncle or an extra father. She shuddered. The thought of Benjamin being a father to anyone was horrifying. It wasn't that he was mean—it was just that he was so serious, even more serious than Papa!

Esther came to the last stitch on the hem of the trousers, tied a knot, then bit the thread off. Benjamin might live in Amsterdam, but Maman still sent him all his clothes. Why could the matchmaker not find him a wife to do his sewing? The matchmaker had suggested many suitable girls, although why anyone would want to marry him was beyond her. Grand-mère said that he was too picky. Esther had overheard Papa say to Maman that *he* was going to choose a wife for his son. Never mind that Papa had said that his children would have some say in choosing their mates. Enough was enough!

Esther peered at her stitching. She was not nearly as good a seamstress as Maman, but she was a lot better than her sister Sarah—a goat had better use for a needle than Sarah!

She stood and held the trousers up against her. They looked to be the right length, although fashion had it that they could be worn anywhere from mid-calf to the ankle. What would it be like to wear trousers? What would it be like to be free of petticoats and corsets and bodices and skirts and dresses and aprons? Imagine having pockets, real pockets, and not the kind that women wore—just bags dangling down from a belt. Think what it would be like to run and not trip over petticoats.

Sarah, the lump, was still asleep. Esther crinkled up her nose and giggled. Who would know?

She pulled on the trousers and tucked in her chemise. The trousers were scratchy against her bare body. She held her hands over her head and twirled around on the tiny rug. The trousers felt wonderful!

"Esther, what are you doing?" Sarah pulled the covers up to her nose. Frizzy black hair poked out from under her bedcap, and two narrow black eyes glared from beneath her thick, bushy eyebrows. It was freezing cold!

"Nothing. Go back to sleep." Esther blew out the stubby candle and slid the trousers down until they formed a pool around her ankles. She stepped out of the circle, scooped the trousers up and gave them three sharp folds.

There was a sound from below. Papa was up. Esther looked over at Sarah. She had fallen asleep again. Sarah snored the loudest just as she was drifting off.

Crouching down, Esther pulled back the rug, popped out a knot in the wooden floor with her fingernail and peered into the room below. Every morning Aaron, the *shamash,* hammered at the door calling all Jewish men to synagogue for morning prayers. But today Papa and Abraham had business with Gentiles in town. They would leave before daybreak, so Papa was saying his prayers alone.

With his *tallit* prayer shawl wrapped around his shoulders, his *tzizit* fringes peeking out from under his shirt and his *tefillin* strapped to his forehead and around his left arm and fingers,

Papa spoke in a low, soft voice. A prayer, Papa said, should be a whisper in God's ear. Women and girls did not have to say morning prayers, but Esther mouthed the prayer along with Papa anyway: "Hear, O Israel: the Lord is our God,* the Lord is One! Blessed is His glorious kingdom for ever and ever."

"Esther, I'm going to tell," Sarah snarled from the bed. Having Esther for a sister was a terrible burden to Sarah. No one liked Esther, and she didn't have any friends—not even when they were little. Sarah grunted and rolled over. There was scarcely a year between them, and yet no two sisters on earth could be more different. Sarah was plump, short, with a face as flat as *matzo*—she knew that was what Esther thought. Sarah described Esther as thin, with a neck as long as a rope and hair and eyes like a witch's. The fact that they had to share a bed was a plague to both girls.

Esther sighed, slipped the knot of wood back into its hole, replaced the rug and hopped back into bed. Her feet were like ice. She planted both on Sarah's back.

"Get them away from me," Sarah growled while Esther giggled. Still, it was very early, and within minutes they'd both fallen back into a deep sleep.

❧

"It's time," said Maman.

Esther's eyes flew open. Maman was standing at the bedroom door, balancing baby Samuel on her hip. She smiled at her daughters, who were curled up in sleep. Samuel squawked and arched his back.

---

* Religious Jews do not say the word *God*. If His name must be read out loud, the name Adonay (the Lord) is said instead. This stems from the deep belief that God's name is too holy to be spoken.

"Hush now." Maman bounced the baby.

"Good morning, Maman." Esther, too, arched her back in a big stretch. Sarah grumbled, but Sarah always grumbled. The sun was up, and though the houses across the street blocked its rays, the room had lightened.

"Esther, a messenger has come from Madame Bendal, the dressmaker, but Papa has already left to do business in the town. After lessons and chores, you must go to Madame Bendal's house with a package of cloth samples. A great lady is coming from Biarritz to be measured for a gown. Hurry."

Maman's smile turned into a frown and her brow furrowed. Her husband owned a shop that sold cloth. It was said that David Brandeau's cloth was the finest in the land. Well, certainly the finest in St. Esprit, and maybe Bayonne, definitely Biarritz, and perhaps the entire west coast of France!

Esther bolted straight up. Madame Bendal lived clear across the Jewish Quarter, very near the gates. Madame was one of the most famous Jewish seamstresses in all of France (at least that was what *she* said). It was also said that she sewed for very wealthy Gentiles. Papa had taken Esther to Madame Bendal's house several times, although she had never actually met the lady face to face.

"May I go alone?" Esther asked her mother.

"You may take Joseph with you," Maman called over her shoulder as she went down the stairs.

Joseph? Esther pursed her lips. Her first time out on her own and she had to take her five-year-old brother. But Esther's disappointment was fleeting; after all, she liked Joseph.

"I'm going out. I'm going to see the world!" Esther bounced up and down on the horsehair bed—which really was not bouncy. If she stretched she could touch the ceiling. At fourteen years of age she had almost reached her full height.

"Stop jumping," moaned Sarah.

"Did you not hear? I am to deliver a package! I am to go out on my own—well, almost on my own." Perhaps she would be invited in for a cup of chocolate! Esther put one foot behind the other and attempted a curtsy. *"Avec plaisir, Madame. Je suis à votre service."* She stretched out her arms so that they dangled with the elegant sway of a willow branch. "Ohhhhh!" She lost her balance and fell down on the mattress. Sarah squawked like a chicken. No matter. Esther leapt up, pulled on her petticoat and laced her bodice over her chemise. "Madame's house is just beside the gates. I'll be able to see everything!"

"So what?" Sarah threw one leg out from under the covers, then, feeling the cold, pulled it back again. "It's not proper for you to be out on the streets. Anyway, I don't see why you want to go." Everything about Esther was odd in Sarah's mind. She was always asking questions, and no book was safe from her prying eyes. Grand-mère said that no man wanted a learned wife. Reading was necessary, but, as everyone knew, there was a difference between being able to read and *reading*.

"Maman didn't even ask *you*," Esther said with satisfaction. Then she laughed. They both knew that the idea of sending Sarah on an errand had likely not even occurred to Maman. Except to go to synagogue, Sarah could hardly be persuaded to walk outdoors. Sarah might have had lots of friends, but she preferred that they visit her, and not the other way around.

Esther finished dressing and ran into the kitchen. "Good morning, Grand-mère." She didn't look over to the chair but assumed that the old woman was at her post, guarding nothing but growling like a guard dog nevertheless. Esther held her hands under a hanging cistern and washed quickly. "When may I leave,

Maman?" She dried her hands and face on a towel that hung beside the basin.

"Sit and have your lessons and something to eat," said Maman. Several braided *challahs* sat ready for a coating of egg yolk and poppyseeds before going into the oven. Maman cast a critical eye over the dough. Satisfied that it would be a good batch, she ripped a lump of dough the size of an olive, threw it in the fire and whispered a prayer that her loved ones might always have enough to eat. "The cloth samples are not needed until noon. Just get your lessons and chores done. Sarah can help me with the bread today."

Esther made a face. All mothers were supposed to teach their daughters how to bake bread, as directed by Jewish law, but Sarah's bread could be used for doorstops.

"It's not right, I tell you. Young girls should not be on the streets alone," Grand-mère grumbled from her chair in the corner.

"Mère, Madame Bendal is our best client. What can I do? I must keep the shop open, and I cannot be in two places at once. No harm will come to her," said Maman, but the look on her face suggested that she was not entirely sure.

"But she will be seen. Isn't it enough that she's already talked about?"

"Hush, Mère." Maman, her face suddenly pink, glanced over at Esther while giving baby Samuel a crust to chew on. He had a tooth coming in.

"The girl should know. It's time to tell her. Even the matchmaker said—"

"Mère!" Maman, who never snapped at anyone, let alone Grand-mère, raised her voice so sharply that baby Samuel let out a wail. Grand-mère, her head bent, muttered something more, then picked up her sewing.

"What does Grand-mère mean, Maman? Tell me what?"

"Nothing, Esther. Sit with Joseph and do your lessons. You may read from Exodus today."

On any other day, at any other time, Esther might have wanted, demanded, to know what Grand-mère had meant, but not today. Who cared what Grand-mère thought, and who cared about the matchmaker? She didn't want to be married anyway, not ever! Esther sipped a mug of warm café au lait.

Esther repeated the *aleph-bet* in Hebrew. Sometimes she spoke in French, sometimes in Ladino and sometimes even Dutch. It was a game they played—to say the letters in all the different languages. But today Joseph was more interested in thumping his feet against the legs of the table than in studying.

"Here, a surprise for you, Joseph. And one for you, too, Esther," said Maman as she plopped down two pieces of bread shaped into the first two letters of the Hebrew *aleph* and *bet*. "Now you may eat your lessons. See how sweet it is to learn?" Maman smiled as she dabbed both pieces of shaped bread with honey. Joseph howled with delight.

Satisfied that the bread was baking as it should, Maman asked Esther to keep an eye on Samuel and went out to the shop, which was at the front of the house.

With the reciting of the *aleph-bet* done, Esther opened the Bible then peered over her shoulder at Grand-mère. The old woman appeared to be napping, and Sarah had yet to make an appearance. One of Sarah's greatest talents was to disappear in a house where there was no place to hide. Esther looked around. Today's lesson was so tedious. Who would know if she cut it short? Tomorrow she would work doubly hard. Her chores, however, had to be done, and the sooner the better.

"Joseph, if you play with Samuel I'll give you my letter."

Joseph did not need to be asked twice, and Esther made her escape.

The chicken coop out back housed twelve lovely laying chickens. Esther *cluck-clucked* to them, calling each one by name, and sprinkled feed over the ground. While the greedy birds pecked at their food, Esther collected the eggs and swept out the coop. She raced up the stairs and aired the beds, swept the steps, emptied the chamber pots—never before had Esther been quite so efficient or so fast. But still the time went slowly. It took forever for the sun to stand in the middle of the sky.

Chapter 4

❧

"Come, Joseph, we're going on an adventure!" Esther held up his new, brightly striped jacket. It was a mild spring day. Even a five-year-old knew that the jacket would be too hot. He shook his little head so hard his sidelocks bounced and jiggled.

"Please, Joseph. Maman said that you must wear it. And you will look so handsome in it."

Maman had made the jacket for him out of the finest silks Papa carried in his shop. It was not like either of them to be so extravagant, or to dress a child in such bright clothes, but it sometimes happened that small bits of cloth were left on different bolts, and so it was that Joseph was made a fine silk jacket.

"No." He scrunched his mouth together and bunched up his hands until they were as small and hard as new potatoes.

"Just put it on until we get out the door, then you can take it off and I'll carry it. Please, Joseph!" Esther blew into his ear until he burst into giggles. With a loud hoot he fell into his sister's lap. The jacket went on.

"You look handsome, Joseph," said Maman as Joseph and Esther ran into the warm kitchen. Joseph beamed. "Wait with Sarah in the shop. I want to talk to Esther. Come, sit," said Maman to Esther as Joseph skipped away.

What now? One of Maman's lectures was sure to come. Esther plunked down beside her mother on the bench.

"You are growing up. Other people's opinions matter, especially now. You must think before you act, Esther. Promise me. Promise that you will always think about the outcome." Maman's beautiful brown eyes were large and round. She seemed to be pleading with her.

Esther nodded, but the truth was that she didn't know *why* other people's opinions mattered, or why *now* was different from *before*. "Yes, Maman," she said softly. She would have agreed to anything—well, almost anything—to get out of the house.

Maman's forehead turned into rows of puckered ridges. She knew too well that the old women of the town gossiped about Esther. She also knew that whispers, given even the smallest amount of fuel, could turn into a raging fire that paid no heed to what it destroyed. Perhaps the cloth samples could wait … But to lose Madame Bendal as a customer would be a catastrophe! If only Papa had not left so early.

Grand-mère tsk-tsked in the corner.

Maman sighed and pushed the package of samples into Esther's arms. "Take the road around the synagogue and head toward the east gate."

"Yes, I know the way. I have waited outside for Papa. I will be fine, Maman, really. And Papa would not want to disappoint Madame Bendal." Esther was growing anxious. She had to leave before Maman changed her mind.

"Here." Maman handed Esther one of her own pockets with two sous in it. "You may need to pay a boy to help you cross the roads. If not, you may buy some roasted chestnuts. Do not dawdle. And hold Joseph's hand."

"Yes, Maman." What joy! Esther tied the pocket's dangling string to her belt, then tucked the pocket into the folds of her dress. She was instantly a lady!

Maman set Esther's coif to rights, for certainly no young girl or woman could be seen in public without a suitable head covering. To be bareheaded would be to declare oneself low-born … or worse, a prostitute.

Maman tilted Esther's head up and looked into the girl's eyes. Her heart could break for this child. Why could she not get her to understand the world in which they lived? Even when she was small, Esther had done things that could not be explained. Once she'd been found perched like a bird on the roof looking up into the sky. She had said that she wanted to fly into the sun. And what of the time she had trailed her father out of the Jewish Quarter? Had the guard at the gate not demanded extra tax, Papa might not have looked back, or seen the child walking behind him. What would become of such a girl? Maman put her arms around Esther and prayed she would always be kept safe.

"Do not talk to strangers, do you understand? Or to *any* young men." Maman straightened up.

"Yes, Maman." Without another word Esther bounced up and skipped down the dim hall toward Papa's shop, where Sarah was keeping an eye on Joseph.

The kitchen and shop were below ground. The shop was at the front of the house, and it was the brightest room, thanks to a small window in the shop door. One could see the window from the kitchen if the door between shop and house was left open. Bright bolts of material sat on the upper shelves, while folded material rested on the lower shelves. Few customers ventured in here, as Papa and Abraham generally delivered the fabric directly to their busy clients.

Esther swung open the shop door. It was just nine steps up to the street. Esther paused. She could not put a name to the feeling, or even explain it, but when she was in the stairwell her heart quickened and her breath was short. It sounded foolish but, when she stood in an enclosed space, the walls seemed to move toward her. This was silly. Freedom, adventure, awaited her! Esther took a deep breath, ran past Sarah, took hold of Joseph's arm and raced up the stairs.

Three young girls, friends of Sarah's, walked down the road toward her. Their arms were linked and they each bore the expression of having swallowed a secret. They gave Esther a hard stare as they passed, and Esther felt a familiar stab of pain. But their rejection no longer grieved her as it once had. On the contrary, Esther had come to like, or at least accept, being alone.

"Come on, Esther." Joseph pulled on his sister's arm.

The streets were crowded. Men were returning from prayers and young boys were coming home from *shul* to take their midday meal. Sullen and pale boys walked in solemn groups. Soon Joseph would join them. It did not take long, Esther thought, for serious study to chase away the playfulness of boys.

Housewives and maids stood in open windows calling out to each other. Everyone looked sickly and grey. The sun was high in the sky, and yet little of its brightness reached the streets. Children grew up in shade and shadows.

The roads were narrow, so narrow that two carts meeting created congestion and sparked arguments. "Go forth and multiply," said the rabbis, but nothing was said of multiplying or expanding homes or land. The Jewish Quarter had to expand. People were getting on each other's nerves. And look at how small the children were! Look at how bent the men were becoming! "We are as full as an egg," the rabbis lamented. Of course there were complaints to the king—after all, the Gentiles had lots of land and space to grow—but Jews did not have the rights of other French citizens, so little heed was paid to their requests. And what did it really matter? It had been this way for hundreds of years. A Jew had to live within walking distance of the synagogue. And rabbis themselves did not want their people mixing with Gentiles. What to do? What to do? It was, as Papa always said, a conundrum.

Today, for Esther, it was enough to be outside, free, with no one to tell her to hurry up or slow down. She squeezed Joseph's hand and took a deep breath before plunging headlong into the street, and straight into the sour Madame Metalon.

"*Je m'excuse,* Madame." Esther made a bouncy curtsy. Madame Metalon was not only the tallest woman Esther had ever met, she was also a busybody and a gossip.

"What are you doing out on your own, Esther Brandeau?" Madame Metalon folded her arms under her ample bosom and peered down from her great height. Her black wig had slipped, revealing tufts of stringy white hair.

"I am with my brother and we are on an important errand." Esther meant to speak proudly but instead she spoke loudly.

Madame Metalon glared down at Joseph and scowled again. Such a ridiculous coat on a small boy. The old woman turned back to Esther. "Bah! Brother indeed. What is your mother thinking? You should not be seen on the street without a *proper* chaperone. Doesn't the matchmaker have enough problems with you?"

Esther's mouth dropped open. That was just what Grand-mère had said. Well, she didn't *want* a husband. Besides, she was too young to marry, so what did it matter? But what was wrong with her? Why couldn't she get a husband? Not wanting a husband and not being able to get a husband were two different things entirely.

"Close your mouth. What have you to say for yourself?" Madame Metalon leaned down closer, then closer still. Esther could see every hair that made up Madame Metalon's moustache. And she could see one especially long, grey hair, which sprouted from a bumpy, black mole beside her nose.

Esther gulped. She couldn't think of a thing to say. No matter, Madame Metalon was not finished.

"Fate has written on your soul, Esther Brandeau. You cannot escape your destiny. Do you hear me? Do you?"

The old woman's mouth was drawn so tight it had lost its colour and looked like a slash across her face. Bits of froth collected in the corners of her mouth. What should she do? Esther curtsied a second time, then grabbed Joseph's hand and ran.

Why were the grown-ups all so convinced that peril lay around every corner? Esther wasn't the least bit afraid of rogues or scoundrels. No one would hurt her in the Jewish Quarter. As for her reputation, well, she just wouldn't talk to a boy, so that was that. Adults made such a fuss about everything.

Toward the centre of the Jewish Quarter stood the grey stone synagogue and the *shul*. Next came the cemetery, the *hekdesh* meeting house and the *mikveh,* the women's bathhouse. The bathhouse was a place where women went after blood flowed from their bodies. Maman had said that one day blood would flow from her body, too. The thought was neither gruesome nor frightening, just confusing. It had something to do with babies. A baby came from a woman's loins, that she knew. Perhaps the blood that flowed from a woman's body was the blood that ran through the baby's body?

What did it matter? What did anything matter on such a wondrous day! Here, in the middle of the town, she could feel the sun on her face. It would be glorious to run, to dance, but modesty prevailed, and for the moment Esther was content to let her heart do the racing.

Esther and Joseph passed peddlers with wagons full of used clothes and cloth, shoe buckles and medicinal cures. There were vendors pushing carts of vegetables—giant cabbages, parsnips and onions. The fishmonger, the butcher, the cake maker, all had special cries that filled the air like birdsong. A tooth extractor had set up shop in a laneway. He stood haggling with a man who had a hand pressed to his swollen cheek. Esther ran her tongue over her teeth and shuddered.

"Look!" Joseph pointed to a man carrying a stove on his back. "He will be roasting chestnuts in a minute."

"We will buy some on the way back," said Esther. The longer she had the coins in her pocket the longer she felt like a grown woman.

Three boys came up the road, one walking a few paces behind the others. Esther sucked in a breath. It was Isaac, the rabbi's youngest son. He had dark eyes, hair as black as night, and not a single pustule on his face. She had seen him in synagogue. It had been hard to get a good look at him, though, since men and women sat separately and his head was always bowed in prayer or contemplation. Even now he seemed to find more interest in the beaten dirt beneath his feet than the world around him. How would he ever see her if he never looked up?

With each step closer Esther's heart thumped harder. It wasn't as if she wanted to marry, but if she were to marry …

"Come, Joseph." Esther reached for her brother's hand again. If she kept looking at Joseph and walked straight ahead she would collide with Isaac. Then he would have to look up at her and *then* she could beg his pardon. To excuse oneself could not be considered the same as speaking, surely. Besides, he was the rabbi's son, not a common boy. She would smile, that was all. No one would think badly of her if she just smiled, and it would be a really little, little smile.

They were coming closer, closer. And then she was upon them. Esther pretended to talk to Joseph. The two boys in front of Isaac parted. Isaac, his eyes still glued to his feet, looked up abruptly. He let out a small cry, then bumped right up against her. The thud sent them both reeling backwards. Books tumbled out of Isaac's hands and fell onto the damp street. He dropped to his knees and frantically gathered them up.

"I'm sorry." And she was, truly! Esther bent down and tried to pick up a book but it slipped out of her hand and landed—oh, no—in a steamy pile of horse dung!

The boy looked up, his brown eyes huge with disbelief. The other two boys did little to muffle their laughter.

"I really am …" Esther sputtered.

Isaac, with a face the colour of a cooked beet, said nothing. He scrambled to his feet, his sidelocks bouncing about his shoulders, hugged the books to him and began to run. The two other boys followed, calling his name.

Esther stood on the street and looked after them. What had she done?

Chapter 5

⌇

Madame Bendal's house, tall and thin like the rest, was the last house near the old gate of the Jewish Quarter. It was said that Madame Bendal was wealthy. Wealthy Jews usually lived in the middle of the town, closest to the synagogue, but not Madame Bendal. Her clients were rich Gentiles who did not want to plunge too far into the Jewish Quarter when they came for a dress fitting, and so Madame Bendal lived on the edge, dangling between two worlds.

Jews and Gentiles got along tolerably well now, Esther's mother would often say. So long as everyone stayed in their places and the Jews paid lots and lots of taxes and fees of all kinds and did what they were told, her father would always add. But not so long ago, the Jews had been put to the rack, some alive in Spain and Portugal. That was where Papa's family was from.

Papa's eyes would fill with tears when he talked about his own father. Beaten, beaten to death, his trousers down around his ankles. It wasn't to prove that he was circumcised, that he was a

Jew, it was to humiliate him in front of his wife and children. "Oh Papa, oh Papa," her own Papa would sometimes cry when he thought he was alone and there was no one to hear. Maman would come upon him. "Stop, David," she would say as she wiped his brow. "The children might hear you. Don't scare the children." All this Esther would watch, sometimes through the knot in the floor and sometimes from behind a curtain. Papa always looked sad, but Maman looked scared.

Esther and Joseph crossed a canal bridge and tiptoed around the dung, garbage and sludge. For a fee, boys offered to lay boards as long as gangplanks across the vilest pools of muck on the road. Esther patted her pocket. No, she would not part with her precious coins. One boy offered his plank free of charge, but Esther would not be tricked. If she accepted the boy's offer she would have to say thank-you and be caught talking to a boy.

"Look! The king!" Joseph squealed. He pointed to a gilded coach pulled by four white horses that stood outside Madame Bendal's house. Esther stopped in her tracks. It was the most magnificent gold-and-white coach she had ever seen. It was the *only* gold-and-white coach she had ever seen! Even its wheels were rimmed in white and gold, and tiny, perfect roses were carved around the windows. The driver and the footman, both wigged and powdered, in gold-and-black livery trimmed with braid, stood at their posts. The stately white horses with black nostrils that flared and snorted had strands of gold and black ribbons woven into their manes.

"It's not the king, but it's someone very important," Esther whispered as they made their way around the back of the coach. The footman paid them no mind.

"Joseph, sit there." Esther motioned to the bottom step of Madame Bendal's house.

Taking a deep breath, she ran up the stairs and rapped at the door. As a maid opened it, a wash of high-pitched and shrill voices flooded out of the house. Esther strained to hear what they were saying. The maid rammed her hand on one hip and, in that triangle of space, Esther caught a glimpse of a swishing blue-and-pink silk dress. Who was that? Oh, look! The walls were covered in silks, and the floors …

"What do *you* want?" The maid spoke with a haughty Parisian accent.

Esther looked up into the flat face of the maid, who really wasn't much older than she was.

"Monsieur Brandeau is my papa. He sent these cloth samples." Esther held up the parcel as if it were an offering.

The girl snatched it out of Esther's hands. "Next time, use the back door." The door closed with a thud.

As suddenly as the opening into this magical world had appeared, it was gone. That was that. Esther skipped down the steps and plopped down beside Joseph. For the moment, it was enough simply to gaze in wonder at the gold-and-white-trimmed coach and the beautiful horses.

Past the house and in the distance beyond the gate she could see a hill. Long yellow grass swayed in the wind; the sun seemed to shine down directly upon it. She would be able to feel the wind on her face up there, to breathe freely. For once, for even a moment, there would be no walls to hem her in. It wasn't so very far away. Not far at all, actually. Why, a person could race up the hill and back again in hardly any time at all. Who would know?

"Come, Joseph." She grabbed his hand.

Joseph sat rooted to the step.

"Joseph, what is it?" Esther asked. But really she knew what was worrying him—he was only five, but he knew as well as she did that Maman and Papa would be very upset if they passed through the gates. "Why don't you take your jacket off?" she suggested. "You'd like that, wouldn't you? I'll carry it. And you want chestnuts, *oui*? I'll buy you some, really, I will." His little face brightened up at the bribe. "That's a good boy. We'll just go to the top of that hill. We'll be able to see everything from up there and no one will know. Come on."

Guards at the entrance to the Jewish Quarter had been replaced with toll collectors. The toll collectors were sluggish men who usually leaned against the opened gates and picked their teeth, but today they were arguing with a cartload of people. They were too busy to notice Esther and Joseph, and so the two dashed under the arches and crossed the road.

The two children dodged between pedestrians, carts and noisy shopkeepers. They ducked around a string of wagons drawn by sloe-eyed donkeys or lumbering oxen. They passed foul-smelling workers heaving great sacks up and onto their backs, men slumped on old livery hacks, carriages and sedan chairs filled with puffed-up men and bejewelled ladies, servants on errands and merchants selling wares. There were women with yellow and red wigs, dressed in bright clothes. There were beggars, too, plenty with only one leg, one arm, one eye. Papa was always talking about the starving people in France. He said that the king should care more for the poor peasants. Maman hushed him, saying that Jews had lived in France for hundreds and hundreds of years but they were still considered "guests" of the king, and it was best not to criticize.

A thin woman, so thin her bones stood out of her face in sharp ridges, sat on the ground holding a baby. The baby, too, looked strange. His middle seemed fat, yet the rest of him was spindly. The woman held out an open palm to passing strangers but none took any notice of her. *Thou shalt neither vex a stranger, nor oppress him; for ye were strangers in the land of Egypt.* Esther had read the passage from the Bible that very morning. Surely she would vex the woman if she passed by without helping her. Esther reached into her pocket. If she gave away one sou, she would still have one left for chestnuts. Esther dropped the coin into the woman's hand, took hold of Joseph and spurted ahead.

They turned a corner and found themselves in a large square. Buildings surrounded a cobblestoned area as big as a pasture. Great, colourful banners hung from poles and gables, and Esther's ears were treated to a jumble of music. Colourful fellows juggled all matter of things; magicians standing at small tables made things appear and disappear. Peddlers sold thin tallow candles, squawking geese and clucking chickens. Pies—there were lots of pies for sale. It was all a wonder to behold. This had to be a fair. She had heard women gossiping about such a thing but never, in her wildest imagination, had she imagined it to be so colourful, so exciting.

Something caught her eye. "Look, Joseph!" Esther pointed ahead.

Joseph, too short to see anything but swelling stomachs and bulging bums, hopped up and down, to no avail. "I can't see!" he cried. Esther lifted him up as best she could. "Ohhh," he squealed in delight.

Joseph was too heavy to hold for long. Esther set him down, took hold of his hand and nudged through the crowd.

"Come, we must get closer." Neither shoving nor pushing, but fully intent on getting a good view, Esther ploughed forward while random elbows and swinging arms nearly knocked Joseph senseless.

Between bobbing heads and hats they could see a stage that had been cut out of the side of a cart. Finally they made it to the very front. "Puppets!" Esther squealed.

A wooden French puppet prince, mounted on a wooden puppet steed, trotted across the stage. He spied a girl puppet. The prince puppet looked down at the lovely girl puppet as she made attempts to lift a puppet-sized bale of hay. It was love at first sight. Alas, the girl puppet was poor, without anything to recommend her except her long, blond tresses, skin the colour of salt and a sweet disposition.

As the handsome prince dismounted to talk with the gentle maid, an evil man puppet came between them. He had a startling big nose and small, beady, black eyes. Tufts of hair escaped the small cap on his head. His wooden arms flailed in all directions.

"Away with you!" cried the evil man puppet.

Downhearted, the prince puppet rode away. The crowd booed. The evil man puppet turned his wrath on the innocent girl puppet. He screamed and yelled and then took a bat to her.

Anguish overcame Esther. She almost cried out, "Stop him!"

But the good prince overheard the girl's doleful cries. With the drumming of puppet hooves, and thunderous applause from the crowd, the puppet prince came to the puppet girl's rescue. As the evil man puppet was lowered into a cauldron of boiling oil, the crowd cheered. Only then was it revealed that the lovely girl was a princess who had fallen under the spell of the evil man. Upon his death, the spell was broken and she was a princess once more.

The crowd cheered. Esther stood amazed and entranced. It was hard to believe that such wonders existed just beyond the gates, that they had been here all along.

A boy rattled a moneybox in Esther's face. He looked fierce and smelled like a privy. Esther dithered. Of course, such great art as the puppet play had to be paid for, otherwise it was stealing.

Reluctantly she parted with her last coin. There would be no roasted chestnuts to eat on the way home.

"Joseph." Esther turned. "Joseph!" She looked down, ahead, then around. Where was he? Oh dear God, where had he got to? He was just here! Small boys did not vanish. "JOSEPH?" No, no, she must not call out, she must not draw attention to herself, she must not let on that a boy was lost, a Jewish boy.

She ran—any direction would do. Evil things could happen to a small Jewish boy on his own among the Gentiles. Sailors, soldiers or roving gangs of boys could set upon him. Maman had warned her, she'd told Esther to hold her brother's hand. Why hadn't she listened? Oh please, please God, protect Joseph. This was all her fault. If anything happened to him, she would be to blame.

Esther sprinted though the crowds, ducking down one back alley, then another. Her coif fell and dangled by a string down her back. Hair escaped its braid and flew about her face. Run, run, run, up and down and back and forth. She came to the end of an alley and bent over, clutching her middle. Only fear kept the tears from running down her face.

"What's this?"

Esther turned. Four boys stood behind her, blocking her only escape.

"Where are you from? You don't belong here." The tallest boy grinned. His front teeth were missing.

"Look at her clothes!" cried another boy.

What was wrong with her clothes? Truly, they were plain and drab, but the cloth was the best. And they were clean. Esther covered herself with her arms and stared ahead, wide eyed. What did they want? She had no coins.

All the boys laughed, some broadly, others with a slow, sly smile. They moved in closer, stalking her as if they were animals and she were prey. With each step they took forward, Esther stepped back. She had been warned that men and even older boys might defile an unprotected woman, but what did that mean? *Help me. God, please.* She needed to pray. But no words came to her. *Get away, get away!*

The boys bared their teeth like dogs. Esther kept moving until her back was against a wall. The boys stopped too. Trapped.

A door opened and out came a wash of filth. An old woman ducked out. Grey hair sprouted all over her head. She took in the scene, then cackled with laughter. Her mouth was empty save for two grey bottom teeth. "What mischief are you boys up to?" The boys turned toward the old woman.

Esther lurched forward and ploughed her way past the startled boys. One made a grab at her, then another, then another. Her dress ripped; her coif was torn away.

Once out of the alley she plunged into the crowd. The sound of the boys howling and whooping followed her. The gate to the Jewish Quarter was too far. She would never make it, and she could not go home without Joseph. *Oh, Joseph, what have they done to you?*

A wagon full of vegetables stood near a wall. Esther slowed her steps, although it pained her to do so. *Step, step*—she must not draw attention to herself. *Step, step.* It took all her will to slow down, all her courage not to cry out. Esther hid behind the cart, then squeezed herself between two stone walls. She would wait until the market cleared and then search for her brother. That was all she could think to do.

&c&

It was near sunset before Esther emerged from her hiding place. On legs that could barely support her, Esther peered up alleyways and down roads. Joseph was nowhere to be seen. Perhaps he was hiding.

"Joseph, come out. It is safe now. Come out," Esther whispered as she poked her head behind barrels and crates. On she went, on and on. It was only when darkness fell that Esther stumbled under the archway and made her way through the Jewish Quarter. There were few lights to guide her, and several times she stumbled. The toll collectors had long since gone home. Now only watchmen patrolled the quiet streets. Tears blurred her vision. What would she say to Maman? How would she explain?

Esther staggered down the dark streets toward the synagogue. *Joseph, what have I done? Where are you?* The world around her seemed to shift. She looked up. Dark, forbidding buildings tilted forward; lights flickered from within; all had eyes that were looking down upon her, judging her. They were moving closer and closer. She turned once, twice, until she was in a spin. Back, get back. She fell but did not feel the falling until a stone slashed her forehead. Blood spilled down her cheek. The fall scattered what was left of her wits. A light fell over her, and behind the light was a dark shadow.

"No, no!" Esther put her hands over her head and shrieked. The boys, they had come back! "No!" Esther screamed.

Abel, the night watchman, looked down at the girl, then he too cried out into the night. "Help! I need help!"

"What is wrong, Abel?" Aaron, the *shamash,* on his way to clean the synagogue, came running. He stopped and peered down at the dishevelled girl. Her head was bare, her hair a tangled heap and, worse, her chemise could be seen through her torn dress.

"Look. It is David Brandeau's daughter." Abel shone his lantern above the girl's head. She was sobbing uncontrollably, her shoulders were heaving up and down. Tears and blood mingled and rolled down her face. "Help me lift her."

With Abel in the lead, his lantern held high, Aaron carried Esther home.

Abel pounded on the cloth merchant's door. First came the sound of footsteps, then the door swung open and banged against the inside wall. Maman cried out.

Blood ran in rivulets down Esther's face and soaked the top of her torn dress.

"Esther," Maman whispered. "Can you speak?"

Esther's thoughts wandered and her vision was a watery blur. The very air around her seemed to bend. She tried to speak but only moans drifted from her mouth.

"Bring her in. Set her down by the fire."

Aaron carried Esther through the shop, down the hall, then gently lowered her into Grand-mère's empty chair.

Esther felt a blanket falling over her shoulders. She heard the voices recede down the hallway. Maman was thanking the men over and over for bringing her daughter home.

"Esther, Esther, your father and Abraham are out looking for you. They have been everywhere. Where were you?" Maman cried as she dabbed Esther's forehead with a cloth.

"Joseph …" Esther reached out and grasped Maman's arm.

"He is in his bed. Stand, we must get you out of these wet clothes."

Joseph was safe. How? How? No, it did not matter how. Relief swept through her and left her breathless. God had been kind. On tottery legs that barely held her upright, Esther stood as her mother peeled off the soiled dress.

"Oh," Maman cried out when she saw Esther's bloodied and battered knees. Again Maman threw a warm blanket around her.

She hugged her and kissed her but Esther did not take her eyes off the fire. Her head throbbed beyond reason and words would not take shape in her mouth.

"Esther." Maman took hold of Esther's hands and whispered, "Did anything happen to you? Did any boy…?"

Esther shook her head. Maman let out a long sigh.

"Has anything happened to her? Is she damaged?" The door banged open and closed. Papa? Was that Papa? He seemed very far away.

"No, no, a cut and a bump on the head is all. Abraham, leave us," said Maman. Esther had neither the wits nor the heart to look up at her brother.

"Where have you been?" The anger in Papa's voice cut like a thousand knives.

Esther dropped her head. Tears rushed up the back of her throat and seemed to drown her from the inside out.

"Think of what you have done, child!" cried Papa. He had never spoken to her so harshly before. "A small errand, that's all that was asked of you. Do you know the damage you have caused to yourself? Everyone will soon be speaking of it."

"Not now, David." Maman's own voice, although thin, was firm. "Get the Sabbath wine. I will fetch clean clothes." Maman and Papa, each to their errands, vanished from Esther's sight.

She would have cried if she could. What had happened? Why had everything suddenly spun out of control? The sick rose in her throat and she turned and vomited into a pail that stood by the fire.

Esther didn't see Grand-mère standing in the doorway. The old woman, wearing her chemise, bedcap and heavy shawl, stood on the doorsill for a moment. She watched Esther shiver and quake. Slowly Grand-mère came upon her, bent low and hissed in her ear.

"Devils are born out of evil. Evil begets evil. How many devils live because of you, Esther Brandeau?"

Chapter 6

⌒∽⌒

A door slammed shut. Esther woke with a start. Why had she been allowed to sleep so long? What was the time? It felt late. And there was no sign of Sarah. For the first time in her whole life, Esther would have been glad to wake up beside her disagreeable sister. At least that would have meant that life was continuing as it always had. Three days had passed since the night she was brought home in disgrace. No amount of explaining could lessen Papa's anger or the gossip that swept through the town.

When Esther hadn't returned from delivering the cloth samples, Sarah's three friends reported that they had seen Esther leave the house. They had confirmed that Esther's little brother Joseph, wearing a brightly striped coat, was with her. The poor child was found much later by Jacob the cobbler. The boy was sobbing about a wooden prince and princess. No one knew what to think!

Madame Metalon announced that she, too, had seen Esther. Just the sight of the girl on the street without a proper chaperone had been proof enough of some wrongdoing. Abel, the night watchman, reported to his wife, who mentioned it to her three sisters, that he had found Esther lying in the street in the middle of the night, without a head covering. Worse, there was mention of blood. Everyone heard through reliable sources that Aaron, the *shamash,* had carried the girl home. Ismahal's name was linked to Esther. To spare the boy any shame that might fall upon his innocent head, his father, the rabbi, had the boy whisked away to Paris to stay with a trusted friend.

All agreed that, even as a small child, Esther had been different. She was trouble, a bad seed. Her poor mother. Her poor sister and brothers.

Esther sat up in bed and swung her legs over the side. Tonight at sunset would be the start of the Sabbath. It was the day to bake and clean and boil water, to rinse all the pots and dishes. Esther usually loved preparing for the Sabbath. But now everything was different.

She heard voices from below and cocked her head to listen. The voices were not loud so much as harsh. Esther jumped onto the floor, but quietly, like a cat. She peeled back the rug and, using her fingernail, popped the knot of wood out of its hole. It was hard to get a good view, but she could see the top of Maman's head. There was someone else in the room.

"It is time she was put out to work, for no good man would have such a thing as *her* as his wife." That was Grand-mère's voice.

"Mère, she is our daughter. She is innocent of all wrongdoing."

"Innocent! Innocent! She is as pure as a pig's tail, that one."

Maman gave a small cry. "How could you say such a thing?"

"She is not your daughter and she is not my granddaughter. She is your husband's illegitimate offspring. How you could raise

her as your own is beyond me. And how you care for her! You
give her more attention than you do me. What would your own
Papa, of blessed memory, say about your attentions to this
wicked girl?"

"That's not true—"

"Look at her! She has her mother's look, no doubt. Do you see
how she turns young men's heads? Even in synagogue I see the
boys try and peek into the women's section. Disgraceful! They
look at her with lust, I tell you. And why? I've never set eyes on
an uglier child—sticks for bones, those demon eyes, and she
walks like she's about to fall through the floor!"

"Mère, stop. You will be heard."

"Do you think the whole town does not know? Do you think
memories are so short? Your own daughter and this one were
born less than a month apart. Any fool can see that they are the
same age, even if their looks are day and night. No decent home
has ever invited that child in. Even girls her own age know to
keep away from her. She has not a friend in the world. And what
of your own daughter? How will she find a good match with such
a thing as that for a sister? She will soon know the truth. No
respectable father will allow his son to marry the daughter of a—"
Grand-mère stopped and swallowed hard. Even she knew that
she had gone too far.

There was silence, and then Maman spoke in low, measured
breaths. "I have often thought that Esther was friendless because
of the whispers. It changes children, changes their very selves
when others treat them badly." Maman's voice was soulful and
soft.

"What do you expect?" Grand-mère sounded triumphant.

"I expect people to care for a motherless child. As for my Papa,
of blessed memory, he would understand that it is my duty to

care for her. Esther is my heart-beloved child. It is true that her eyes are a strange colour, but man judges by the look of the eyes, God judges by the depth of the heart. She is kind and she has a good heart. And Mère, I do not neglect you."

Esther could hear Maman's footsteps as she crossed the room. She must have reached the door and turned.

"As for my husband, the man who provides a home for you, he made a mistake and he has atoned for his behaviour. Esther's mother is dead. He could have let the child be raised by strangers. He did right to bring her to me. He is a good man who once went astray. Do not speak ill of him again."

A door opened and closed.

It was as if she were bewitched, for Esther could no more pull her eye away from that hole in the floor than she could unhear what had been spoken.

Grand-mère stood and paced up and down the small room. Her mouth curled in distaste. "Osnath," she uttered. "Osnath."

Esther drew in a breath. Osnath was the daughter of Machlan, the creature who could leap from chimney to chimney, who had fiery breath and fiery hair? Esther grew cold. Did Grand-mère mean that she was Osnath?

It was good that Esther could not hear the old woman's thoughts, for it was Sarah, sweet Sarah, that the old woman treasured. Sarah had been a baby to love. Milky and docile, Sarah had mewed and purred in her mother's arms. And when Sarah was a month old, out of the night had come David Brandeau with a scrawny brat in his arms. "Its mother is dead," David Brandeau, the adulterer, had announced. Grand-mère shook her head. Think of the humiliation that her poor daughter was made to endure. Not only did she discover that her husband had taken another woman into his bed, but then she was saddled with his crime. Grand-mère hissed and spat as she lumbered back and forth across the room.

As for the scrawny, screeching brat they had called Esther, she could not be comforted. Night after night she had watched her beloved daughter pace the floor while cradling this creature. Exhaustion overcame the household. No one could escape the cries of the child howling for its dead mother. But it would not do to blame David Brandeau. He was but a man, and all men were foolish. Besides, he provided a roof over their heads. No, the fault lay with the brat, Esther, and its dead mother.

"She has brought yet more shame onto this house and my own daughter's good name!" Grand-mère lamented out loud. The old woman raised her eyes to the ceiling and caught sight of the hole. Grand-mère's and Esther's eyes locked. The look of hatred from Grand-mère sent Esther scuttling backwards.

Esther slipped the knot into the hole in the floor and pulled the rug over it. She clutched her stomach and shoved her hand in her mouth to stop the moans from escaping. *Someone who was not Maman had given birth to her.*

❧

It seemed a long time before Esther could rise and dress herself. Had she fallen back to sleep, perhaps she could have convinced herself that it had all been a bad dream. But Grand-mère's words were still with her, hanging over her head like a dark cloud. *Illegitimate.* She had another mother, one who was now dead.

Esther crept down the stairs and walked into the kitchen. Where was everyone? Papa would be at synagogue, but where were Joseph and Sarah? Esther turned and looked at the empty chair in the corner. Even Grand-mère was missing! Baby Samuel sat clapping his hands and making baby sounds on a horsehair pillow. The rocking chair squeaked. Esther jumped. She spun around and spied Maman.

"Maman?" Esther spoke softly. The name seemed to stick in her throat.

"Esther, are you well?" Maman spoke softly. She looked tired. Dark circles were under her eyes and even her wig, always so carefully brushed and put on, seemed dishevelled.

Esther nodded, yes, she was well. "Where is everyone?"

Samuel howled. Esther scooped him up and kissed his downy, golden hair.

"Papa went to synagogue early, and then ..." Maman's voice trailed away.

"Then what, Maman?"

"Then he is going to the matchmaker."

The matchmaker? This made no sense.

"Is he going to see about a wife for Benjamin?"

Maman shook her head.

"Abraham?"

Maman shook her head.

"Is Sarah to be married?" Esther whispered. Even as her words were uttered her heart began to pound.

Again Maman shook her head. So, Papa must be going to the matchmaker about her. But she was just fourteen! It was true that many girls were betrothed by twelve years of age, and some did marry at fourteen or fifteen, but Papa had always said that such an age was too young to marry.

Esther's head was spinning. She did not want to be married. Not even to a prince. She turned, and the room seemed to turn with her. Marriage. Babies. That's what awaited her. She would never be free. Never, never. Could walls move? Certainly at that moment they were closing in on her, closer, closer, so she could hardly breathe! Baby Samuel wailed in her arms. Oh, she had not meant to hold him so tightly.

"Esther, sit down." Maman took the baby from her.

A thought came to mind. She might cry out for the pain it caused. Her family wanted to be rid of her. They didn't want her any more. That's why Papa was trying to marry her off.

They both heard the door of Papa's shop open and close. Papa, his face long and dark, came into the kitchen.

"We have a match." He sank down into a chair by the table.

Maman, her eyes suddenly bright with expectation, sat with the baby on her lap across from her husband. "Who? Tell us quickly."

"Red Mordecai," said Papa quietly.

"The rag-picker?" asked Maman in a small voice.

"He is the only one."

Esther looked from Papa to Maman then back to Papa. No, this could not be happening. Why didn't Maman say something?

"Papa," Esther whispered. She hugged her middle as though she'd been punched.

Papa held up a flat palm. "Wait—there are conditions. Mordecai has agreed to a betrothal of one year if Esther goes to live with Benjamin and my sister in Amsterdam. There she must lead an exemplary life. She will cook and sew and not leave the house except to attend synagogue. Once the gossip has died down, she will return home and they will marry," said Papa. "And there is more."

Maman's shoulders snapped back as she drew in a deep, angry breath. More? How could there be more? How could it be that such a man as Red the Rag-picker could make demands of the child of David Brandeau, respected merchant? She said nothing, but her thoughts were plain enough.

"The dowry must be tripled."

"Tripled?" Maman gasped. "But as it is, Esther's dowry is large."

Papa shrugged. "He says that he has his pride."

"His pride?" Maman, who seldom raised her voice, slammed her hand down on the table. The baby let out a startled cry. Esther had stopped paying attention. Why was her dowry large? That meant they would pay anything to be rid of her. It was true. It was true, true, true. They didn't want her. Esther didn't move, she couldn't move. Her hands were bunched into fists. She wanted to cry out, but instead she sat as still as any girl had ever sat and said nothing.

"I have booked passage on a ship sailing for Amsterdam. Esther, you leave the day after Sabbath on the afternoon tide."

"In two days!" Maman let out a small cry as she grabbed hold of Esther's hand.

⸙

Esther sat by the window not touching the hamper of sewing at her feet. For the first time her family had gone to synagogue on the Sabbath day without her.

She looked around her little room. It was a lovely, comfortable room. Did Red Mordecai live in a house like this one? Did he keep chickens? She said his name out loud. "Red Mordecai." She said it again and again. It wasn't a bad name, but it wasn't a name she would have chosen. She had seen him many times, even spoken to him when he had come to the shop door. Once, maybe twice, she had sold him small squares of material left on a bolt or as a sample. Maman had said to sell him the remnant at half its value, less than that sometimes. It was a *mitzvah,* a good deed. He was poor. Once she had heard Madame Metalon say that he owned nothing and was very generous with it.

He was old—not as old as Papa, but old. His beard was long and black with sprigs of grey, and his hair sprouted out in peculiar spots—beneath one nostril, in his ears. And he had been married before. Had his first wife died? Had they divorced? He seemed kind, like Papa—but to be married to such a man! What would it be like? She had no idea! It was all a blank.

Esther listened to Maria, a *shabbos-goya,* moving about in the kitchen below. It was against Jewish law for people to work on the Sabbath so Maria, a Gentile, would lay out the meal before Maman and the children returned from synagogue. Maria was a stout woman who walked with a heavy foot. Maman said it was because her heart was heavy, but why would a Gentile feel sad? They all had such freedom.

Why think of that now? Esther closed her eyes and tried to stop hot, sticky tears from rolling down her face.

Her head bobbed against her chest. Something, a sound perhaps, roused her. The room was almost dark. She must have fallen asleep!

"There you are. It is almost sunset." Sarah stood at the door with crossed arms and a puckered mouth. She tapped her foot. The Sabbath would soon begin.

Esther followed Sarah down the stairs. The smells from the kitchen were warm and inviting.

"You must wash your hands, Esther. Hurry," said Maman as she placed a loaf of bread in front of Papa. Esther held her hands under the cistern, then took her place at the table. Grand-mère, Sarah, Abraham, Maman, Papa, Joseph and baby Samuel, in a small chair, all waited for the sun to dip below the horizon. The candles had to be lit before sunset. It was a desecration to light the Sabbath candles after the sun had set.

Sabbath dinner was usually Esther's favourite time, but tonight was different. Hardly anyone had spoken to her since Papa had announced to the family that Esther was to be married and would soon be leaving for Amsterdam. Even Joseph seemed to avoid her.

Esther's brother Abraham dropped two coins into the *tzedaka pushka,* the charity box, then took his place beside Papa. Maman, with a square of delicate lace covering her head, lit the candles then cupped her hands around the flame. With a look of calm on her face she closed her eyes and sang, "Come, my beloved, to meet the Bride. Let us welcome the presence of the Sabbath. Come in peace … and come in joy … Come, O Bride! Come, O Bride!" Maman sang sweetly, and when she opened her eyes she beheld the Sabbath lights.

Papa said the *kiddush* over the wine. Everyone, even Joseph, had a sip. Then Papa said the *ha-motzi,* the blessing of the bread, while holding up one of Maman's fine loaves. Papa tore off a piece, ate and passed torn pieces of bread around. Only Sarah dared to snicker as the bread reached Esther.

Grand-mère watched Esther with obvious satisfaction. Her old, milky eyes seemed extra bright that night.

Esther hardly tasted Maman's delicious chicken soup with rings of fat swirling in the bowls. A roast chicken followed, along with platters of baked eggplant, artichokes and zucchini, spicy food cooked in the Sephardic style. But to Esther the food had no taste. She could hardly get it down her throat.

"You may begin, Abraham," said Papa. Just before the prayer to end the meal, Papa would always ask each child to say a *mitzvah.* Abraham, silent and studious like their older brother,

Benjamin the rabbi, said, "'You may only eat animals that have cloven hooves and chew cud.'"

Papa nodded. "Sarah, it is your turn."

Sarah seldom made time for religious studies, but tonight she gave Grand-mère a sideways glance, smiled a sly smile and said, "'It is against the law for a woman to wear men's clothing.' I saw Esther try on the trousers meant for Benjamin," she announced, positively beaming. Startled, Esther looked at her sister. Sarah stuck out her tongue.

"That's enough, Sarah. Esther, it is your turn." Papa motioned to her.

"'To honour father and mother,'" Esther whispered to her empty plate.

There was a silence before Papa said, "Joseph, do you have one?"

"Be a good boy!" He laughed and threw his hands up in the air. His sweet laughter made everyone smile, and for a moment it was like old times.

"That will do nicely, Joseph. I shall say one for Samuel." Papa smiled at his youngest son while Samuel, hearing his name, let out a shriek and banged his hand on the table.

"'It is the law that we not stand idly by when a human life is in danger,'" said Papa.

"I have a treat!" Maman stood up and fetched a loaf of honey cake from the sideboard. It was Esther's favourite. It was supposed to be served on Rosh Hashanah and Yom Kippur—a sweet cake for a sweet new year. Why had Maman made it today? Esther looked at Maman but her gaze was not met.

Joseph squealed his delight and Samuel joined in. Everyone but Esther gobbled down the honey cake. Then came the *birkhat ha-mazon,* the prayer to end the meal.

"Esther, you may go to bed." Maman, too, sounded tired and drained.

"So soon?" Grand-mère said, bristling.

"Esther leaves for Amsterdam tomorrow. I think it would be best if she rested."

Without looking at anyone, Esther left the warm kitchen and wearily climbed the stairs. She fell into her bed and, despite the turmoil that whirled around inside her, she fell asleep.

Chapter 7

⁓

Morning came but there was no sun. The day was dark. Esther sat on the edge of her bed and watched as Maman filled her trunk. What of her other mother, the one who gave her life?

"You will like Amsterdam." Maman folded a blanket over Esther's two good dresses.

Amsterdam was a city of great art and science, grand buildings, canals and manicured parklands. But Esther knew that all of this would be lost to her. She could expect to see nothing but walls.

"Did you put the coins in your pocket?" Maman asked gently.

Esther patted her hip. The pocket was well concealed under the folds of her dress.

"Good." Maman sat beside her and took up Esther's hands. Her beautiful brown eyes brimmed with tears. "My darling daughter," she whispered. "'If I take up the wings of the morning, and dwell on the ocean's farthest shore, even there Your hand will lead me. Your right hand will hold me.'" Tears shaped like raindrops cascaded down her face. "You must always remember that I love you, and your Papa does too. He wants what is best for you. I cannot interfere. He is … Papa." Maman's voice trembled. "Now come, we must finish packing."

Esther and Maman, one at each end, carried the trunk down the stairs and stood it by the door. Papa called out to a man on the street waiting with a cart. The trunk would be taken on ahead and put into the ship's hold. Esther would sail on the noon tide.

"You must eat before you leave." Maman put her arm around Esther.

How could she eat when the life that she knew was coming to an end? Esther shook her head. It was just as well. The kitchen was being cleaned for Pesach, the Passover festival. Every nook and cranny would be cleaned and swept. The only small pleasure Esther had at this moment was knowing that Sarah would be left to do the cleaning, and Sarah really, really hated cleaning.

"It is time to go, anyway," said Papa.

Esther pulled her shawl around her shoulders and kissed Maman goodbye.

"Be brave, my daughter. Always be brave," whispered Maman.

Sarah had a momentary bout of sisterly feeling before remembering that the whole bed would now belong to her alone. Abraham, who had endured much teasing because of Esther, had mumbled a hasty goodbye earlier. As for Grand-mère, a wave of the hand (although it was more of a *shoo*) was all the parting the old woman would spare.

"Don't go." Joseph's big brown eyes filled with tears. Esther picked up the five-year-old and whispered, "Take care of Samuel. You are his big brother." She held him tightly, as if to imprint the feel of him, then set him down and twirled his sidelocks in her finger.

On this windy April day, Esther and Papa went by cart to the port of St. Esprit. Father and daughter sat in the back of the mule-drawn cart. A carpet bag crammed with food, a blanket and gifts for her aunt and brother sat at her feet. The cart rumbled through the Jewish Quarter, past the thin, tall, shuttered houses and shops and, in the distance, the slaughterhouse.

With every lurch and jolt, every clop of the mules' hooves, the port grew closer. Esther fingered the fringes of her shawl and tried to think of what to say.

"Papa?" The cart knocked the two together and apart, together and apart. "Papa, I do not want to marry Red the Rag-picker." She caught herself. "I mean, I do not want to marry Red Mordecai." Her voice quavered. A great bubble in her throat made it hard to talk.

Papa sighed. "Esther, I despair of you. Do you want to lose what is rightfully yours in the world to come? You must marry and have children. What other life is there for you, or for any woman? Once you have had children, a blessing to any woman, you will be happy. Moses told us to follow the good ways. The choice is ours. He said, 'I call heaven and earth to witness that I have set before you life and death, the blessing and the curse; therefore choose life.' You must choose life, my daughter. Marry, have children. You will find happiness in that. You will see one day that I am right." He did not look at her as he patted her hand.

Happiness? Esther looked at Papa out of the corner of her eye. Was he happy? She had never thought to ask such a question. He did not seem happy. No adults seemed happy, not even Maman, and certainly not Grand-mère. Why did parents want their children to be like them, when they themselves were not happy?

"Papa, why is it all women must marry? I wish—"

Papa raised his hand. "God wants, man wishes. God gives us love, knowledge and ability. It is enough."

Esther turned her face away from Papa to prevent him from seeing the tears streaming down her cheeks. *Why, Papa? Why do you not care?*

They were at the gates. Papa paid the body tax and again they drove on. The gates were no longer closed, although many a rabbi wished them locked each night, as they had been in the old days. All the better to keep curious Jewish boys from roaming into the Gentiles' district and maybe meeting Christian girls! To the French king the walls hemmed Jews in, kept them in their place. To Papa, and perhaps all Jewish men, they prevented the outside world from crashing down on them. But how Esther loathed the walls. Yet on this day, it felt as though she was being cast out, made not welcome in the only world she knew.

"What of the other world?" she murmured as the cart passed under the arched gate.

"What is it that you say, daughter?" Papa turned to Esther.

"Nothing, Papa. I didn't say anything."

The cart rumbled through the Gentile part of town, carving a path through the throng. Would now be the time to ask Papa about her birth mother?

"Papa, the woman who gave me life, did she die because of me?" The question spilled out of her, the words half spoken, partly whispered. What would Papa do now that the secret was out? As much as she did not want to cause further distress, this was her chance. She braced for his anger.

Papa turned and stared at his daughter. Disbelief was abruptly replaced with a grim look of resignation. He did not ask Esther how she came upon this knowledge. "No, you did not cause her death. Although I did nothing to hasten her demise, I alone am responsible for … everything. She asked me to care for you. She was a brave woman and she loved you. Do not speak to me of her ever again."

The shock of Papa's answer left Esther winded. She almost cried out with joy. Not for a moment had she imagined that the woman who birthed her had loved her.

"Jew. JEW!"

Esther turned to see a boy bend down, pick up a pebble and, with a smirk on his face, take aim at their mule. The stone landed on the old beast's thick hide and bounced off. His skin barely felt the flick of a whip, let alone the tap of a pebble. The mule, Papa and the driver, too, paid the boy no notice. The boy tried again, and again, but they were soon out of his reach. And so they plodded on, molested perhaps, but undisturbed. Now was not the time to ask Papa about her other mother.

"Papa, why do they hate us?"

Papa sighed. "Too many reasons for me to explain in this short time."

"Try, Papa."

"Well, we all come from Abraham—Christian, Jew and Muslim. It is the Christians who believe that Jesus is the Messiah. Jews believe that Jesus was a prophet and the Messiah has yet to come."

"Jesus, he was a Jew?"

"Yes, of course," said Papa.

"And his mother Mary, she was a Jew?"

"Yes, of course Mary was a Jew, as were all the Disciples."

"Then why do Gentiles hate us if their Messiah was one of us?" Esther looked about her. Except for the odd hard scowl, none of the surrounding crowd gave them any notice. They were not invisible; they were ignored.

"The Christians believe that Jesus was executed by a Jew."

"Was he, Papa?"

"Jews never had such power in Rome, and Jews never, ever put a man on a cross. Perhaps if the Jewish people at the time had had any power they might have prevented hundreds of thousands of Jews from dying on the cross as Jesus did. No, no, to kill a man in such a manner was a Roman custom." He spoke slowly, sadly and softly.

"But Papa—"

"Not now, Esther. This is no time to talk about such things."

Following a stream of carriages, wagons and pushcarts, the cart slowed to a crawl as it approached the wharf. Screeching gulls sliced through the air overhead, swooping down to pluck up fish guts and entrails. Merchants shouted, children chimed in, dogs barked. Ladies of breeding, who otherwise would not raise their voices above polite conversation, bellowed at their servants and children. There were Muslims, too, nodding, talking, trading. How exotic they looked, how fine in their flowing caftans. Only an elegantly dressed black slave guarding his master's trunks was silent. There was so much to hear, to see, to take in, that for a moment Esther forgot her worries.

The cart pulled alongside a ship tethered to the pier. The bow of the wooden ship looked strong and mighty. Yet it was not a large brig, not as large as the others that were tied up farther down the pier, and certainly not as big as the ships anchored out in the bay. It was a Dutch vessel under the command of Captain Geoffrey. Esther had imagined a large, bearded man, fully in command, roaring orders from the deck. All she could see was a toady little fellow shaped like one of the wooden barrels common seamen were loading into the hold.

Papa leapt up in the cart and waved to a stout woman who stood on the deck of the ship. Madame Liebe Balmont was to be Esther's chaperone. Her sprawling family of three boys and four girls, plus servants, darted about her like a school of fish. Madame Balmont returned Papa's wave and smiled at Esther. Nothing would induce Madame Balmont to believe that the girl had the devil in her. She was an unfortunate child caught in unfortunate circumstances, that was all.

Father and daughter climbed out of the cart and walked through the throng toward the good woman and her brood. "All aboard." The crowd surged forward.

"Remember that actions are more important than belief," Papa called out quickly as the momentum of the crowd moved them forward. "Remember to be kind. Remember to keep *kosher*. Follow God's commandments and all will be well." He was pushed aside, and suddenly father and daughter were parted.

"Papa!" Esther cried. She clutched her carpet bag with one hand and reached out to her father with the other. "Papa, don't make me go away. Please, Papa, don't send me away." Did he hear?

"Remember, God is near to all who call unto Him." Even from a distance she could hear his voice tremble.

The movement of the crowd carried her toward the foot of the gangplank. "Papa!" she cried. She jumped up and down, bobbing over the heads of the pressing crowd.

The gangplank underfoot swayed as she gripped the rope-railing and made her way up to the deck. Picking her way around trunks and bags, coils of ropes and barrels, adults and children, she found a place at the rail and looked down into the crowd. She caught a glimpse of her father's hat.

He didn't want her, no one wanted her. Her life as she knew it was over. She would go to Amsterdam and live like a prisoner. She would return and marry an old man she did not love. She would have his children. She had no choice.

"It is your faith that gives you roots, my daughter," Papa shouted from below.

"It's not roots I want, Papa," Esther whispered. "It's wings."

Part 2

Chapter 8

⁓

*H*uge hemp ropes, uncoiled from iron anchorages on the wharf, were flung from shore to ship. They soared up into the air, arched into elegant loops and were caught by sailors on the run. The bare feet of common sailors smacked along the deck as their massive arms and callused hands coiled up the ropes. Other ropes, thicker still, were cranked onto giant tumblers.

Esther cupped a hand over her eyes and looked up. Sailors hung off the ship's rigging like grapes on a vine. One sailor, perched high above them on a small shelf, appeared no bigger than her thumb. How wondrous! What must it feel like to look out over the whole world? For surely that was what could be seen from such a height.

Orders from the captain were passed from sailor to sailor then shouted down into the hold of the ship. Two towboats came alongside, with pairs of men at the oars. A pilot called out the depth of the water as the ship moved away from its berth. There was a fair wind, and in no time the only sounds were the soft slap of feet on the wooden planks and the grunts and groans from sailors as they hoisted the sails up the masts. Canvas bellied out and cracked as the sails caught the wind, and the ship leapt forward. Cheers rose up from crew and passengers alike. They had set sail.

Esther looked back. Papa was nowhere to be seen. She leaned out over the rail and peered down into the water. Near the shore it was a percolating stew of filth, but as the ship ventured out toward the setting sun, the sea turned blue. At first the waves were small, like ruffles on a child's shirt, but as they sailed on, the bow slicing through the water sent up whitecaps that curled like a waving hand.

Away went the putrid stench of the town with its unwashed bodies and overflowing outhouses. Away went the stink of animal dung and rotting carcasses. Away went the confines of house and home, disapproving looks and cruel words.

The coast grew smaller until the land was but a thin line. No matter how isolated she might be from the world, she knew her place in it. The great mountains of Spain were to the south. They would fade from view as the ship headed north through the Golfe de Gascogne. Soon they would pass the red, rocky shore of the great commercial port of Bayonne, a city so important it minted its own money. In a day's time, with a fair wind, they would pass the city of La Rochelle. Then, up, up, past the city of Nantes, which though not far from the coast, was not a coastal town. Then they would sail around Brittany, through the English Channel and on to Amsterdam.

Esther closed her eyes. Her hair had blown loose from its cap and swayed and swirled about her face. She would have to hope, hope beyond reason, that fate would intervene and she would not have to marry.

Her eyes flew open. In front of her, and not farther than an arm's length, she beheld the broad, smiling face of a sailor. He had light blue eyes, white teeth and flaxen hair. He was handsome beyond measure. Their eyes locked.

What was she doing? He was a boy, and a Gentile boy, too! Shame came upon her so quickly it was all she could do to lift her hand and hide her reddening face.

"Esther, Esther, over here!" Madame Balmont waved. Esther raced along the ship's rail, dodging passengers and their bags, coils of rope and working seamen, until she stood beside the plump chaperone.

Esther bobbed a curtsy and dared not look over her shoulder, in case the sailor was still watching her. "*Bonjour*, Madame."

The good woman smiled weakly as she lurched back and forth with the ship's motion. Her normally ruddy face was as pale as a biscuit. "Travel for the young is about education and experience. But, for a mother such as myself, it is about arrival." Madame Balmont abruptly stopped talking. She didn't dare open her mouth again for fear something other than words might tumble out.

"Maman, Maman!" Two small children clutched Madame Balmont's grey dress.

She waved them away, momentarily lost her balance and then clutched the rail as if her life were in peril. "I do not feel well. I must lie down."

"Maman, I want to stay and watch the waves." A boy, not much older than her brother Joseph, bounced by Madame Balmont's side.

"I will take care of him," offered Esther.

Madame Balmont's brow crinkled. She had faithfully promised David Brandeau that she would keep an eye on his daughter. The woman reached for her servant girl. Seasickness won out over concern.

"That would be kind," Madame Balmont uttered as she and the maid swayed from side to side. "I shall retire." Madame Balmont, accompanied by children and servants, descended into the bowels of the ship.

"What is your name?" Esther asked the child.

"I'm not telling," shouted the boy.

"Perhaps you do not have a name."

"No name! No name!"

"Then I shall call you Joseph, because you remind me of my little brother." Esther was shouting now, too. The gentle wind had turned blustery as the ship left the shelter of land.

"Joseph. Joseph. Joseph. I like that name. He has a coat of many colours. I would like such a coat." The boy stamped his feet on the deck and laughed.

"I like the coat you have on," said Esther.

"It's only a purple coat. I wish it had more colours."

"You are lucky to have a purple coat." She pushed thoughts of her own Joseph and his coat out of her mind. Esther plunked herself down on a coil of rope and pulled a blanket out from her carpet bag. A small, wooden overhang gave them shelter from the wind. "Come. We can wrap this around us and watch the waves."

The boy did not protest. It was getting chilly. Esther wrapped the blanket around the two of them, closed her eyes and willed away bad thoughts. There was nothing in her past that gave her comfort and nothing in her future that gave her hope. But there was *now,* and for now, that had to be enough.

The sun set and night enveloped the ship. The air made them sleepy, why else would the two have dozed off? A cry roused them.

Esther jolted forward, brushed aside her hair and looked up. The ship's mast rocked back and forth as if grasped at the tip by a careless hand. Great flashes of light streaked through the sky followed by claps of thunder. Another flash came after that, then another and another. The wind grew fierce. A lightning bolt streaked across the sky and hit the ship's mast. Then came a crack of thunder and a splitting of wood, and then … nothing.

"Fire in the hold!"

Within moments the empty deck was filled up with stampeding people. They were running, or yelling, or both.

"What's wrong?" Joseph woke abruptly and rubbed his eyes with balled-up fists.

"I'm not sure." Holding the boy tightly Esther pulled her knees toward her chest.

"Maman," he cried. "I want my Maman!"

"Hush now. Your mother is safe, and she knows that you are with me." Esther's heart beat wildly. Where to run? Smoke began to drift up through the hatches. Passengers continued to race up the steps from below deck. They grabbed at each other, pulling each other down, crawling over one another like crabs in a pail. Their eyes were wide with fear as they stormed back and forth, pacing, scanning the dark sky. Mothers shrieked for their children, husbands shouted for their wives. Their screams were shrill and desperate. The boy struggled in her arms. It was like holding on to a cat who wanted to break free.

"Come, come here." Esther hugged the child harder.

The ship rocked. Passengers and sailors alike were sent sprawling across the deck. A man crashed down over Esther and the boy with the weight of a felled tree. Esther screamed. More timbers cracked. Sheets of sail came loose and flapped madly. The smoke grew thick. Among the cries and yells were the sounds of a winch lowering a small boat over the side.

"Maman!" The boy slipped from Esther's grasp, leapt up and flung himself into the crowd. He dodged between legs, manoeuvring his small body in odd directions.

The press of people left Esther spinning. She beat her hands against backs and chests. "Come back!" He was gone.

A flame shot out of the hold, sending Esther hurtling through the air and down the deck. Feet stomped her; flying hands and arms hit her. She tried to stand but managed only to cling to a twisted rail.

White light skimmed over dry canvas sails and raced toward the main boom. Fire consumed the topsail, running the length of the spar, leaping over lifts, sheets and halyards. The topsail tumbled and smashed against the ship's rails. Wood, rope and iron plummeted from above, slamming into the deck. The deck erupted into slivers of splintered wood as bits of sail and iron tumbled into the black water. The rigging, already in tatters, was suddenly engulfed in flames. The very deck beneath her rose and moved in one continuous wave. It was as if a grey carpet were rolling down the deck. Rats! The rats were abandoning ship.

"Every man for himself," cried a disembodied voice.

No amount of gasping could get air into her lungs. Smoke seared her nose and stung her eyes. A hand caught her arm and pulled her forward. The hand became an arm, the arm a body. She fought against it. Slapping, pushing.

"Get into the boat!"

Esther, still screaming for the boy, flung her head back and looked into the blue eyes of the sailor. "No!" She planted her hands on his chest and pushed as hard as she could. Her feet left the deck as she was hoisted up, then tossed over his shoulder like a sack. Smoke blinded her. She could not open her eyes for the pain. "Let me be!" and "Let me down!" Then came a thud as her body crumpled against the ribbed wooden bottom of the small boat. It bobbed with her falling weight. A rough hand shoved her to one side. Oars hit the water.

Esther gripped the edge of the boat and pulled herself up to look back at the ship. Smoke had formed a forbidding wall around it. The hull vanished in the thick haze. She looked around. The little boat was filled with sailors. *No, no!* The passengers had been left to die. The screams of the almost-dead cut through the dark.

Sailors yelled to each other. The ship would soon keel over, causing a swell that would envelop and swamp the little vessel. Esther curled and braced herself at the bottom of the wooden boat.

The craft crested with the waves, then plummeted down into a swirling valley. Sailors gripped the oars and fought to gain control. Up it went, then down again. All who sailed these waters knew of the rugged and rocky French coast that was before them. With sure knowledge, they knew that this small boat would be smashed against red, jagged rocks. And still the rain had not started.

A great crack echoed from the ship. Esther lifted her head. The ship was in flames fore and aft.

The passengers wailed, each shriek ripped from their throats. Gentile, Jew, Muslim, rich, poor, slave—all equals in death, and all crying out in despair to the same God, the father of Abraham. The ship rolled, the sea gulped and the calls of the dying were abruptly muted. The ship became a stone, and the stone ship sank.

Ahead, waves broke against the rocks, sending up purple pearls of water. Giant boulders rose up like the backs of whales. For the smallest of moments, rocks floated. And in a flash Esther's boat burst like a bubble. It splintered into a hundred pieces, hurtling each soul on board into the sea. The cold water enveloped her. Down she went.

A hand reached for her. It grabbed for her body, her clothes, an arm, a leg. The arm hugged her waist. Darkness surrounded them. Down and down they went. Her arms sliced through the water. With the force of a ball fired from a cannon she shot up. She gasped. She might explode with the suddenness of air that filled her chest!

A wave caught her and flung her against a rock. Seawater washed down her throat and was retched back up. She heaved as she struggled to breathe, then pulled herself onto the rock. Again a disembodied hand grasped for her in the dark. Esther caught the hand and pulled.

Strength, strength, give me strength.

The hand, then the body, fell over her, and the two lay draped over a rock not a stone's throw from shore.

The rain started.

*C*hapter 9

*E*sther lifted her head. Sand stuck to her face, hair and hands. She licked her cracked lips and tried to take in her surroundings. It was early morning, yet she had no memory of washing up on the beach. Wreckage from the ship littered the sand as far as the eye could see. Waterlogged timber, swaths of blackened sails, trunks, wooden casks and barrels, all matter of objects washed in with the tide. Bodies, bathed in the pale-yellow light of a new day, rolled in and out like flotsam.

"Get up." His voice was low and sharp. Esther gazed up into the blue eyes of the young sailor who had saved her. "Scavengers will come! We must get off the beach. Hurry!"

Esther was half pushed, half dragged into a cluster of rocks that stretched across the edge of the beach. Sharp stones pierced her bare feet. Her ripped dress fluttered around her legs. Beneath it, a white chemise billowed like a flag.

"Get down." He pulled her arm so roughly she nearly cried out.

They crouched on the beach's edge behind sparse bushes and rocks. A small scream caught in Esther's throat. She covered her mouth with her hand and bit down hard.

The purple coat. The boy, the one she'd called Joseph, was among the bodies at the water's edge! His small, twisted corpse lay face down in the sand. Tears and sick mingled in her throat. She should go down there. She should go to him. Esther lurched forward on hands and knees, clawing her way back through the bushes and over the rocks.

"Stay back! Look there!" He pointed to distant sand dunes. Esther squinted. Human shapes tumbled and slid down the dunes onto the beach. There were frenzied shouts, screams and whoops. Men, women with baskets, dogs, even children swarmed over the debris.

It was to the corpses that the scavengers went first. They ran as fast as rats, and for good reason. If caught they would be taken away and hanged, if not killed on the spot. The smaller bodies, those of children, were ignored. Jewels were ripped off men and women alike. A woman's dress was torn away, leaving her body bare. A scavenger found her hidden money pouch, held his booty aloft and howled. Esther patted her side and felt for her own pocket. It was still there.

A body moved on the beach. Yes, yes! Someone was alive out there! *It is the law that we not stand idly by when a human life is in danger.* Esther lunged forward. As she was about to cry out, a scavenger came upon the man. He pulled out a pistol, lifted it up in the air and bashed the half-alive man in the head with the handle. She felt herself crumple to the ground as the scream in her throat dissolved into a sob. Could such cruelty, such evil, exist?

She turned to the young sailor. He was scanning the rock face behind them, looking for safe passage. A trumpet sounded.

The king's own men were on the march. Like black beetles, the barbarous scavengers scattered and scurried across the beach and over the dunes.

"Come. We must leave or be mistaken for looters. Justice will be swift." The sailor pulled Esther to her feet. There were sand dunes at the back of the beach but cliffs, at either end, loomed as large as mountains. Without another word, the sailor led her up a steep path. They scrambled over sharp, red rocks as best their bare feet would allow. The sailor was faster, more sure-footed. Esther's soft hands bled as she repeatedly gripped rocks, long grass and thorny bushes. And yet the pain of her bloodied hands and stubbed feet were hardly felt, so urgent was the need to flee.

Up and up they climbed. They reached a bend in the path. Esther turned back. The view below was piteous. The grey, charred hull of the ship had drifted toward shore and lay, mostly submerged, on a sandbar. It resembled a thing once living, a whale, perhaps. Waves pummelled it as if attempting to reclaim it for the sea.

The king's horses were making their way up and down the beach. A soldier, with a spyglass pressed to his eye, scanned the beach, dunes and soaring cliffs. Esther ducked farther into the thorny foliage. Several soldiers at the far end of the beach had rounded up a handful of scavengers and were herding them toward the soldier with the spyglass. One luckless scavenger made a dash for freedom. He ran up the dunes, scrambling against the sand. A soldier on horseback levelled his musket and fired. The thief's arms were flung out. He wavered, then fell and rolled down onto the beach, trailing a stream of blood behind him.

She grew cold, so very cold.

The sailor touched her arm. "My name is Philippe. I mean you no harm."

Philippe—a Christian name. Esther sat on her haunches. She didn't reply, just puffed.

"I know your name. It is Esther."

"How? How is it you know who I am?" Her voice sounded meek but in truth she was becoming suspicious.

"I heard a man—your father, I think—call out to you as the ship set sail. And that woman, the one with so many children, I heard her say your name, too."

Esther nodded and felt something like relief. But what did names matter? She had to get home. She felt feverish, and the scratches that laced her arms and legs were beginning to itch. "Please, tell me the name of the nearest village?"

"We are near Biarritz."

Biarritz! They were not half a day's journey from her home in L'Esprit. Surely they could reach there by nightfall! She gazed down at her torn dress. It looked as if animals had attacked her, and worse, she was without a head-covering. She had neither coif nor bonnet nor hat to wear, nothing to show her reverence for God. She needed a moment to think, and yet her head was spinning.

Esther took hold of a nearby rock and pulled herself upright. The pain of her torn and battered feet shot up her legs and made her knees buckle. Her arms reached out to steady her but it was too late. Esther toppled forward and fell. Her head came down upon a sharp rock. Her old wound was opened. Blood poured out of the gash like red dye from a vat. It ran into her eyes and down her face.

The boy gasped. He had seen many an injury on board ship—and much worse ones, too—but this one seemed startling on one so young and so … beautiful. He reached for her chemise and tore off a long strip. Esther sat childlike and speechless as he wrapped the material around her head. But no sooner had he bandaged her head with the cloth than the blood seeped through it.

Philippe scooped Esther up into his arms. She attempted to protest. It was a feeble gesture. They set off along the rocky path toward the town. The road beneath Philippe's feet was steep and cobbled. He stumbled occasionally, caught himself and staggered on.

Esther tried to lift her head and look about but the sun was blinding. Large houses, on either side of the road, were mostly hidden behind pale walls and high fences. There was a smell in the air. What was it? Lemons, perhaps, and other fruits besides. Trees swayed in a honeyed breeze.

How beautiful. Trees were a luxury in the Jewish Quarter. There was no space for them to spread their limbs.

Philippe paused to catch his breath. He set Esther down by a small, plain building with a steeple as sharp as a pin. Esther, her thoughts still scattered and her vision not right, looked up at its sand-coloured walls. And it was there, on the steps of the parish Church of Saint Martin, in the town of Biarritz, that Esther closed her eyes at last and succumbed to exhaustion.

◦◦◦

Philippe burst through the back door into a warm kitchen and dumped his burden on a daybed by a small fire.

"*Bonjour, ma tante.*" He turned and grinned at a woman wearing a cook's cap and apron.

"Saints above! Have the *Anglais* arrived?" The old woman crossed herself twice. Philippe looked down. A smear of blood ran down his chest. "It's not my blood, Aunt," he said cheerfully.

"Take it off you, and be quick," said Cook as she flung open the doors of a large armoire at the back of the kitchen. It was empty save clothes on the upper shelves. She pulled down shirts and shawls and trousers, vests and clothes of all sorts. It was an old, well-established house, and when someone died or was run out, Cook claimed all they owned, and none dared question the seizure.

Philippe yanked his torn and bloody sailor's shirt over his head and stood bare-chested by the open fire. Cook flung him a shirt, which he caught and pulled over his head. That done, she turned her attention to the girl.

"What have you brought us this day, Philippe? A fish it isn't!" Cook peered down at the girl.

Esther moaned softly. The bleeding had stopped, but she was shivery and weak.

"A fish it might be, Aunt, for it was in the sea I caught her."

"Don't tell me, Philippe—was that your ship that went under just last night? Fire, was it?" She asked the question in a matter-of-fact manner and did not seem overly concerned that her nephew had nearly met his maker. A woman of some fifty years, she was stout, plain and grim. If there was any joy in life, she had yet to find it, and at this late date she didn't expect to.

Philippe nodded. "Hit by lightning and caught on the sandbar, too. Most souls lost, I fear."

The woman bent down over Esther. "Was she on the ship?"

"She was, and had a bump to the head after that." Philippe had thought twice about bringing Esther to his aunt. Her temper flashed like fire, and many had been singed by it. No one would have called his aunt either goodly or kind, but Philippe was her nephew, and well he knew that she held him in some regard.

Cook laid her hand on Esther's forehead. "She's feverish." She called over her shoulder, "Girl! Where is that useless thing?" she snarled. "GIRL!"

A small girl, hardly more than a child, hovering between the open kitchen fire and the firedogs, cautiously stepped out into the kitchen's light. She was a feeble thing, pretty, perhaps, had her face not been ravaged by the pox, leaving it pitted and scarred.

"*Là voilà*. Stop hiding and get me a cloth. Useless girl! They give me an indentured servant to assist me. What use is the little slave to me? I'd turn her out if I could."

The girl came running with a cloth. Cook snatched it from the girl's hand and then pulled off the bloodied bandage that Philippe had wrapped around Esther's head. "Burn this." She flung the bandage at the girl's feet. Cook dipped the cloth, filthy though it was, into a jug of water, then mopped Esther's brow. She was rough, and her touch was anything but motherly. Satisfied that the cut was closed, she crossed the great kitchen to stand above a bubbling pot. "A cup of broth will do her some good," she declared as she ladled a paltry amount into a mug and handed it to her nephew.

Philippe knelt down and gently held the mug out to Esther.

Esther sniffed. There was an aroma in the air. It was spicy and tantalizing. With blurry eyes and an aching head she looked away from Philippe and his offerings toward the great fire. A beast was turning on a spit. Its juices ran clear and sizzled on the logs that burned beneath it. Was the broth made from the bones of such an animal? From this vantage, it was hard to tell whether the thing was pig or cow.

"I am not hungry." She shook her head. The small movement caused waves of pain.

"You must be. Why do you not eat?" He spoke softly into her ear while watching his aunt in the distance.

"I … I am Jewish," she murmured.

"And Jews do not eat? I have heard many a strange thing about Jews, but what miracle is it that you do not need food?" he whispered.

"It is not … kosher."

"What does that mean?"

"It is not … clean."

Philippe's head snapped back. "Not clean? How is a freshly made cup of broth not clean?"

"Please, please, I meant no offence. I … I do not know …" Try as she might, Esther could not make sense of all that had happened.

"Might it not be best…?" Philippe paused, again looked over at his aunt, then bent to Esther's ear and whispered. "I mean, perhaps it would go better if you were not to mention that you are … Jewish."

"What goes on in my house under my very nose?" The booming voice startled both Esther and Philippe and sent kitchen staff scuttling to various corners of the room. Standing at the far entrance of the gigantic kitchen stood Catherine Churiau, widow (although neither husband nor corpse had ever been produced to prove it).

Philippe snapped to attention. Esther did what she could to rise but succeeded only in lifting up her shoulders and then thumping back on the pallet.

"We have a guest, Madame," Cook stated plainly as she continued to stir her pot of brew.

Catherine, a beguiling woman of no apparent age, dressed in the attire suited to a woman of the king's court, glided across the stone floor. Her fan fluttered at such a speed that Philippe felt its breeze as she passed by. It was uncommon for the lady of the house to frequent the kitchen, but then there was nothing common about Catherine.

"What is this—a street urchin? Cast it out. It is diseased!" Catherine's painted red lips curled as she regarded Esther with the same distaste as one might a maggot-ridden animal.

"No, Madame, she's been hurt," Philippe tried to explain.

"NO, MADAME? NO, MADAME!" She turned on the boy and bellowed. "WHO MIGHT THIS BE?" She snapped her fan shut and jammed it into his muscular chest.

"I am …" Philippe clutched the mug to him. Brown soup sloshed down his shirt. He stared ahead with a vacant look. Evidently he had forgotten who he was.

"His name is Philippe. He is my dead sister's boy. He and his little brother Mathieu are all the family I have," said Cook from a distance.

Catherine took a second look at the hale and hearty fellow. She moved closer still, until she was but a breath away. She bounced her fan off his chest, narrowed her eyes into cat-like slits and gazed directly into his. "How old are you?" she purred.

"He is a boy of sixteen, Madame. Away with you, boy. Tend to your little brother. I'll look after this one until you return." Cook walked across the room, ladle in hand, and motioned to Esther, who lay like a sorry lump of wax. "She'll be right with a little food in her. Away, now."

Philippe tried to move but his feet appeared to be hammered to the ground.

Catherine smiled at the boy, then caught a whiff of the broth. "What is that swill?"

"It is for your good mother, who sits alone in that great room of hers with hardly a soul to talk to. A good broth means the world to her and her constitution." Cook plucked the mug from Philippe's hand.

"Her CONSTITUTION?"

"Yes, Madame. Her CONSTITUTION!" The two women stood eye to eye, glaring at each other.

Catherine's mother, Marie de La Grange, a courtesan of some fame, had hired Cook when Catherine was a child. Cook's skills in the kitchen matched Marie's in the salon and bedroom. Thus, the house of Marie de La Grange—shared with her daughter, Catherine Churiau, who also became a courtesan—grew in renown. It was Cook's status within the household that allowed her to take in the girl over the objections of the lady of the house. But Cook was no fool. Many a servant who stepped out of her place found herself without a roof over her head. France teemed with poverty and starvation. Cook had no intention of finding herself homeless in her old age. Nevertheless, she wasn't about to let Catherine get the upper hand—not yet, anyway.

Catherine shrugged. She consoled herself with the thought that once her mother passed on, Cook would find herself out on her ear. Catherine relished the thought of the old goat in the poorhouse.

"The Duc de Richelieu will be dining, along with Count Benoit. There will be eighteen in all." Catherine's voice was riddled with contempt.

Esther could barely make out what was real and what was a dream. Who was this strange woman dressed from head to toe in mauve silk with the miniature pink roses racing up and down her dress? She turned her head ever so slightly and grimaced as the pain shot up her neck and into her head. Where was Philippe?

Among strangers, a familiar face, no matter how new, is a friend. Esther tried to say his name but all that issued forth were dry gasps.

"Hear that! She is ill, I tell you. I'll have no plague brought into my house." Catherine leapt back, extracted a handkerchief from her sleeve and covered her nose.

"There is no plague. I'll see her right." Cook shook her head in disgust.

"Philippe," Esther whispered as she tried to lift her head. Her eyes bulged and her ears knocked with the beat of her heart. Even her teeth ached.

Catherine turned her attention again to Philippe. Her eyes lingered over the boy, exuding a gushing warmth that turned Philippe's legs to jelly. "I should like to see you again—when you are twenty."

Philippe mouthed an inaudible sound and nodded. Try as he might, he was unable to extract his eyes from Catherine's creamy bosom.

Defying earth's natural pull, Catherine glided across the room as if she were riding a soft breeze.

"Philippe!" Cook snapped at her besotted nephew. His eyes still rested on the empty space that Catherine had just occupied. "Philippe!"

"Yes!"

"Attend to your little brother. Mathieu still boards with Madame Boucher and her growing brood. It would seem that her husband's boots need only be under the bed for her to be with child yet again. Poor France. Do we not have enough people in this country? Still, it is not a happy arrangement for your little brother. And take him this." Cook passed Philippe a loaf of hard bread and a lemon. "See that lemon right into his mouth. Those urchins of Madame d'Frome's will steal it as he chews. They will hang for theft one day, mark my word."

A squeal went up! It was a great, loud cry that made Cook leap. The little maid, who had done her best to make herself inconspicuous, huddled by the fire and howled. A burning ember had landed on the feeble girl's apron. The girl grabbed the crimson ember and flung it back into the fire, then let out a wail as her flesh sizzled.

"Foolish girl," said Cook as she marched over to the child, snatching a jug of water as she went. She doused the sorry girl with cold water. The shock of the fire, the burnt hand and then the cold water left the girl gasping.

"That apron will cost you!" Cook scowled.

The girl continued to sob, whether from pain or humiliation one could not tell. She thrust her whole hand into her mouth and licked and sucked.

"Philippe?" Esther called. She struggled up on her elbows. What was happening? Why was the girl in the corner crying? Where was she?

Philippe bent down and whispered into Esther's ear, "No fear. My aunt is as tough as an oxhide but she means no harm. I will be back."

What? He meant to leave her there? Esther was suddenly as alert as a cat. "No, take me with you," she cried.

He almost laughed. "You are not well."

"I can't stay here!" Even as she spoke, Cook screeched at another servant for yet another misdeed.

"Then I shall send word to your family. They can come and get you."

Esther's whole body lurched forward. No, they wanted to be rid of her. She would not go back—not yet, anyway. But what should she do? If only her head did not ache so. "Please, please take me with you." She tried not to cry.

"No girl can go where I am going. A girl cannot work, and without work, you cannot eat." Philippe pitied her, but what could he do? She was ill, and she was a lady, or at least very much like a lady. Her hands were soft and she was well spoken. He'd bet his last coin that she could read, maybe write, too.

"I will not be any trouble, none at all." The room seemed to spin as she tried to stand. She fell back with a thump.

"Stay here, just for a while. I promise that I will return." He didn't know what else to say. It wouldn't do for her to be out on the streets. No girl with her looks would last long out on her own, that was certain. He turned away. Those eyes of hers seemed to bore right through him.

"What's this? You still here?" Cook turned on Philippe. If she held him in any esteem it was not reflected in her voice at that moment.

Philippe gave his aunt a hearty grin, then ducked out the door.

"Wait!" Esther cried, but he was gone.

Chapter 10

⁓

The smell was beguiling. It brought her up, up, up out of a sleep so deep, no dream would have dared intervene. It wasn't a smell … it was a fragrance, an aroma, a scent so powerful that her mouth watered, and though half asleep Esther licked her lips. She awoke hungrier than she had ever been in her life.

She lifted her head and tried to make out the shapes and sounds that surrounded her. It seemed as if she was forever waking up in a muddled state. The rocks piled beside her were warm. There was a hard bed beneath her. It was not a bed at all, really, but a pallet of wood covered with straw, and a rag that might once have passed for a blanket lay on top of her.

"You are awake at last."

Esther cried out. The girl standing above her was covered in blood. It dripped from her mouth. It was on her hands. Her apron was streaked with a deep red.

The girl's eyes grew round. Her hands flew to her face as she too screamed. The child leapt back and, shaking like a frightened puppy, she cowered against a wall. The two could only stare wordlessly at one another.

A moment passed, then another. The girl looked down at her red-splattered dress. "It is my day to pit the cherries, Mademoiselle," she explained.

Esther's head fell back on the pallet. Cherries. The girl was covered in cherry juice. She would have laughed if she'd had the strength.

"You have been asleep a day now." The girl crawled forward. She shoved a bandaged hand under Esther's head and drew a mug to Esther's parched lips. Broth dribbled down her throat. One gulp, two, Esther coughed up the third and sent the liquid spewing through the air. The liquid splattered over the girl's tattered, stained and badly mended apron.

"I'm sorry." Esther's voice was raspy. She ran the back of her hand over her mouth.

"No matter." The girl shrugged. How could a few more spills make a difference?

"That broth, what is it made of?"

"Broth is made of broth!" replied the simple child.

"From what bones?"

"Chicken bones."

Esther nodded as she sat and slumped forward. That was probably all right, although, truth be told, keeping kosher mattered little to her at that moment.

"Would you like more?" The girl held out the mug. Esther took it gratefully.

The child was a filthy little thing. One could hardly tell where the dirt of her clothes ended and the dirt on her person began. And her hair, what colour might it be? Perhaps flaxen if it were washed. Maman would make short work of her, that was certain. Maman's pocket! Esther bolted straight up. The few coins, everything she had in the world, were in the pocket. Esther patted her skirt with a flat hand, then lifted the blanket. Her pocket was gone.

"I hid this." The girl reached under the pallet on which Esther lay and shyly pulled out the pocket that had dangled from Esther's belt. Esther sighed and flopped back. "It was me who cared for you while you were sleeping." The girl spoke with a mixture of eagerness and pride. "Cook says you are to get your strength back, for she'll not have a corpse lying about her kitchen." The girl pushed the mug back under Esther's chin, then leaned in close and whispered, "Even a corpse must work in Cook's kitchen." Esther smiled. "No need to laugh at me, Mademoiselle. They say Cook would think nothing of turning a dead body into stew."

"What are you saying, girl?" Cook's voice reverberated off the walls. She crossed the room and towered above the two.

The girl went mute. She clutched the mug to her belly and before Esther's eyes seemed to dissolve into the wall.

"Wipe your mouth. The next time I catch you eating the cherries I'll have your eyes, you hear me? Go and change that apron. You look like a butcher. As for you—what is your name?" Cook snarled. She was not a fat woman, as most cooks seemed to be, but sharp and pained looking. Her face was broad, with eyes like mouse holes burrowed in the dirt and eyebrows thick enough to make do as two moustaches. And her nose was so pointy it could no doubt have cut the rind off cheese. "Do you not know your own name?" Her snarl had turned into a growl.

Esther clutched the thin blanket to her with one hand and struggled up onto two wobbly feet. "Esther Brandeau," Cook snarled.

"You are a friend of my nephew's. It is for his sake that I offer you my kindness. Girl, where are the dress and sabots?"

The girl, now wearing a cleaner but equally shabby apron, scurried across the room and flung open the doors to a kitchen armoire. She pulled down a pair of small sabots, an apron and two dresses.

"What keeps ya?" bellowed Cook. The girl quickly chose the dress with fewer holes. She ran back and gave the lot to Esther.

"Idiot! It is the other one," screamed Cook. She flung the dress back into the girl's face. The girl, perhaps fearing a whack, scuttled back and forth, then placed the second dress in Esther's hands instead.

Cook's pea-sized eyes narrowed as she leaned down toward Esther and hissed in her ear, "You have taken advantage of my Christian charity for two days, so it's four days' work out of you I expect. You are to scrub down this floor. Can you cook?"

Esther paused. It was said that Gentiles gave little thought to what went down their gullets. Why, she had heard that they would eat anything with legs, including a table if it be covered with sauce.

"I can bake bread, Madame."

"Bake, you say? Then bake you shall. Get this one to help you." Cook pointed to the beleaguered maid. "Bake!" Cook threw her head back and laughed.

"Madame, the boy, Philippe—will he return soon?" Esther asked tentatively.

"He is a sailor. He comes and goes with the tide. There is little to hold him here except his small brother."

"Has he no other family?" Esther pressed for every bit of information. At that moment, he was her only contact with the outside world.

"His parents and seven brothers and sisters are all dead." Cook, making the sign of the cross over her chest, offered her words up grudgingly. She was no talker unless it suited her. She turned and walked away.

"Madame?" Esther called after her. How should this woman be addressed? But she was gone.

Esther stared down at the poor clothes in her hands. The homespun linen was of the worst quality. Papa would never have had such cloth in his shop, and Maman would not have used such stuff even for sacking. Esther might be indebted to this house, but she had not asked to be brought here, and she was not a servant. Still, she couldn't go on wearing her own tattered dress.

She looked about her. Although the kitchen was half below ground, sunlight streamed through high windows. It was an immense room, not small and dark like the rooms in her house in the Jewish Quarter. She had never been in such a room before, never even thought it possible that rooms could be so big and airy and filled with light.

Esther ducked into a corner to slip on her new (although it was neither new nor clean) dress, apron and sabots. She would have to account to Papa for these missing days and nights. Think of what the neighbours would say when they heard that she had spent the night in a Christian house, and that a Gentile boy had helped her. Everyone would find out, Sarah would see to it, even if it meant that her own reputation would be tarnished by the telling. There would be more snickering, more finger-pointing. Time, she needed time to think. What would it matter if she spent one night or two, or ten, for that matter, in a Christian home? Her problems could not get worse. Besides, it was Papa who had sent her away. She looked around again. She would stay, at least until Philippe returned.

"What is your name?" Esther asked the girl.

The girl shrugged.

"You must have a name!"

"No, I do not think so. Leastways, I forget it." Her eyes dropped to the floor while her hands twisted clumps of her dress. The girl had a bird-like quality to her, as if a slight wind would pitch her into flight.

"How did you come to this house?" Esther spoke softly, half expecting the girl to flutter away.

"My father left me here. I tend the fire and turn the spit." The girl pointed to the fireplace and a long rod that stretched across the open flame. As she extended her arm, the sleeves of her dress fell back. The tips of her fingers were stumps, and the few nails left to her were blackened shells. Copper-coloured burns ran up and down her swollen arms. There were blisters and boils, too, some threatening to burst. She was covered in bites, and lice were making a meal of her. Still, her arms were big and strong from turning the spit day in and day out. It was possible that she could pound and pummel bread dough.

"Let me see your hand—the one you burned," Esther asked gently.

Slowly, like a trusting dog offering up a wounded paw, the girl lifted her bandaged hand. Esther unwrapped it and sniffed the wound. Despite the filth, there was no sign of puss.

"We must find a clean bandage."

"Oh no, Mademoiselle. I must not use anything new." Her eyes widened with panic.

Esther looked around. "Well, we shall wash out my old chemise and tear it into strips. That way you can have a fresh bandage every day until it is healed. Come, let me run water over your hand." The child, overwhelmed perhaps, only nodded. "We might even run some water over you."

"Me? Oh no, Mademoiselle. That would open the pores and expose me to sickness. 'Tis well known that washing brings on the sickness. My mother told me so."

"Where is your mother?"

"She is with the angels, Mademoiselle. God wanted her, and my baby brother as well."

Esther said nothing; there was nothing to say.

"Do you want to learn how to make bread?"

The girl looked up. Her eyes brightened, and she nodded. If she made bread there was a chance she could eat it, too.

"If you want to be a bread-maker, you must be clean. Where do you sleep?"

The girl pointed to the corner of the room. It was alive with lice, any fool could see that. And it was infested with mice and stank of rotting vegetables. Esther could think of nothing to say to that either. She could only look at this sweet child and wonder why God had abandoned one so helpless.

"Philippe told me to care for you." The child smiled a thin, small smile.

"Philippe—what of him? Is there news?" Esther nearly leapt at the girl. He was the key—if he brought her here, he could take her away again.

"I know nothing, Mademoiselle, though it is said that he may be back on the ships."

Esther slumped down on a bench and pondered her fate. What would Maman be doing right now? Would Papa be searching for her?

The girl sat beside Esther, her head again drooping like a dead flower. "It wasn't my Maman's fault that I was given away."

Esther put an arm around the girl. "We are the same, you and I."

～⁓～

"Philippe!" Cook yelled to the boy who filled the doorway. Esther's heart jumped. She had bided her time these past three days, but impatiently so.

"What news have you of your brother Mathieu? Does he fare well?" Cook charged across the stone floor and pinched Philippe's cheeks until tears welled in his eyes. Esther looked up at Philippe but made no move to speak to him. It was best she wait for Cook to cease her prattle.

"Not as well as I had hoped, Aunt. For certain he is with a hard family. They want more than I earn to keep him. I gave them a coin for now, but I will have to take him with me soon." Philippe looked around the room before resting his eyes on Esther. His smile faded as he took in her sorry state. His aunt had wasted no time at all in turning her into a drudge.

"He's too young for the ships, Philippe. I can have him here for a year or two. No more than that, mind. There is work here for a small boy. Take this. Eat." Cook handed him a crisp apple. The old woman looked past Philippe to a kitchen maid who was attempting to baste the hind of a cow. "What is it you are doing? Fool! Fool! Have I not taught you better than that?" Cook stomped across the kitchen, grabbed the spoon out of the maid's hand and then smacked her with it.

Esther leapt toward Philippe. "What news have you?" It was all she could do to contain herself.

"There is much to tell, but are you well?"

"Well enough. What of my father? He must be looking for me. We are not far from my home. Well you know that St. Esprit is just a few furlongs down the coast."

Philippe's mouth pulled tight across his jaw. Esther searched his face for clues of things to come. "What is wrong? Do you not recall my father? He came to see me off on the ship. He is tall—"

"Esther, you are listed as deceased. All the passengers on the ship are believed to be dead. No one is looking for you."

Dead? The word had no place to settle in her mind. *Dead?* Her knees grew weak. She stumbled back until she felt a bench then sat with a thud. Would they have said *kaddish*? Would they, even now, be sitting *shiva*? What would they feel? Joseph would miss her, but he was young, he'd soon forget, and Samuel was but an infant. Benjamin, the rabbi, might pretend to miss her, although he would not. She and her brother Abraham had once been close, when they were little, but now he was busy doing the things boys did to prepare for manhood. As for Sarah, she would now be the only daughter, a jewel. Esther sighed. Grand-mère would go to her grave happy. As for Papa, if Grand-mère spoke the truth and she was illegitimate, then might he think that her death was a blessing in disguise? *Oh Maman, dear Maman, only you will truly grieve.*

It was as if a wave washed over her. Esther Brandeau was dead. Dead to the world, alive only to God. Esther drew in a breath. She would not have to marry Red the Rag-picker. She would not have to go to Amsterdam and be shut away in a room with only the walls to talk to. Never again would Maman weep over her bad behaviour. Never again would she disgrace her family.

Esther looked up at Philippe and might have said something had Cook not bellowed, "Off with you, Philippe. Your friend Esther makes the bread." Cook shook with laughter.

Chapter 11

⁓꧁⁓

"**M**adame Catherine wants you to attend her in the main salon." Cook made the announcement from the doorway that bridged the baking room and the kitchen. Catherine's personal maid stood behind Cook. She folded her arms across her chest and tapped her foot impatiently.

Esther looked past the three masonry ovens, several kneading troughs and two trestle tables and felt herself grow pale. Did Madame Catherine not like the new breads and cakes Esther had introduced? Had she perhaps gone too far? Esther had no intention of remaining in this house forever, but she was not yet ready to leave.

"Hurry! Are you deaf?" Cook bristled.

"I cannot …" Esther held out two dusty hands. She could not be seen in a salon as she was. Every part of her was covered with flour.

"Do not keep Madame waiting. GO!"

Esther plunged her hands into a bucket of water and turned

to the girl beside her. "Quick, fetch me a clean apron."

The girl's feet seemed riveted to the floor. Tears filled her eyes. In her new role as baker's assistant she had found, for the first time in her sorry life, someone who neither kicked nor beat her. But there were changes afoot, the girl could feel it. And then what would happen to her? She'd be forced to spend the rest of her life banking the fire and turning the meat.

"Do as you are told, girl!" Cook charged across the room, and with a swipe of her hand the girl was sent sprawling on the stone floor.

Esther winced. It wasn't the first time Cook had used such force.

The girl scuttled across the floor like a crab on a beach, then scrambled up onto her feet. She skirted Cook's long reach and returned with a clean, blue apron.

Esther donned the apron. There was no looking glass in the kitchen, no way of telling if her hair was smoothly combed under its dusting of flour. Esther trailed the silent maid up the stairs, out of the kitchen and, unknowingly, into a new world.

⤛⤜

"What took you so long?"

The maid curtsied, mumbled an apology, then turned on her heel. Esther stood in the middle of the most magnificent room she had ever seen. The colours were pink, plum and white silk and the furniture was fat and soft. Great paintings of women in various stages of undress graced each wall. Was this how Gentiles decorated their homes? How amazing! What would Grand-mère think?

"What are you looking at? I am speaking to you." Madame Catherine stamped her foot. She and Cook had much in common.

"Yes, Madame." Esther curtsied.

"Do give the girl a chance, Catherine."

Esther turned to find the source of the voice. There, languishing in a mellow posture on a far chaise longue, sat an odd-looking insect of a man. In one hand he held something long and thin. She had never seen snuff or cigars before, let alone cigarettes. The man drew smoke into his body while sloshing golden liquid around in a glass. He took a puff, then a long sip. His black eyes peered at her all the while.

"Are you the new baker that old trollop has employed without my permission?" Catherine spoke to Esther in a loud, commanding voice.

What was an old trollop? Who was an old trollop? She couldn't think of a single thing to say.

"Do you not speak?"

"I have baked the bread in your kitchens for three days now."

"Three days, is it?" Catherine regarded Esther as if she had just been discovered on the bottom of her shoe. "Ah, I know who you are. You are the misery I saw in the kitchen." Esther nodded. "Well, the bread is ... good. You may stay."

Stay in the kitchen? Did she want to stay?

"Thank you, Madame." Esther curtsied then dithered. Was she dismissed?

"Wait. What is your name?"

"Esther Brandeau."

"Esther? What kind of name is that? Esther? Where are you from?"

"St. Esprit."

"Who is your family?"

This was it. The moment had come sooner than planned.

Esther squared her shoulders and looked her new employer in the eyes. "I have no family."

"No family! None at all? Have you lost them? Forgetful, are you?" His voice was high, but falsely so, as if he was speaking through his nose on purpose. How was Esther to know that such a nasal manner of speaking was the fashion in Louis XV's court?

A powdered blue wig was perched upon his head, a paper mole graced his cheek and his lips were painted a scarlet red. He was a profusion of colours: striped green silk shirt, red vest that no doubt sparkled in the lamplight, yellow sash, purple woollen breeches and copious ruffles at the neck and sleeves. Polished brass buttons ran up his embroidered waistcoat. He wore pink stockings and stubby, high-heeled shoes topped with red silk bows. Mostly he was oily; even his tongue seemed coated in grease.

"My parents are dead," said Esther. The lie tripped off her tongue. Maman used to say that a lie was a never-ending road with no way off and no way back.

"You may go." Catherine waved her away while refilling her glass from a crystal decanter.

"Wait!" The man, if he could be called a man, jumped up. He walked toward her like a grasshopper, with knees and forehead seemingly determined to arrive before the rest of him. His long spidery fingers grasped Esther's chin and tilted her head up. He smelled of fruit, pomegranates perhaps, and dust. "Look at her eyes! And this face! It's too long, of course, but it's interesting. And how fashionable, a delicate mole in just the right place." The man peered at her upper lip. His small black eyes seemed to bore a hole right through her. "Open your mouth, girl."

Esther clamped her mouth shut and stepped back. She took another step back, then another and another.

"What's wrong with you? Do as Monsieur Bernard says. Open your mouth," snapped Catherine.

With her back imprinted on the silk-covered wall, Esther parted her lips.

Monsieur Bernard stuck his dirty finger on her lip and pulled down, then up. "Ahhhhhhh," he said with satisfaction. "Perfect teeth." He sniffed. "Sweet-smelling breath, too."

How dare he! But he was not finished. He poked his finger deeper into her throat and, by sheer reflex, Esther bit down.

"Oh!" he squealed. "The little beast bit me!"

Catherine screamed with laughter. "Serves you right!"

"I think her talents may be wasted in the kitchen, my dear Catherine." The man plugged his wounded finger in his mouth and sucked, leaving Esther trembling with humiliation.

"What are you suggesting, Jean? Have you changed your tastes? Do you fancy my little bread-maker?"

Monsieur Bernard dismissed Catherine's barb with a snort. "Were you not saying that you had no daughter or protegé to mould? That you had no one to care for you in your old age?"

The man had Catherine's attention, for she stopped and cocked her head. "Surely you are not suggesting that a scullery maid be turned into my protegé?"

Esther watched them both intently. What was a protegé?

"She has no family. She has a quality about her, a natural elegance, shall we say. And she is clean. Think of her, dear Catherine, as a lump of clay, or perhaps bread dough. She is yours to mould, or bake, as you see fit." That said, the revolting man threw himself down on the chaise longue and tapped his long fingers against his bowed, scarlet lips. "Walk," he commanded.

Esther stood still.

"I said walk. Shall I take a whip to you?"

Esther took one step, then two.

"See? A natural. She walks like a princess!" The man appeared to take credit for Esther's ability to put one foot in front of the other. A baby cutting milk teeth could walk. What did he mean?

"Get out." Catherine, suddenly bored, waved her hand in Esther's direction.

The door she had entered was now clear across the room. Esther opened the door nearest her instead and ran down the hall. Which way was the kitchen? She turned and charged down another hall and another after that. Her heart was beating wildly, although she knew she was in no danger. A set of stairs led up, but none down. Maybe if she went up a flight, she would come to other stairs that would lead back down three flights. This was silly. How could she get lost in a house?

"Can I help you?" The voice came from a room to her right. Esther stopped short, turned and looked tentatively into the room. An older woman, though still beautiful, wearing a soft green dress and holding a book, sat by a window. Her dark hair was wound around her head in a soft roll. A black ribbon bound a long curl that draped over her shoulder. In its simplicity, it was pure elegance. Her only adornment was a bejewelled cross that hung around her neck.

"I am … lost, Madame." Esther curtsied.

"Lost!" She spoke gently, kindly, too. "My goodness. Has my house grown?"

Her house? Esther had assumed that the house belonged to Catherine Churiau.

"What is your name?" asked the woman.

"Esther."

"Like Esther in the Bible?"

Esther nodded.

"Do you know the story of Esther?"

Of course she knew the story, but should she admit it? Esther shook her head.

"I should think not. The biblical Esther was a mistress of disguise. She is not a proper example for a young girl. She was Jewish, and yet she hid her true identity from her husband and his kingdom."

"But it was for a purpose, Madame. Esther saved her people and ..." She stopped. She had revealed too much.

"In the end she saved her people, but what of her reasons in the beginning for deception? Of course you would not know the answer to that. Did you not just say that you do not know the story of Esther?"

"I ... I was confused, Madame." Her face coloured.

"Can you read?"

"*Oui,* Madame."

"Well, you should content yourself with the New Testament. What do you do in my house, Esther?"

"I am the baker."

"Then it is you who is responsible for the delicious bread I have been eating of late! You should be congratulated. It has been many years since I have tasted challah. But is this how my daughter dresses our servants?"

Her daughter! Was this Catherine's mother?

"Cook ..."

"Ah, Cook! Cook runs that kitchen like an army captain. Ask her to give you suitable clothes immediately. No, tell her to come and see me. I will tell her to outfit you properly."

"*Oui,* Madame." Esther curtsied.

"The stairs to the left will lead you to a hall. At the end of that hall are more stairs. You'll find your way. And Esther, when you are settled, come back and visit me. I am alone most often and would enjoy the company."

"Madame, how may I address you?" Esther knew the question was impertinent, and so she asked it in the smallest of voices with her eyes cast to the floor.

"My name is Marie de La Grange. This is my house." The woman's laugh was not harsh like Catherine's but soft, like a gentle rain.

Esther received two blue aprons, a skirt, blouse, chemise, a new pair of wooden sabots and two caps, one for the night and one for the day.

"Good work." Esther spoke kindly to the girl who stood over the kneading trough pummelling the dough. The girl looked up and smiled. She, too, was the happy recipient of a new smock and cap. She had smiled more in the last three weeks than she had in her entire life.

Esther had been right about the girl's arms. She might have been tiny, but after years turning the spit over a hot fire her arms were strong and well suited to kneading bread dough. As for her hands, they were scarred but well healed.

Esther surveyed the trays of risen dough. Yes, they were to her liking. She pulled off a piece the size of an olive and tossed it into the oven fire.

"Why ... why do you do that?" the girl asked.

"It is a tradition my mother taught me. The first of the dough must be given unto the Lord as a gift. And these," Esther took a good-sized lump of dough and divided it into three thin strands, "are to symbolize truth, peace and justice." She braided the three strands, making one large challah loaf.

"I have never heard of such a … tradition?"

Esther paused. She should not have revealed herself so. Who knew what the girl might repeat? It wasn't that she had set out to hide the fact that she was Jewish, it was just that it had been easier in the beginning not to say anything, and now … and now?

"It is nothing, not really a tradition, just something my mother does," murmured Esther. The girl, who never really knew her mother, nodded her head knowingly.

Esther prepared a tray for Madame de La Grange. She wrapped a special small challah loaf in a linen napkin. There had been no chance to thank Madame for the clothes, as Cook would not allow kitchen servants to venture to the top of the house. But Madame would know that the bread was from her, of that Esther was certain.

Esther slid the last batch of bread for the day into the oven and looked to the girl to gain courage. She took a deep breath. Esther was ready to challenge Cook. The upstairs servants had reported that Catherine and Madame de La Grange were well pleased with the bread. Cook would not get rid of her easily if the ladies of the house were pleased. Still … No, to dither was to falter. She must confront Cook now, before she lost heart. She took another deep breath, then barged through the doors into the main kitchen. Air escaped from one room to the other and kitchen staff and house servants, awaiting their noon meal, breathed in the bread-scented air that wafted through the doors.

Cook stood above a copper pot sipping soup. Esther paused and then spoke plainly. "I want a proper room to sleep in."

The chatter in the kitchen hushed. The only sound left was the sucking slurp of Cook as she tasted soup from the pot.

"Cook, I ..." Esther faltered.

"I heard you. A room, is it? Miss High-and-Mighty wants a room!"

The staff snickered nervously. Unnoticed, the girl had followed Esther into the kitchen and now leaned silently against a far wall.

"I will no longer sleep behind that!" Esther pointed to the great fireplace.

Cook's eyes narrowed and her forehead creased. She put down her ladle, turned with the deliberate speed of a man-o'-war and stared hard at Esther.

Be brave, thought Esther. *Be brave.* Her heart beat so loudly in her ears she could barely hear, which was fine, since there was only silence to be heard.

Time passed, an immeasurable amount of time. Finally, the old crow jutted out her lower jaw and said, "I want double the loaves for the next ten days."

It was a silly request. What would it matter how much bread was made? A household could only consume so much. Simply, Cook did not want to appear to be cowed in front of the staff. Esther nodded. She would double their production, triple it if necessary. But Esther was not finished with her demands.

"And ... I want her to have a bed in my room, too." Esther pointed to the girl, who had now shrunk into a small ball against the wall.

"She's an indentured servant here to tend the fire. It's well that she learn the baking trade, but I'll not have her out of her place!"

If Esther backed down now, the girl would forever be tucked up by the fire, a slave to the whims of others. She took another deep breath and stood her ground.

Cook sighed. "Very well. Philippe's brother, my nephew, will be here soon. He can tend the fire. Just as well he has something to do. But I'll not have any interference with market day. The girl will carry a basket along with the rest."

Esther agreed. Two or three servants always trailed Cook on market day as she paraded about the square like a chicken on parade. It was the only time the girl saw more than these walls, felt the sun on her face or met those who did not look upon her with scorn.

"But you mind me, it will do no good to have that girl think she's better than she is," Cook carried on, wagging her finger in front of Esther's nose. "Now get to work."

"There's one more thing," said Esther.

"Grrrr," she growled like a beast.

The kitchen staff scattered. Gently, ever so quietly, the butler reached across a table and pulled a butcher's knife out of Cook's reach.

"The girl has a name," said Esther.

"A *name*?" Cook twisted and reeled as her hard black eyes darted around the room. She spied the pathetic creature, and with lips curled in disgust she pointed and bellowed, "WHAT IS YOUR NAME?"

The girl opened her mouth. Nothing came out, not a word, not even a squeak. Her sorrowful face and soulful eyes looked helplessly at Esther.

"Her name is Pearl." Esther spoke so that all could hear plainly.

"*Pearl!* What kind of name is that for a waif? Why, a shadow has more weight. We shall call her Shadow." Cook laughed and sneered at the same time.

Miracles happen. The girl, who had never quibbled with the world's judgments, never questioned her lowborn place, stood as tall as her battered body would allow and said, "My name is Pearl."

*C*hapter 12

༺෴༻

E sther and Pearl moved into their new room that very night. It wasn't so much a room as a wardrobe, and the beds were not so much beds as straw-covered pallets, and the room was bare except for two hooks and a candleholder. But it had one adornment that Esther treasured—a window. True, it was high up on the wall and only an arm's length in width, but it was nevertheless a window.

Exhausted beyond measure, they tumbled into their beds. Pearl's teeth chattered as she pulled her thin blanket up over her shoulders.

"Here, sleep beside me," said Esther. They curled up like two spoons in a drawer, and then both were warm. "Have you not seen your family since you came to this house?" Esther asked.

"My Maman died birthing her ninth in ten years. The baby was laying crosswise inside her and there was nothing I could do." Pearl spoke in a matter-of-fact voice. "Papa married again soon after Maman was taken away. Our new mother would have none of us. I was put out to work and told not to darken her door no more."

"And what of your younger brothers and sisters?"

"I know nothing of them," Pearl whispered.

Joseph and baby Samuel—what if she never knew what happened to them?

"We shall be each other's family now." Esther gave her a hug. "You shall be my little sister. I have never had a little sister, not really." Esther did not mention that she had never had a friend, either.

"Why did you call me Pearl?"

"Because you are a treasure, a *petit bijou*." Esther spoke in a voice heavy with sleep.

Pearl, too, closed her eyes but not before tears, as round as pearls, had rolled down her face.

⁓

Days and nights passed, and not unhappily. Once Cook felt sure that Esther would not try to usurp her position, the rhythm of the kitchen continued uninterrupted.

Every morning Esther and Pearl awoke in the dark and prepared the morning loaves. They worked side by side, sharing secrets and singing simple songs. Esther had to teach Pearl how to sing. The girl balked at first, as though the sound of her voice was frightening, but as each note was connected to a word, and the words were strung into a tune, the girl found the pleasure in it. Counting and the alphabet followed. They ate well, and with a loaf of bread in Pearl's belly each day, the girl was gaining weight and even had a little colour in her cheeks.

A day came when Pearl giggled. It was such a foreign sound to the girl's ear that she came to a standstill. Her eyes grew round and her face took on a look of such astonishment that Esther nearly fell over laughing.

It was weeks before Esther set eyes on Philippe again. But one day the door between the kitchen and the baking room banged open and there he was, grinning.

"You look fit," said Philippe.

"As do you."

For a moment they stared at each other. She was still the most beautiful woman he had ever seen, though *beautiful* hardly seemed the right word. But where would a sailor such as himself find lofty words to describe her looks?

"I came to say goodbye."

Goodbye? Esther's eyes grew round and her mouth gaped open. But why should Philippe's announcement take her by surprise? The life of a sailor was to come and go. "Where are you going?"

"My ship sails at first tide. We sail to Spain and on from there. It may be that I do not return for many months."

Months? Up until then she had given little thought to the future. No, that wasn't true. She was always thinking about what had been, what might have been, and what was to come. It was just that she had not *decided* about the future. To *not decide* was to stay suspended in time. As long as Philippe was close at hand she could return home at a moment's notice and explain away her absence by saying ... by saying what? If only she could go with him.

"Will you be here on my return?" He looked eager, his blue eyes bright and wanting. She needed to make a decision. She thought of Pearl, the few hard-earned coins in her pocket, her small room and the satisfaction of pulling the bread out of the oven each day.

"The work is hard, but I will stay awhile longer."

Philippe grinned. If her look was dark and mysterious, her scent was light and airy. He thought he might kiss her … but he pulled away, half ashamed, partly embarrassed. She was of a higher class and not for the likes of him.

The upstairs maid poked her head into the bread-making kitchen. "Madame wishes to see you in her boudoir."

"Why?" Esther looked up from the kneading table, but the maid's face was blank. There had been no complaints—Esther was sure that Cook would have passed along any criticisms happily. What could Catherine want with her? There were ten loaves in the oven, and while Pearl could be left to knead, she was not ready to take on the entire bread-making process. Mind, if worst came to worst, there would still be time to put in another batch.

Esther sighed, gave Pearl some instructions and rolled down her sleeves. She peered about the main kitchen. Cook was nowhere to be seen. Good, perhaps she could get back before the old woman even knew she was gone. The maid was tapping an impatient foot.

Esther followed her to Catherine's boudoir and gently scratched at the door.

"Enter," shouted a voice.

She pushed open the door and stood in the main bedchamber. This house, and its furnishings, continued to astonish Esther. Catherine's boudoir was not one room but a series of connecting rooms. Esther's view took in several chambers beyond. In front of her a great, canopied bed stood in the middle of the room. Tall, blood-red velvet curtains were tied back behind an immense carved oak headboard. Rumpled pink silk sheets and a goose down quilt lay across the bed. There were many chaise longues, chairs and pillows in the room. A kennel, decorated to match the fabric of Catherine's bed curtains, stood against a far window.

Catherine's small dog ran up to Esther and danced about. It had brown, curly, heavily perfumed fur, floppy ears and a short snout for a nose. She wasn't the least bit afraid of it. Why, it was hardly a dog at all, more like a silly, long-haired cat. Esther reached down and patted it while peeking into a small room that housed a canopied bathtub. Beyond that was what some called the "English place"—a water closet or foreign toilet, imported from England.

While attending to her toilette, Catherine languished in a long, velvet wrapper in front of her dressing table. The front of her hair was done up in curling papers while Jeanne, Catherine's personal maid, stood behind brushing her tresses with long sweeps. Without rouge or powders, Esther thought Catherine a great beauty.

"Don't stand there. Come where I can see you," Catherine snapped.

Esther walked across the room and stood near, but not too near.

"Enough." Catherine flicked her hand at Jeanne. "Open the windows and leave us."

Jeanne dutifully put down the brush and opened a far window that stretched from the floor to the ceiling. A sun as yellow as churned butter stood in the sky and birds twittered in the trees of Catherine's enclosed garden. The scent of lemon blossoms soon filled the room. Such was the life of a courtesan, although, beyond giving elaborate parties that seemed to last for days, it was not really clear to Esther just what a courtesan did to achieve such power and wealth.

"I have been thinking about you." Catherine sipped her chocolate and paused. She spoke in measured tones, as if each word were heavy.

"Me, Madame?" Why would Catherine give a girl such as herself a moment's thought?

Catherine picked up a puff, dipped it in a shallow dish and dusted her face with sparkly, speckled powder. "I have been thinking about what my friend Monsieur Jean Bernard suggested." Esther recoiled at the mere mention of the oily man's name. "I am told that you can read and write. Is it true?"

"Yes, Madame."

"Do you know your age?"

"I am almost fifteen years, Madame."

"A perfect age." Catherine smiled.

Perfect? Perfect for what? The only thing fourteen was perfect for was—

"No!" Esther backed up. The dog, sensing something, began to yap.

"*Viens ici,* Poppie," Catherine called to the little dog. "What is wrong with you?"

"I will not marry him." Esther felt the door behind her.

"Marry?" Catherine's eyes widened. Her mouth fell open and out came peals of laughter. "Marry Monsieur Bernard? Wait until I tell him! Oh, oh!" Her laughter continued unabated until tears rolled down her face. "He does not *like* girls, my dear." Catherine laughed all over again.

Esther's brow furrowed. What did she mean, "not like girls"? Why was it that they spoke the same language but she understood so little?

"If you are to become my protegé, you have much to learn." Catherine hiccuped, then dabbed her eyes with a lace handkerchief.

Esther stood still and sullen against the door. It was the same word that the odious man had used—protegé. What did *that* mean?

Chapter 13

❦

"*I* will not." Esther clutched her hands into two fists and glared.

"You will do as Madame tells you or leave this house." Cook's face was contorted with rage and her thin body wavered as if in a wind.

"What does she want of me?" Esther hissed. Catherine was a mystery, but not one Esther cared to solve. And now Catherine had asked—no, demanded—that Esther move upstairs.

"What does it matter? You are nothing but a servant. You will do as you are told." Her anger exhausted, Cook plopped down on a bench and ran her apron over her sweaty brow.

Esther stood at the far side of the table and leaned on her knuckles. "What of Pearl?"

"PEARL?" Again fury reared its ugly head. "That skivvy will go back to tending the fire," Cook snarled.

Neither saw the girl crumpled into a mound of rags with her fist crammed into her mouth.

"Pearl is a good baker. She can learn. She can almost read."

"Read? READ? She can no more read than that mangy cur I toss the table scraps to. Reading is for ladies and gentlemen, not for the likes of her. No good comes of encouraging her sort. No good!" Cook's temper took on a more ominous tone.

Esther considered. Having lived in this house for only a short time, she already knew that, no matter what, Catherine would have her way.

"I shall go upstairs, if ..." Esther's words were measured, "you can assure me that Pearl will carry on with the baking and get paid for her efforts."

"Paid? She is indentured. She has been paid *for*. I paid her father myself," Cook hissed.

Pearl's own father had sold her? But there was no time to digest this news.

"I shall go to Madame de La Grange. I shall tell her about Pearl and how you abuse her. She will listen." Would she? It was a gamble.

Cook sputtered. But this time her rage was suddenly snuffed, like a fire smothered with sand. "Very well. Pearl, as you call her, may carry on as you say. But be careful that your precious jewel does not pay for your arrogance!" Spittle flew out of Cook's mouth.

⁂

"You must not talk to the servants. They are here to serve, nothing more. You will rise at seven in the morning, dress, drink your chocolate and begin your lessons at nine. You will not have any contact with my friends, with the possible exception of Monsieur Bernard. I want your entrance into society to be a surprise."

While Jeanne dressed Catherine's hair, Catherine herself sipped chocolate and flapped a pink fan with such velocity that Esther could feel its breeze.

Esther shifted from foot to foot, waiting. What did that mean, "entrance to society"?

"Stay still. Are you a boy in the street? Look up, shoulders back. *Mon Dieu,* there is work to do! You will now be called Camille." If Catherine noticed Esther's confusion she did not acknowledge it. "Monsieur Bernard tells me that Esther is a *Jewish* name. What were your parents thinking? Jeanne, up, up. I want more height to my hair." While the maid bobbed about, Catherine peered into her mirror, then pursed her lips, as if to kiss her image.

"I like my name," Esther whispered.

"My dear girl, you do not want to be taken for a Jew, now, do you?"

Esther looked down at her feet. She was ashamed. She should shout out loud, "I am Jewish. I am proud to be Jewish." She said nothing.

It had never occurred to Catherine that Esther might be Jewish. Jews were excellent merchants, especially in the trade of cloth. They were good with money, or so it was said. But the idea that a Jew—or a Gypsy or a Protestant, for that matter—might live in her house and benefit from her benevolence? No, not possible.

"Madame." The downstairs maid stood at the door and curtsied.

"What is it?" Catherine snapped.

"The dressmaker awaits, Madame."

"Ah, yes. Jeanne, take my blue gown down to her. *Vite!* As for you, Camille, I have ordered you several simple dresses, nothing too extravagant. I can sell them if you prove to be unsuitable." Catherine hummed as she swept out of the room.

Esther turned and looked in the mirror. Who looked back, Esther or Camille?

~

"Camille."

Esther, her head bent to her sewing, did not look up.

"Camille!" Catherine marched into the room bellowing for a second time.

Oh that hateful name. No, it wasn't a hateful name, it just was not *her* name.

"Yes, Madame." Esther, or rather Camille, put aside her sewing, stood and curtsied.

"A portrait painter will arrive today to begin your likeness. I have chosen your dress. Hurry and change."

An artist was to paint her likeness. Imagine! Esther nearly flew down the hall.

"Walk!" screamed Catherine.

Dressed and trussed, Esther posed. It was a tedious process, boring in the extreme.

It took many weeks for the portrait to be completed. Esther was allowed only a brief look before it was whisked away. It was odd to see oneself on a piece of canvas. Were her eyes really that colour? Was her look really so fierce?

~

"What is the news below stairs?" Esther asked the maid who came to turn down her bed. "Has anyone heard from Philippe? How are Pearl and Philippe's brother, Mathieu?" Esther would have had better luck talking to a stone. The maid could not be induced to speak more than a word or two. She would have to find out for herself.

Twice before, Esther had crept down into the kitchen in the small hours of the night. Only when she had passed Cook's bedroom and heard the snores of the woman would she dare tiptoe to Pearl's door. It wasn't only Cook that Esther feared. Spies were everywhere. Anyone might tell Cook, or even Catherine, of Esther's nocturnal visits. Only the boy, Mathieu, Philippe's little brother and Cook's own nephew, escaped the woman's wrath. But no one begrudged the motherless boy his favoured status, for by all accounts he was a sweet and gentle child.

With the small light of a candle to guide her, Esther stood at the door of Pearl's room and peeked in. Pearl now shared their old room with three other servants. She had been allotted a corner, a space not long enough to lie flat. Her blanket was a thin square of sacking.

As often happens between friends, the need of one is heard in the heart of the other. Despite a long day that would have done in a grown man, Pearl was awake, her eyes wide open. The girl crept out of the room and stood shivering in her chemise. Esther slept under a goose down quilt. If only she could have shared it without being found out.

"How are you faring?" Even in the dim light Esther could well see that Pearl's eyes were dulled with overwork and her skin had taken on a yellow pallor.

Pearl smiled; there was little to say.

"Did Cook do this to you?" Esther touched a purple mark beside Pearl's ear.

Pearl shrugged. "It is not as bad as it looks."

"Here, I brought you food." Esther thrust a roll of paper into Pearl's hand. "Go on, eat."

Tears brimmed in Pearl's eyes as she unwrapped the paper and stuffed her mouth with sausage.

"Come, I have found a place under the stairs where we can hide things."

Esther put her arm around Pearl's shoulder, held the candle high, and the two conspirators trundled off into the dark.

In the early mornings, while Catherine slept, Esther visited Marie de La Grange. Each found it agreeable to be in the other's presence. It was the quietest of times; not even maids or servants intruded. Esther was not to know that explicit instructions had been given that no servant or intruder of any kind was to set foot near Madame's rooms before noon.

Esther loved these rooms more than any in the house. While Catherine's rooms were cherry red, rosy purple, startling pink and a blinding orange that assaulted the eyes, Marie de La Grange's rooms were elegant, the colours muted and bathed in a soft yellow light. The chairs and settees were deep and lush and there were soft blankets to wrap oneself in. Best of all, there was always a fire burning in the fireplace and fresh flowers on the mantel.

While Madame played her harpsichord, Esther curled up in a great chair with leather-bound books. Never before had Esther guessed that such books existed. Some were penned by a fellow named Voltaire. There were plays by Molière and Racine and translations of the English story *Robinson Crusoe*. The meaning of many of the great works was not within her understanding, but the idea that she could read them, that no one would say they were unsuitable, was intoxicating.

"Might you join me in prayer?" Marie de La Grange turned away from her harpsichord.

A prayer?

"Come, come, child. I know that you say your prayers every morning. Of course one must *kneel* when saying one's prayers."

What did Madame mean? Esther said her prayers every morning, standing, as was her tradition. But how would Madame know such a thing? But then, spies were everywhere.

If Madame took note of the look on Esther's face, she ignored it. "I know of the circumstances of your arrival. No doubt your rosary was lost at sea. You may have my childhood rosary." Marie de La Grange dropped simple wooden beads into Esther's lap. Delicately, yet firmly, she cupped the girl's hand around the cross that dangled from the bottom of the beads.

"I shall say the prayers. Repeat them after me. It is important." Marie de La Grange stared into Esther's eyes. There was a tone to her voice that was urgent, as if danger were near.

Esther, too stunned to do more than nod, riveted her eyes to the carpet. "I believe in God, the father Almighty, Creator of heaven and earth; and in Jesus Christ, His only Son, Our Lord, Who was conceived by the Holy Ghost, born of the Virgin Mary, suffered under Pontius Pilate, was crucified, dead and was buried ..." It went on. The prayers were in Latin. It was a hard thing to memorize a prayer in a language she did not understand.

"Now, repeat again," said Marie de La Grange.

Esther repeated the prayer. Again, again.

"Your accent is poor. I think your lessons should include Latin. Remember, my dear, beauty offers no protection from those who are bent on doing harm."

Neither Esther nor Madame Marie de La Grange mentioned these visits to Catherine.

⌒

"Walk!" Catherine sat on a silk chair and shouted.

For the hundredth time that week, Esther practised the "Versailles Walk"—tiny, tiptoed steps that from afar gave the impression of a woman floating over the ground. "I said walk!"

It wasn't the walk that was hard to master, it was performing it in copious amounts of fabric! Esther wore a pink-and-purple dress of silk flounces supported by hoops of whalebone. Under the dress were body linens—petticoats, camisole, corset— although none covered her most private parts.

"Again!" Catherine shouted from across the room.

Esther practised the walk until at last she could make it from one end of the ballroom to the other without her dress so much as fluttering.

"You shall learn the harp," announced Catherine. And so a music teacher was engaged. Did no one but Esther notice that he was deaf?

A dance teacher was employed. A bored violinist sat in the corner murdering one tune after another while Esther twirled about with her hand poised in the air, imagining the man who would one day be her partner. It was hard not to laugh.

"You must learn to gamble." Shuffling was the worst. A pack of cards flew out of Esther's hands and soared into space before fluttering to the floor.

Monsieur Bernard offered to teach Esther several card games. As often as not, cards went up his sleeve. When shuffling, Esther realized that one of the hand-painted cards in the deck was ever so slightly larger. Ah, so that was how he knew which card was the ace. Esther might have said something, but she thought perhaps it was rude. After all, he always let her win a few coins. Besides, watching him drop cards on the floor and hide cards here and there was entertaining.

A tutor arrived from Paris to teach court protocol. If she was to be presented at court, her curtsy had to be flawless. The curtsy would be her defining moment. This, above all things, would separate her from the rabble.

"No, no, no, you imbecile. Again, again, again," shouted the tutor. Like Monsieur Bernard, he too would toss his arms in the air in frustration and then demonstrate the correct method. It was amusing to watch a man execute a *flawless* curtsy. More than once Esther twisted her foot the wrong way, bowed too deeply, sank too far back or down, just to watch the little man do it *correctly*. Of course, recovering from a fit of giggles took time.

Esther quite liked the idea of riding a horse, though the reality of it was very different. The French allowed women to ride both astride and sidesaddle. Nevertheless, Esther flew out of the saddle again and again and again.

"Again!" yelled the riding instructor.

How she had come to hate that word, *again*.

"Your French is too common." Elocution lessons were added to Esther's schedule.

"No! Raise the food to your mouth. Do not bend your head forward. Do not look at your food at all." The etiquette teacher was a formidable woman of a rare age who walked like an empress yet had the body of an ox.

It seemed that her natural good looks were not enough. Hair that had once been tucked away under coifs and hats was now washed in concoctions of rose petals, egg whites and lemon and combed out with nettle juice. On sunny days she was bundled up to sit under a winter sun while wearing an odd-looking hat with no crown in the middle. Her hair, black with streaks of auburn, was spread out over the hat's brim to catch the sun's rays. To Catherine's satisfaction, the auburn streaks gradually took on a more reddish hue. Extra lemon was added to the washing concoction.

While the changes of colour were subtle, the feel of her hair was not. Esther swished her hair from side to side. It was as soft as the finest silk in Papa's shop. At home in the Jewish Quarter, hair was hidden under wigs and hats. In Catherine's world, hair was a woman's crowning glory. Esther patted her hair. She felt wicked, but delightfully so!

Not everything was as pleasant. Esther was made to wear gloves made of raw chicken skin to bed. The smell made her want to retch.

Mashed fruit was applied to her face. It was a regimen that left her sputtering and sticky. Flies liked the concoction, too.

Catherine went to great lengths to stay healthy. While winters were mild in that region of France, the damp often caused phlegmy chest congestion. To fortify the system, all meals were accompanied with ass's milk. As an added precaution, an electuary of dried figs, rue leaves and nuts, rolled in honey and shaped into egg-sized pieces, was to be consumed each morning along with a glass of heavy French wine.

Catherine also feared illness through over-bathing. She believed a bath once a month to be more than sufficient. "A man must enjoy a woman through all his senses. He does not want to inhale soap but the pungent aroma of a woman." At Esther's insistence, Catherine allowed her to bathe once a week as long as she wore a light chemise to protect her skin from the metal tub.

After the servants had filled the tub, Esther was left on her own when in the bath. It was one of the few places where she had time to think. All this attention was baffling, but it was exciting, too. Just think what Sarah and her friends would say if they saw her being attended to by maids and tutors and dressmakers!

Of course the day would come when she would have to explain everything to Papa and Maman, but that day seemed far away. They would be angry with her at first, but she hadn't done anything terribly wrong—not yet, anyway. She tried hard not to think of home, and she tried equally hard not to think of *why* all this was happening. Perhaps she would be sold off like a horse at an auction as a wife. Hadn't Papa done what Catherine was doing? Didn't the matchmaker do exactly the same thing? Were not all women in some way bartered to men?

Papa and Catherine—Esther almost laughed out loud. They both wanted to make her into something that she was not. How funny to think that such different people had something in common.

⁓

Esther stood at the bottom of the grand, spiral staircase. Earlier, Catherine had given her instructions as to which dress to wear. Esther now wore a simple, although elegant, blue dress with a rather gay hat over pink-ribboned, trussed hair. It must be for a social visit, but Catherine had not mentioned the name of the host—nor would Esther have recognized the name if she had.

"I did not want to introduce you to society until you were more accomplished. But it is time. My mother, Madame de La

Grange, will accompany us." Catherine pulled on gloves and stood, allowing the butler to cover her shoulders with a long cape made of the pelts of an animal called a beaver.

"Camille, pay attention," Catherine snapped. "I will introduce you as my niece, Camille d'Lauseur, from La Rochelle. You are recently orphaned and have now come under my care. Say no more than that for now. Ah, Maman, you are here." Catherine walked out the door to her waiting carriage.

Madame Marie de La Grange, dressed in black silk and lace, descended the stairs with the elegance of a dowager queen. The jewel-encrusted crucifix hung on a chain around her neck, and in her gloved hands she carried her own ebony-and-pearl rosary beads, a black fan and two small black prayer books. Madame gave Esther a regal nod. "Do you have the rosary beads?"

Esther curtsied and nodded. "*Oui,* Madame."

"Good. I thought perhaps you might accept the gift of my childhood prayer book as well." While pressing the book into her hand, Madame de La Grange raised her fingers and, with a gesture as gentle as a mother's kiss, touched Esther's face. "Remember, Esther, at the end of your life it will not be happiness that you seek, but peace." Marie de La Grange turned and glided through the door.

Prayer book? Esther looked at the leather-bound gold-embossed book. Imagine carrying a prayer book on a social visit, but Gentiles had many strange customs. Dutifully, Esther followed Madame out into the light. There, on the top steps of Madame de La Grange's house, she gaped at the waiting coach. It was the very same coach she and her brother Joseph had seen those many months ago in St. Esprit, outside the home of the dressmaker, Madame Bendal. Esther wavered. She'd have run back into the house if she could.

"Come, Camille." Catherine snapped her fan shut. "It suits no one to be late for church."

Church?

⌑

Esther recognized the tall spire that jetted up into the sky. It was on these very church steps that she and Philippe had stopped to rest before carrying on to Madame de La Grange's home.

The Church of Saint-Martin was charming, small, almost humble. As they alighted from the gilded coach, Catherine waved her hand in greeting to a clutch of elegant men and women standing on the steps.

"Be nice to your friends," Catherine whispered into her ear. "But be nicer still to your enemies."

Catherine's *friends* nodded and waved back, but all eyes were on Esther. Their gaze felt like pinpricks, but whether they approved or not Esther could not tell. Her own eyes were riveted to Madame's back. Monsieur Bernard had obligingly leaked tantalizing snippets of gossip about an amusing young thing who had come under Catherine's protection. The girl might yet prove to be Catherine's successor! Tongues wagged.

Above their heads, church bells pealed. Madame de La Grange entered through the tall wooden doors, then Catherine and finally Esther. *Hear, O Israel: the Lord is our God, the Lord is One! Blessed is His glorious kingdom for ever and ever,* Esther recited in her heart while attempting to breathe normally.

No one noticed that an unbeliever had entered the church. But that wasn't really true. She wasn't an unbeliever. She believed in God, and was not the Abraham of the Jews and the Abraham of the Gentiles one and the same? Rational thought did not help.

Esther's legs wobbled. She felt faint. Daylight streamed in through stained-glass windows and sprinkled the congregation with colour. Above, soaring buttresses met like hands pressed together in prayer. Statues stood in carved hollows in the walls. She noticed a pleasant smell to the church. Only then did she see the incense wafting up from silver holders. Unlike the synagogue, in this church men and women sat together. It seemed, rather it felt, wicked.

As they walked up the centre aisle Madame de La Grange reached out and pulled Esther toward her. "I am getting old, child. Let me lean on you." Madame de La Grange was not old and certainly not ailing, and yet she slipped her arm through Esther's and by sheer will propelled them forward.

They stopped beside a bench. Madame de La Grange made the sign of the cross. Esther did likewise. Had the church fallen down on her head at that exact moment she would not have been in the least surprised.

Nothing happened.

They sat on the hard bench. They kneeled. Madame de La Grange closed her eyes in prayer. Esther followed her every move, as though to do otherwise would leave her exposed and unmasked. She was sick with fear.

The priest, dressed in richly embroidered robes and vestments, walked down the aisle holding a jewel-encrusted Bible aloft. One young, bright-eyed altar boy held up a wooden cross while another swung a silver pot that released yet more sweet-smelling puffs of incense into the air.

A small statue, no bigger than a child, stood in an alcove near the altar. It had to be Mary, Mother of Jesus. *She looks kind,* Esther thought. *She's like me—a Jewish girl among the Christians.*

Chapter 14

Clutching a leather-bound translation of the *Essay Concerning Human Understanding* by an Englishman named John Locke, Esther made her way to Madame de La Grange's rooms.

"Madame?" Esther softly scratched at the door.

"Come, my dear. Ah, have you finished that book already? Sit, sit beside me. I would like to talk to you."

Marie de La Grange placed her ebony-and-pearl rosary beads on a three-legged table and gave Esther a long, steady stare.

"I think perhaps we have assumed too much." Madame's tone suddenly changed. Her voice became businesslike as she picked up a pearl-studded silk fan and whipped it back and forth.

"Pardon, Madame?" Esther curtsied, then sat gracefully upon a stool at Madame's feet. What did she mean? Who was "we"?

"Do you know why my daughter is spending so much time training you, my dear?"

Esther nodded her head slowly. "I am to marry?" she whispered.

Madame de La Grange closed her fan, rested it in the palm of her hand and studied Esther carefully. It was Madame's opinion that while there might be safety in naïveté, in ignorance there was only danger. It was time that Esther fully understood her destiny. With folded hands, Marie de La Grange spoke simply and plainly.

Esther's name was now Camille, and Camille, Madame assured her, was to become a courtesan. With Esther's quick mind and natural beauty, she might well become one of the greatest courtesans France had ever produced. Think of the admirers! It would be a wonderful life. Hadn't she, Marie de La Grange, been a courtesan herself? Look at her now. Didn't she have all that could be expected in this life? And what choices did a woman have? Married women were obliged to produce many children, one every two years at the very least. Death in childbirth was expected. Food, clothing and shelter were provided at the whim of her husband. It was true that a woman might take the veil and join a convent, but that would require a dowry, and Esther had no such thing.

Make no mistake, a courtesan was not a prostitute. It was a fair trade. A woman gave her charm, her mind, her wit and her body and a man paid her handsomely for it. Did Esther understand?

Esther sat as still as a stone in a brook allowing Madame's words to wash over her. Slowly, slowly, slowly, as if her mind were far, far away, Esther came to understand the meaning of Madame's words. She nodded and bowed her head. Tears collected in her eyes although she allowed none to dribble down her face.

Marie de La Grange frowned. Surely it was understood. How could it not be? Think of the time and effort Catherine was putting into her. Why else would she have bothered? As for tears, what sadness was there in such a future?

Madame misunderstood. Esther's tears were not those of sadness but of shame. If she had been doused with cold water she would not have felt more foolish. It was true, what gain would Catherine have if Esther were to marry? How could she have been so simple-minded?

Marie de La Grange patted Esther's hand. "Do not look so sad, my dear. Sadness is a blessing if happiness is its outcome. You will see one day that I am right. Now why don't you pay a visit to my daughter?"

Esther nodded. Perhaps here, in all the open space that Christians enjoyed, the walls did not hem her in, but she was still not free. Esther curtsied and left Marie de La Grange's rooms to wander the halls.

A courtesan—a great beauty, admired by all. Would that be so terrible? It was not the same as being married off to an old man. She was not being cast out, treated as if she were a burden to all whom she loved! Besides, would it not be wonderful to have a carriage at her beck and call? Was there not some freedom in that? She might have two horses, or four—why not six? And riches—think of the riches. But what if Maman found out? Or worse, Papa? Well, she might send money back to the Jewish Quarter. She could buy books for study. She would be like Esther in the Bible. The Esther of the Bible told no one that she was Jewish and married a great king. In the end, she saved her people. The idea that she, too, might help her people was thrilling.

Yet, she would be expected to entertain many men, all kinds of men, spidery-looking men like Monsieur Bernard. Slimy men. Oily men. Wolfish men. Men with spittle in the corners of their mouths. Men who smelled like a privy.

What to do? Esther paced the hall. She was young yet. Maybe she did not have to do anything. Perhaps she could return to the kitchen and decide later, next year or even the year after that. After all, she hadn't minded baking, and she did miss Pearl. Perhaps if she just *talked* to Catherine, if she just *explained* how she felt. True, Esther had heard that Catherine sometimes played cruel tricks on people, small things like spreading gossip or delaying a dress from a dressmaker so that a friend missed an important ball. But she was not a monster. If Esther explained how she felt, Catherine would surely understand.

Esther looked up and was amazed to find that she was in front of the door to Catherine's boudoir. But standing at the door and announcing her presence were two different things entirely. Should she? Maybe she should think about it further. No, this was silly. She reached out and scratched the door.

"Enter," Catherine hollered. Out of earshot of visiting gentlemen, Catherine screeched like a fishwife.

Esther opened the door and stood on the threshold. Catherine sat at her dressing table surrounded by onyx jars, golden compacts, lapis lazuli, dusting powders and all manner of weaponry to attract the opposite sex … and bugs. All powder attracted bugs, especially lice, but such was the price of beauty.

Catherine went back to dabbing her face with a large puff sprinkled with vermilion and gold, leaving her skin, her neck and her bosom glittering. She turned and faced Esther.

"What do you want? I did not send for you." Catherine gave the girl a long, hard glare. "Ah! So, my mother has told you of your future. You are an innocent little one. From what protected world do you hail that you did not understand my expectations from the outset? Are you not pleased?"

"I do not know, Madame." Esther stared at her feet. It was as if a cork were stuffed down her throat, for certainly it was that hard for words to escape.

A dark, foreboding look, like storm clouds on the horizon, crossed over Catherine's face. She spun around and faced Esther. Her eyes narrowed. Her lush, painted lips puckered. She flung the powder puff down, cracked a tortoiseshell comb in two and glared at the girl she called Camille.

"What do you mean, you do not know? What is there to know? You ungrateful wretch! Maybe you want to return to the kitchen." Catherine jumped up, raised her hand and made ready to strike.

Esther cowered but there was no need to fear Catherine's fist. Catherine would not bruise her investment, and, make no mistake, Catherine intended to make good on the time and money she had spent on this miserable creature. Esther would be her passport into the world of the court, but more than that, once the king was finished with her, the girl's value would soar. Ha! She almost laughed out loud. Men would stand in line to be where a king had once been. Catherine would orchestrate it and, in the end, would claim a large portion of all Esther earned. No, Catherine would not strike Esther. Instead she thumped back down at her table, lowered her voice and delivered a life lesson that felt like a beating.

"What are you but a fish pulled from the sea? You haven't even the value of a slave. A slave has been paid for. A slave must be kept and fed, but a servant can be turned out onto the street at a moment's notice. If you were dismissed without reference, what would you do? Get a job in a trade, perhaps, or work in the textile industry? You will starve to death." Catherine wagged her finger at Esther, then carried on with a torrent of words. "After ten, twelve hours standing over machines you will stagger home to share a bed with two or three other people. They will steal from you and give you diseases for which there are no cures. Lice and fleas will chew and gnaw at you until your skin turns black."

Catherine stood and paced.

"Perhaps you will become a *grisette*. She is one who waits at dance hall doors for men to take her home—only then will she feel the warmth of a blanket. Maybe you will become a *lorette*. A *lorette* might have a man to support her but, alas, not well. He may give a pittance for a room where he avails himself of her, but food and clothing are not in the offering. A *lorette* still must take in other customers. Sadly, many of these men are riddled with disease.

"A *grisette*, a *lorette*, what does it matter? Both will grow old quickly and die sick as despised prostitutes. Such women are buried in common graves. This is the life of a girl who is without family and means. You will be nothing without me. Nothing!"

Catherine, seething with anger, stopped and pressed her moist mouth to Esther's ear. Her voice, suddenly a whisper, dripped with disdain.

"I shall teach you how to live a life of enormous wealth and luxury. The great men of Europe will be at your beck and call. If you learn your lessons well, you will never know a day's hunger or a moment's want. Now get out."

❧

"Pearl," Esther hissed down the dark stairs. "Pearl!"

When no response came she groped her way along the hall. The candlelight was poor and hardly cast a glow. She heard soft footsteps. Esther held the candle high as the girl approached.

"Oh, Pearl!" Esther muffled a cry. The girl's face was beaten to a yellow-and-purple pulp, her lips were thick, and one eyelid was a swollen ball. Worse, she dragged a leg.

"I have news." Pearl suddenly lit up. "Cook told the bone-setter at market that Philippe was on a ship. It will not return until spring."

Spring! That was months away. "Did you hear the name of the ship?" Pearl shook her head. "Was it a French ship?" Again Pearl shook her head. When first she heard this nugget of news, she treasured it in the hopes it would make Esther happy. She had failed.

"Do not cry. You did well." Esther put her arm around Pearl's shoulder. The girl winced in pain. In this condition, Pearl could not run away, she could not even walk away.

"I will think of something," said Esther.

⌒⌒

"I have a surprise for you."

Catherine was perched like a large bird on a nest of swirling satin sheets in the middle of her bed. In one hand she brandished a letter and in the other a small velvet pouch.

"The Duc de Richelieu is the First Gentleman of the Bedchamber to the king *and* he is a dear friend of mine. He is in a position to bring certain information to the king's notice." Catherine threw her head back in a fit of hysterical laughter. "The king has seen your portrait! This is for you. It is from the king of France!" Catherine dangled the velvet pouch from her fingertips before flicking it toward her.

Carefully, as if unwrapping eggs, Esther opened it. Out tumbled an exquisite, gold-framed miniature portrait of King

Louis XV. He gazed out at Esther with piercing black eyes. His small smile seemed wicked, as if he were about to share a secret. Esther stared at it in disbelief.

"Why did the king send this to me?"

"Idiotic girl, he is interested in you. Look, the frame is solid gold, the portrait original. It is worth a fortune! There is still a great deal you must learn before you go to court. You will need a new, grand wardrobe. I shall send to Paris for a dressmaker and cloth—yes, I shall buy lots of new cloth. Only the most exquisite will do. I have excellent connections. And we must work on your card playing. I am going to court, and you, a common scullery maid, have provided the introduction." Once again Catherine burst into laughter.

Esther stood, wide eyed and wide mouthed, at the edge of Catherine's bed. She peered down at the portrait. Why would a man, king or not, be interested in her? Slowly she handed it back to Catherine.

"Silly girl, keep it. It's yours! There is more to come, pearls, emeralds, diamonds." Catherine bounded out of bed, pointed to her red-and-black silk wrap and snapped her fingers. Esther held it up as Catherine slipped it on.

Like a high priestess poised on a throne, Catherine resumed her usual position at her dressing table.

"Court is a treacherous place. Sit the wrong way, acknowledge the wrong person, even give a poorly executed curtsy and all we have worked for will be lost. There is so much you must learn. Listen, listen carefully. You must keep your own counsel. Telling your sorrows only increases the enjoyment of the listener. Trust no one, least of all those who attempt to become a friend. Do not speak badly of your enemies, they are the only ones who will tell you the truth. Take what you have and discover its worth. Your beauty and your youth have value. And when they are gone, you will be left with experience, guile and intelligence—all eminently more valuable."

Catherine reached for a puff and dabbed copious amounts of powder on her nose. Glittering dust filled the air. Esther coughed. No matter, Catherine carried on, her voice growing lower and lower until her words were mere hisses.

"Mystery may be visible, but magic must never be revealed. Wit and charm are the two greatest assets of a woman. A lie well told is a woman's best defence. But to tell the perfect lie one must be as truthful as possible. Truth must surround the lie and then, and only then, will you succeed. And the greatest advice of all—listen now, *ma petite,* and heed my words for what I have to tell you may save you many times over." Catherine's voice was so low Esther had to bend forward to hear. "Never, ever, appear desperate."

Too shocked to move, Esther only nodded.

◦◦◦

Esther waited in the dark on the back stairs. Twice now Pearl had failed to claim the food left for her. She fingered the coins won from Monsieur Bernard at chemin de fer, a card game she had come to enjoy. Of course, she would have won more often had he not cheated so much.

All week she had thought of her life to come. She was to go to court. There was no place for such an idea to settle in her mind. The thought both rankled and intrigued, sometimes both at the same time. But if she did become what Catherine said she would become—a famous courtesan—then might she not ask, no, *demand,* that Pearl come with her? At the very least she could buy Pearl's freedom. Perhaps she could become a courtesan for a short time. Then once she had money she and Pearl could live on their own. The more Esther thought, the more ideas came to her.

"Oh Pearl, where are you? I need to talk with you," Esther whispered into the dark.

There were voices coming from below. Esther pulled back the rug. She pushed the few coins she had into the cubbyhole then scampered up the last few steps and ran down the hall.

❦

"You will attend a small dinner party tonight." Catherine made the announcement while examining her own face in a looking glass. "Wear the yellow silk dress."

"Tonight?" Esther was speechless.

"I am inviting only thirty or so of my *closest* friends for dinner. But know this, the king's spies are everywhere. Be assured that what happens tonight will reach his ears! Once we have returned from the opera, you will join us."

The colour drained from Esther's face. Catherine took note.

"It's not the rack. No one will boil you in oil. Stand up straight." Catherine studied the girl. "No jewellery, I think. Innocence will be your adornment. Go now and have your hair dressed."

Catherine had sent word that Esther's hair was not to be powdered. As Esther sat in her own boudoir, and at her own dressing table, she watched as her hair was swept up into a small tower. She could only wonder why the king would have spies in Catherine's house. Surely the king had affairs of state to consider. And what of the poor and the starving? The king must be like the rabbi—on a much larger scale, naturally. All rabbis fretted and worried. The king, too, must suffer deep anxiety about his people, especially since the country was in such dire circumstances. It was all so very odd and confusing.

A maid carrying a leather box entered Esther's room. She opened it to reveal two finely carved ivory combs for her hair. Esther took a deep breath and stared in wonder. Before coming to this house she had never dreamed such things as these existed.

Catherine had also given directions that Esther's corset be cinched tightly. The maids pulled on the strings until Esther thought she would faint. They were not satisfied until the smallest maid's hands could meet around her waist. The corsets pushed up her sorry excuse for a bosom, which, left unattended, hardly made two bumps on her chest. Bits of cloth were added to give a bustier look. A padded, boned undergarment gave Esther's otherwise petite derriere a voluptuous boost. Then came the petticoats and finally the yellow dress. Her lips were made red and her skin was speckled with gold. As Esther disappeared, Camille emerged.

Esther stared at herself in the looking glass. "Camille," she whispered. "I am Camille."

The results left the servants speechless. Some bitterly resented attending a girl who, until recently, had toiled alongside them. But after this night, no one would quibble with the fact that Camille, formerly called Esther, was a great beauty of France.

Chapter 15

༄

"Camille," Esther whispered to herself as she paced in her room and fluttered her fan. "Camille," she said again and again.

"Madame says that you are to attend her." Jeanne stood in the doorway and curtsied.

In silk embroidered shoes Esther glided down the hall, descended the stairs and stood on gleaming Italian tiles outside the doors of the main dining room. *Breathe,* she commanded herself. Her heart beat so wildly that it felt as if it might leap out of her body entirely. She nodded to the two footmen. With a flourish the doors were opened wide, and with practised grace Camille walked forward and stood on the threshold.

The room was painted the pink of sunset. Great mirrors adorned each wall, allowing three huge, sparkling candelabras with hundreds of lit candles to multiply their effect a thousand times. The ceiling was white and gold, the wood furnishings smoky and dark, and the chairs were dressed in emerald greens and ruby reds. Delicate candlesticks and gilded porcelain graced the table, while cut crystal winked in the flickering light. The aroma of dozens of flowers arrayed in giant vases was overwhelming. Added to the smell was a profusion of perfumes all mingling to create a sickeningly sweet fug.

One head, then another, and another, turned toward the door. The well-dressed rabble (who until this moment had been behaving more like unruly children than aristocrats) paused. A hush descended. With an air of perfect poise, Camille surveyed the room.

Catherine's needle-sharp eyes travelled from person to person, noting the reaction of each. She was pleased.

"Ah, there you are, my darling Camille. May I present Camille d'Lauseur, formally of La Rochelle?" Catherine motioned to a far chair. Camille followed her gaze, moving her eyes but not her head. Her heart might have skipped but not a trace of trepidation crossed her face.

A grinning man, with a head like a cabbage and wearing a riot of velvets and silks, bounced up beside an empty chair. Was she to sit beside complete strangers? Would Catherine throw her to the wolves so easily? Panic swelled and rose like a wave. If she could have crawled into the curl of that wave and hidden she would have. But then the panic subsided. The guests could only wonder what this exotic creature was thinking.

Camille walked over to a chair held by a footman. Eyes followed her every move.

The cabbage-head man gave the footman a sharp shove with his elbow. "Allow me, my dear," he said, with the slur of a man well on his way to being drunk. Camille eased herself down into the chair with the grace of a princess. A glass of champagne appeared at her elbow.

"Ladies and gentlemen, attention!" The obnoxious Monsieur Bernard, wearing excessive make-up and a black beauty mark on his cheek, held his glass high. "A toast, to a new flower of the Empire. May its plucking bring happiness and wealth." He bowed, then winked at Camille. Peals of laughter went up as the blood rose in Camille's face. Esther, not Camille, cast her eyes down.

As the guests drank heartily a door opened and in walked a parade of servants bearing huge platters of sumptuous food. Pheasants dressed in glaze and decorated with elaborate feathers and jewels; pink salmon with shimmering gems for eyes; an entire hind of beef; a pig with an apple in its mouth and sliced oranges embedded in its skin—all were laid on the table. Champagne flowed in an unstoppable stream.

How was it that most of France was starving and yet such excess existed?

"Drink, drink, drink, my dear." The cabbage-head man pushed her fluted champagne glass up to her lips. She sputtered and swallowed what she could.

"More champagne," he yelled, waving his arms like windmills.

Camille shook her head, yet still her glass was filled. The meal went on forever. Course after course. Guests left the room only to return with bits of puke on their clothes. The stink of vomit now mixed with heavy perfumes and body odour. The thick make-up on men and women alike was melting. Red lipstick dribbled down chins, and the gold in the vermilion powder rolled down skin on trickles of sweat.

The hour grew late, and yet the eating and drinking continued unabated.

"Did you know that my little protegé inquired about marrying my dear friend Monsieur Bernard?" Catherine, her eyes rolling in her head, banged her hand on the table and burst into laughter. An eruption of hysterical hooting and howling followed.

Monsieur Bernard, *the one who did not like girls,* climbed up on the table. Dishes and glasses scattered and smashed, to the delighted screams of the guests, Catherine's loudest of all. This insect of a man loped down the tabletop and stopped in front of Camille. He dropped down, landing one knee squarely in a terrine of foie gras, and held up his champagne glass.

"My darling Camille, would you be mine?" His black beauty spot fell into his glass.

The heat, the wine, the humiliation all conspired against her. Hot, sticky tears brimmed in her eyes.

Monsieur Bernard drained his glass then dropped it on the table. He caught her chin in his long, spidery fingers and pressed his painted lips against her ear. "Fear what you desire," he hissed, then melted into hysterical laughter.

"Try as you may, old friend," cried Catherine from the far end of the table, "my little protegé's destiny lies not with you. She will not only bring me into court, but provide for my old age!" Catherine banged the table and howled with jubilation.

Monsieur Bernard laughed too, then leapt off the table, landing on all fours like a predatory beast.

"Our little bird does not have an appetite!" The cabbage-head man's words flew out of his mouth on a gust of garlic.

"Eat! Drink!" screamed Catherine, and the lot of them dug in yet again.

"Open wide, my little bird," hissed the cabbage-head man. He popped something soft into her mouth.

"What is this?" The wine made her head spin. And the walls— they were closing in.

"A specialty from Bayonne, my dear. A French delicacy."

Whatever it was melted in her mouth. It was, to her amazement, tantalizing, like nothing she had ever tasted before.

"It is delicious," Camille uttered. But enough, she must leave, must catch her breath.

"Amazing what a brilliant chef can do with a ham."

Pig? Vomit rose in Esther's throat.

Chapter 16

꧁

That part of the night that was not spent expunging the poisons from her body was spent sobbing. Twice food had been brought to her rooms and twice she had waved the trays away. Now, in the harsh light of midday, Esther's head pounded and her stomach quaked. She rang for more water and drank the carafe dry.

As the sun rose to the middle of the sky, Esther dressed. She was expected to ring for a servant to help her, but instead she opened her wardrobe and chose a simple day dress of the softest cotton. It was an impractical choice, but she could not bear the thought of a stiff dress with too many slips. Quick movements made her dizzy. Even her fingers ached as she tried to tie her hair back with a ribbon. She could not avoid her reflection in the looking glass, try as she might.

Who was she?

A traitor.

A liar.

A fraud.

A prostitute—*almost* a prostitute.

A pig-eater.

"Mademoiselle, the cloth merchant has arrived. Madame wishes you to attend her in the main salon."

Esther nodded to the maid. "I am coming." She picked up the miniature portrait of the king and turned it over in her hand. It was a valuable thing. She would give it to Catherine for safe-keeping. Esther slipped it in her pocket along with the coins she'd won at cards. Perhaps she would have the chance to leave them under the stairs for Pearl. *Oh Pearl, Pearl, what should we do? How will we ever escape?*

Esther descended the stairs and stood on the bright tiles in the main hall that led to the salon. The doors to the salon were slightly ajar. There was not a footman in sight.

Catherine's voice rang out. "Extraordinary! Quite magnificent. You are the best cloth merchant in all of France, Monsieur. Camille, come, hurry. This is too beautiful."

With her usual light step, Esther pushed through the door. Gangly, ugly Monsieur Bernard stood knee deep among huge bolts of fabric. Damask, silk, tulle and velvet were strewn carelessly across the floor. Neither table nor chair was spared the adornment of the exquisite fabrics.

"Splendid!" crooned Monsieur Bernard. He held up a spectacular length of blazing red silk, billowed it up into the air like a flaming sail, then looked toward Esther as she stood in the doorway. "Come, come, Camille. Wear this and even the king will delight in ripping it off you. No man will be able to resist you! That is … no man other than myself!" His laugh was hysterical, like an exotic bird in a cage. The silk fluttered to the ground.

"Camille, do not stand on the threshold. How many times

must I tell you that it is bad luck." Catherine's voice was unusu-
ally shrill that day.

The cloth merchant, dressed in sober black, his hands clasped
respectfully behind his back, turned in Esther's direction. She saw
first his profile. Dignified, reserved, so out of place in this house,
with these people.

Papa!

Esther fell back behind the door.

"Camille, what are you doing?" Catherine called out.

Esther spun around.

"Camille!" Catherine hollered. Her voice ricocheted off the
walls like shot from a rifle.

"Mademoiselle?" cried a servant as Esther flew past with the
speed of a hunted bird. "Where are you going?"

She threw herself down one set of stairs, then another. One
hallway became another, then another, then another. She landed,
breathless and bewildered, in the kitchen. Neither Cook nor
Pearl was anywhere to be seen. She flung open the back door that
led to the street and stared into the face of her brother Abraham.

～

Hours passed, but there was no telling time in the dark. Esther
crouched in the bottom of the armoire in the kitchen. She had
heard the search, the thumping of boots, plaintive calls up and
down the hallways. She had even heard the servants talking
among themselves. "The girl has run off!" they'd said. Most had
laughed.

Nine months had passed since the shipwreck, and now her
brother did not recognize her. True, he had not looked at her
directly, at least not into her eyes. He'd stood on the stoop holding

bolts of cloth and, as was the custom of a good Jewish young man when confronted by one of the opposite sex, he'd looked down and mumbled an apology. Esther, numb with shock, had stepped back and let him pass. He hadn't seen her because the Esther he knew was dead. He didn't know her because she had lost her modesty. Shame crawled over her like an army of ants.

Despite the cramps in her neck, back, legs and feet she waited. Yet she was unsure of just what it was she was waiting for!

Dear God, can you hear me? What must I do? But would God listen to a girl who defied her family, her religion?

There was no telling the exact time, but the afternoon had come and gone. Twice she had peeked out to see if she could spot Pearl. Supper had been served at midnight. The kitchen had been cleaned, the servants had wafted to their rooms or pallets, and soon a new day would begin. Still, she waited. The idea came to her suddenly, although perhaps it had been there all along. She would run away. She sat quite still, as if allowing the thought to find a place to settle.

Run away.

From everything.

If she was to leave this house, she must do so now. It did not matter where she went, it only mattered that she get away.

There was little room to move about, yet Esther managed to reach into the pocket that dangled from her belt. She fingered the five coins and the portrait. On hands and knees, her ears perked like a dog's, she crawled out of the armoire, stood, stretched, then tripped over her dress. How could she escape wearing such a thing as this? It was too light and feminine for the street, but she dared not chance running up to her own boudoir.

The lamps had been turned off but a small, banked fire burned in the grate, giving off just enough light to take in her surroundings. She spotted the clothes that sat on an upper shelf of the armoire. These were Cook's bounty—the clothes she had stolen from all the past servants who'd had the misfortune to cross the threshold of her kitchen. Esther touched a thick linen shirt, then pulled away as if her fingers had been singed. Dare she? Could she? A surge of energy ran through her like lightning. Maman had said to be brave. But Maman would not approve of what she was about to do. She could not think of that now.

Dress, corset, underclothes of all sorts fluttered to the ground. She pulled, yanked and twisted herself out of layer after layer as fast as possible. A servant wafting through the kitchen at this hour would have been unlikely, but in the house of Catherine Churiau what was unlikely to happen often did happen.

Nearly naked, she reached up and pulled down a bundle of clothes. A skirt landed on top of the heap. Esther grabbed it, caring nothing about the holes or the poor quality of the cloth. She stepped into the simple skirt and pulled it up to her waist. Then her eyes fell upon the breeches. Boys' breeches. A girl cannot work, and without work, you cannot eat. Those were Philippe's words. Catherine, too, had said that girls on their own could not survive. To run away as a girl would invite trouble at every turn. What of the day she had lost Joseph? Think of the boys who had cornered her, who had meant to hurt her. But boys could come and go as they pleased. Boys could work. If she could become a boy, she would be safe.

The thought was so perfect that she nearly cried out. The skirt fell into a pool around her ankles. She picked up the breeches and slipped them on. They felt wonderful! In no time, Esther stood in a boy's shirt and breeches.

Somewhere outside the house a dog barked. The sound spurred her on. She pulled the pocket containing the portrait and her few coins out of the tumble of petticoats. The belt went around her waist. The pocket hung down under the breeches between her legs. Well she knew the anatomy of a boy. She had two big brothers and two little brothers, after all.

Wooden sabots lined with leather sat on the shelf. She undid her satin slippers and threw them on the heap of clothes, then swooped down and gathered the pile up and rammed everything into the armoire every which way.

Her red-streaked hair was too long and too thick to hide under a cap. It would have to be chopped off. The idea was terrifying and thrilling. Catherine had gone to such lengths to turn Esther's hair into her "crowning glory." There would be no turning back once she had cut it.

Esther reached for a knife. She held it up toward a window and watched the moon's light dance on its edge. She gathered her hair into a bundle and, in a single stroke, lopped it off. The strands of hair fell onto the stone floor. How many times had she sat at her dressing table in Catherine's house and been bored with her reflection? What she would give for a looking glass at this moment.

Footsteps! She placed the knife on the table and darted underneath. How small and quick she felt in boys' attire. The footsteps came closer. A door opened and a lantern cast a meagre pool of light. The hank of hair on the floor looked like a dead animal, a rat, perhaps. Two black leather boots were now beside her. If she were caught, it would be over. The pool of light veered away. The footsteps receded.

Think. She must cover her tracks, but how? She must take the hair with her. No, no, she would burn it. Esther leapt out from under the table and flung it into the grate. It crackled and hissed. Pearl? She must get a message to her, but how? The risk was too great for both of them. Later she would find a way to get word to her. *Forgive me.*

The sun was coming up. She grabbed a cap, slid into one jacket, then another, then settled on the first, and just as she was to open the door she reached into a bowl and stuffed her boy pockets with apples and lemons. With the wooden shoes clasped against her chest, Esther closed the door behind her and set out toward the market and, beyond it, the sea.

Chapter 17

❧

*D*aybreak was on the horizon as Esther left Catherine's house and darted across the courtyard. Dew had left the lemon trees and the olive branches shiny, and the air was sweet with the smell of morning flowers. She opened the gate. The streets of Biarritz were deserted.

At the crest of each hill Esther looked down toward the sea to find her bearings. She rushed past the Church of Saint-Martin and headed for the market. There was no time to rethink, to ponder what she had done.

As she came to the top of another hill she could see merchants setting up their stalls and booths in the market square. With a heart that would not be stilled, Esther made her way toward it.

Baskets of muddy onions, parsnips and vegetables of all kinds were being laid out for display. There were wheels of cheese, sausages, fish (fresh and salted) and berries. Hens and pheasants cackled in crates and rabbits nibbled on hay in hutches. Despite the early hour, vendors were already calling out greetings, abacuses rattled and coins clinked. Servants waved to one another and then plunged into gossiping, chattering like birds. A woman in all her finery stepped out of a grand carriage to haggle with a fragrance seller. It was too delicate an enterprise to leave to a mere servant. A blood-soaked butcher held up the head of a boar and claimed its purity. No matter which way she looked, no one so much as glanced back. As Camille, her every movement had been scrutinized. But no one noticed a scruffy boy in peasants' clothes. It was magic. She was invisible.

The sun was warm and the sea air was salty and fresh as she made her way through the market and down the hill to the beach. No corset, no hoops, no dress, just a light, airy feeling—she believed she could fly if she put her mind to it. The wooden shoes were ill fitting. She cast them off and wiggled her bare feet in the sand.

The sea, the sand dunes, red rocks, a collection of fishing huts and, in the distance, piers jutted out into the sea. Curling rollers washed up against the shore, taking away bits of sand and leaving seaweed in their path. Day fishing boats were on their way out and night fishing boats were coming in.

Esther looked to where the shipwreck had been. Months and months had passed, a fall, a winter and now a spring. Nothing remained of its battered hull. Scavengers, human and otherwise, had picked its bones clean and the battered wood had been dragged away for fuel. There were now only two classes in France, the fed and the starving.

Twice she watched a troop of blue-coated soldiers tromp by. Would Catherine have reported her as a runaway? She'd be safest down by the wharf, and besides, that was where she was most likely to find Philippe.

Tall ships were moored at the pier. The wealth of the Indies had come home. Harlots and pickpockets stood on the wharf beside beaming merchants awaiting conversations with the captains. Great ladies, with their well-dressed black slaves in tow, were arriving in droves. They alighted from their carriages and commenced parading up and down the wharf, perusing Persian and Chinese silks, porcelain from China, Korea and Japan. Spices were dumped into bowls, and the air was filled with the aroma of cloves and cinnamon.

A cheer went up. Esther turned. A caged tiger, its skin streaked with open sores from too many whippings, was being unloaded. For a moment the wooden cage dangled over the heads of the crowd. The tiger, its eyes wild, hissed and spat, to the delight of those gathered. As a hoist lowered the cage onto the wharf, adults and children alike thrust sticks through the bamboo bars of its cage. Esther turned away. Once caged, nothing lived long.

Esther jumped up on a stone seawall and looked out over the harbour. The surf sent up sprays of water that turned into crystals of light under the sun. In front of her, ships of all sizes bobbed about at anchor like seabirds on open water. Some brigs dwarfed others, their high-ended hulls rising above the waterline, their masts pressed against the sky.

A good-sized brig out in the harbour was having a wash day on the top deck. Women had been brought on board to do the work. Their hair was wrapped in turbans and their skirts were tucked up into waistbands, revealing fine, sturdy legs. Their laughter wafted across the water as they bent over cauldrons of washing water set to boil over fires lit in iron vessels underneath. Esther shaded her eyes and looked up to the ship's rigging. Young sailors hung on the lines like cocky perched birds. She followed their gaze back down to the top deck. It was the big bottoms of the maids they were dreaming about.

What world had she stumbled upon? Esther threw her head back and let the sun shine down on her face. A light wind blew through her hair and a salt spray dusted her smiling lips. Sooner or later Philippe would be on one of those ships. Meanwhile, she would watch the dappled white-and-blue sky and thank God. A prayer came back to her as she looked out to sea, Maman's prayer: "If I take up the wings of the morning, and dwell on the ocean's farthest shore, even there Your hand will lead me. Your right hand will hold me."

I am fine, Maman. I do not have the life you might have wished, but I will remember God in all that I do and will forever thank Him for all that I have. And at that moment Esther owned the world.

Absentmindedly she reached into her breeches and pulled out her pocket. She tipped the contents into her hand. Five, six coins. No! She squeezed the pocket between her fingers. The portrait was missing! Esther leapt up and searched the ground around her. How might she have lost it and not the coins? She ran back to the market, scouring the ground as best she could. She retraced her steps as far back up the hill toward Catherine's house as she dared. Back she ran to the water only to thump down on the seawall. It was gone forever. It was the only valuable thing she owned, yet Esther felt no great loss. It came from a world she did not want to be part of.

A rock came hurtling her way and nearly knocked her out entirely.

"Hey, boy," a man yelled out. "Get down from there and help me move these barrels. I'll pay ya for your trouble."

Esther looked down at a face pitted by the pox and ravaged by drink.

"Are you deaf?" The man—likely a peddlar, since he wore no smock—reached for another rock.

"Me?" Esther jumped off the wall.

"I'll not have an idiot working for me. Are you an idiot?"

Esther shook her head vehemently. He'd said he'd pay her.

"You aren't much to look at. What age be you?" The man jutted out his hairy chin and looked her up and down. A weakling was no use to him.

Esther was considering, too. Her real age was fifteen years, but without so much as a sign of hair on her face she'd best say she was younger. "I am twelve years old."

The peddlar lifted an eyebrow. "Off with you. You're too small." He sniffed and turned away.

"I can count. Read, too."

The man came to an abrupt stop. Well, that was something! The truth of it was, he was as strong as an ox, but could not count past ten. Many was the time he'd been cheated out of a box or barrel because he'd counted up wrong, and there was that hag of a wife ready to pounce on him like a demented cat to add to his troubles. But counting was a miserable thing. It was remembering which word went with which number that confused him like the devil. Why should *three* mean *three*? Why should *three* not mean *five*? It was a word, no more. All this he pondered while Esther stood waiting.

"What be your name?" asked the snooty-faced fellow.

What was her name? She hadn't thought of one.

"What name do you go by?" He shouted this time.

Of course she would need a name. "P-Pierre?" she stammered. Pierre was a common enough name.

"Are ya asking me or telling me?"

"Pierre." This time she spoke with assurance. There had been a footman in Catherine's house—what was his last name? "Pierre Mausiette," she announced.

"Well, Pierre, count to fifty."

Esther counted to fifty.

Whether the lad got it right or wrong, the man could not tell, but it sounded good. "You can help me move these barrels and do my counting, and if you cheat me I'll see you hanged! I'll give you grub and one coin and a place to sleep. Take it or leave it." He wiped away the snot that had collected on his upper lip, then put his hands where his hips might have been had he not been so fat.

"Grub and *two* coins and a place to sleep," Esther retorted. She felt brave and bold.

They had a bargain. She was given a room to sleep in at the back of a warehouse. It wasn't much—a dirt floor, straw for a bed, a barrel cut in half and overturned to make a table. But it had what Esther craved most of all, a door secured with a bolt and a hole in the wall that made do as a window.

One day's work turned into two, then three. The labour was hard. Her arms and legs ached, and she was so exhausted that each night she fell into a dreamless sleep. And yet, excitement rose up in her every morning as she pondered the day to come. It was an excitement fed by fear. A wrong move, a wrong word and it would all be over. But what life there was around her! Adventure was at every turn. It was not that she had forgotten Pearl, but it was her own survival that she was concentrating on now.

⌒

The peddlar's work was done, and now Esther was without employment, but with more coins in her hidden pocket she was not overly concerned. There were plenty of odd jobs about the docks. Besides, she wanted to stay near the water, all the better to keep an eye out for Philippe. There was no sign of him; still, she searched the harbour day and night without fail.

The captain of a middling-sized ship heard that there was a boy looking for work who could read and count. The captain sent his cabin boy to search out this Pierre Mausiette.

"Be you the boy who can read and count?" asked the cabin boy, who himself could not have been more than seven or eight years old. Esther sat on the stone wall chewing an apple and nodded. "My captain wants a word with you," said the boy. She tossed the apple core into the water and followed him.

The captain was a grizzly sort, rough and dirty. "Where might you have learned to read?" he snarled.

"I was apprenticed out to a baker, and the baker's wife taught me." Esther, standing on the ship's deck, spoke easily and convincingly, having given the matter some thought.

"And where might a baker's wife have learned to read?"

"She worked as a lady's maid before she married. It was the lady of the house who taught her." Stories and lies were coming more easily to Esther now. Catherine was right, her life did rely on her ability to lie.

Satisfied, the captain employed Esther to write down and deliver messages about the town.

❧

It was Philippe she wanted to see, but it was Pearl she sorely missed. Weeks passed, and despite frequent visits to the market she had not laid eyes on her friend. Of course she had seen other people of her acquaintance. Such sightings were frightening at first. On one occasion she'd stumbled headlong into the belly of the cabbage-head man. He'd scoffed and would have had her pilloried had his attention not been directed elsewhere. As it was, he mentioned to his walking partner that there were too many filthy boys on the street and they should be done away with. To think that this man would have paid a king's ransom just to be in her company not a few weeks ago! It was enough to make her laugh out loud.

On market day, Esther sat on a high perch on a stone wall. It was from this lofty height that she spotted a wisp of hair under a coif. The walk was familiar, too. Could that be her?

Esther jumped down, tossing aside a half-eaten apple, and made her way across the crowded market. As the girl changed directions, Esther dove and ducked behind a wagon, a water barrel and a cart. Had anyone paid her any mind, they might have taken Esther for a pickpocket stalking an intended victim.

The woman in front of the girl thrust cheese, sugar and spices back into the girl's basket. She haggled with the butter merchant before accepting a slice of creamy butter wrapped in a lettuce leaf. Each purchase made the girl slump forward a little more, then pull back, as if to balance her burden. A greeting was called. The woman turned. It was Cook! Her face cracked into a hearty laugh as she caught sight of a friend. In no time the two were deep in conversation, trading in the currency valued by servants—gossip.

Esther looked at the girl. Pearl gripped a large, handwoven basket with both hands. The weight of it caused Pearl to grimace. Esther looked about. A small alley was behind her, a wagon loaded with cabbages off to one side. Another household servant stood scratching himself beside a pickle barrel. Somewhere a lute played and a boy announced to the crowd that a puppet show was about to begin.

She crept as close to Pearl as she dared and crouched behind a cabbage wagon.

The time was right.

Esther leapt out from behind the wagon and grabbed Pearl from behind. She cupped her hand over the girl's mouth and pulled. It was a tussle of flying arms and scuffing feet. The basket fell to the ground as the two girls stumbled back into the alley. Esther shoved Pearl up against a wall. The child screamed.

"Hush, hush. It's me." Esther rammed her arm across the girl's mouth, pushing hard, all the while whispering in her ear, "Esther. I'm Esther. It's me."

Pearl's arms flailed about in all directions. Esther had under-estimated the strength of a child who pounded dozens of loaves of bread dough every day, who lifted more than her weight in sacks of flour, who hauled water up stairs and down. Pearl's foot flew out and the contents of the basket spilled into the gutter. Her large eyes rolled back into her head and she cried out, making the yelping, breathless sounds of a trapped beast.

The merchants within earshot turned. It took a moment, and then they laughed. Lovers having a spat. And if the boy was up to mischief, what of it? Many a young lass had her virtue taken thus. They turned away.

"It's me, Pearl. It's Esther," Esther hissed into Pearl's ear. "It's me. It's me."

Pearl's body went limp. Esther pulled back and looked into Pearl's liquid eyes. It was a moment she would regret. Pearl shoved hard and made her escape.

"No, no!" Esther cried as she fell. "My maid, it is me—the one who named you!"

Pearl swivelled in her tracks. She reached out to a wall to steady herself, all the while staring intently at the boy on the ground.

"You be dead. They told me that you were dead." Pearl fell onto her knees and threw her arms around Esther. For a moment, however brief, it was enough to hold on to each other.

"Your hair? You are dressed as a boy!"

Esther grinned as she snatched up the cap that had fallen on the ground.

"Quick, the basket."

Esther pulled her cap back over her head and began scooping up the packet of sugar and cheese and dumped them back into the basket. The butter was covered in dirt and the rare spices were spilled out on the ground.

"We do not have time. You must listen. I will come back for you. You are my friend. Have you the coins I left under the stairs?" Pearl nodded. "Use them if you must. Here, I have more." Esther reached into an outside pocket in her jacket and held out two gold coins.

"And what is this?"

Both girls, on hands and knees, looked up as Cook stared down. The woman's eyebrows cast long shadows over her eyes and face and her mouth was pursed as if pulled tight by a drawstring.

Pearl scrambled up onto her feet. Whatever wits God had chosen to dole out to Pearl came to her now.

"This is my brother, Cook. The shock of seeing him made me drop my basket."

Cook might have lashed out at the girl but instead she paused and stared at the boy still on his knees. "Stand up, boy." The woman growled like a dog.

Esther stood up on quivering legs, but it was not for herself that she was afraid. She kept her eyes riveted on her feet. Well she knew that the colour of her eyes and the delicate mole above her lip might give her away yet.

Cook paused. Something was amiss, but what? "Are you this miserable girl's brother?" she snarled. Her nose crinkled as though she smelled something rotten.

Without lifting her head, Esther nodded, not trusting her voice.

"He is, really. A half-brother. My father's bastard." Pearl piped up.

Cook nodded. It was possible. But …

"It was the shock of seeing him, the shock." Pearl's voice waned.

"Hold your tongue, girl. What's in your hand?" Cook spoke directly to Esther. There was something about the boy, something …

Esther opened her hand, revealing the two gold coins.

"Ah, this is to replace the spoiled goods." Cook snatched away the precious coins and turned her back on the girls. She put one, then the other between her teeth and bit down hard. They were real. "And where would the likes of yourself…?" Cook turned back. Pearl stood with downcast eyes. The boy was gone.

Esther flew. It was easy to hide in the market. She dodged wagons, carts, sedan chairs, peddlers and the like and made for the wharf. Finally, when she was sure that she had put enough distance between her and the marketplace, Esther leaned against a wall to catch her breath.

"Jew! Jew!"

Jeering voices, laced with scorn, came from behind. She turned. Had she been found out? How? Her disguise was complete. What could have given her away?

"JEW!"

The taunting voices grew louder. They were coming toward her. Boys—a gang of them.

"JEW!"

Did they think her a Jewish *boy* or a Jewish *girl*? She had been careful to wrap a length of cloth around her chest to flatten her small breasts. And how would they know her to be Jewish when the likes of Catherine did not? It made no sense, but panic was upon her. There was no time to think. She had scarce got over meeting Cook, and now this! Esther peeked around the corner of the wall.

Six, maybe more, boys stood with their backs to her. She made ready to run again when she stopped and followed their line of vision. Over there, cowering beside an old cart, was a young boy. They were not after her, they were after a child! His dark coat, his sidelocks, his hat—he was Jewish, to be sure, but what was he doing on his own? Where was his father? His brothers? Jewish children never walked alone outside of the Jewish Quarter.

The biggest boy picked up a stone. He would heave the first and then the others would follow until a hail of rocks showered down.

Fear, as bright as fire, stood in the little boy's eyes. He couldn't have been more than seven or eight years old. Esther's eyes darted in all directions. His family must be nearby, they must be!

The rock sailed through the air. The child raised his small arms across his eyes. As the rock hit, the child cried out. Esther screamed. It was a cry so loud, so fierce, it burned her throat. Head down, eyes up, Esther curled her hand around a fair-sized rock and held it up over her head. The rock sailed out of her hand. One of the boys howled in pain. The rock had hit its mark. They looked about, confused, then gazed in amazement at this new boy who stood a distance away. Why would one of their own defend a Jew?

A long, dirty finger was pointed at Esther. A cry went up. Esther turned on her heels and ran. The pack charged like hunters in pursuit of their prey. Sweat rolled down her face as her heart hammered away in her chest. A prayer would be good, if she could think of any words beyond *please, please, please*.

She came to the top of a hill and looked down over the wharf. Where could she hide? A rock clipped her shoulder. She slipped. The run was now a tumble. Over and over she went. She slammed into something. There was shouting. A horse reared. She scrambled onto her feet and set out again. The shrieking voices of the boys behind her were gaining. That's when she saw him.

"PHILIPPE!"

Chapter 18

Philippe had not meant to be away so long. Poor weather and the ship's cook had hampered the journey. Putrid meat and stagnant water—the result of water casks not properly cleaned and meat not properly salted and stored—had reduced the ship's crew to a motley lot bent on spewing, not sailing. No sooner had the ship docked in Biarritz than the cook had scampered ashore like a rat. This hasty exit was a wise move, for certainly Captain Belleville would have had the cook pilloried, had he himself not been ill beyond measure.

Philippe stood on shore and heaved his seabag over his shoulder. He was one of the lucky few who, although sick for a short time, had recovered quickly.

"PHILIPPE!"

He turned to the sound of his name.

"PHILIPPE!"

He dropped his seabag and looked around. A boy ran toward him. His short black hair flew around his face. Gasping, the strange boy crumpled at Philippe's feet. Philippe stepped over him. His eyes scanned the pier.

"It's me, Esther!" She lay on the ground panting, but Philippe was not paying her any mind, nor was he even looking her way.

He'd heard his name, and damn him if it wasn't Esther's voice, but where was she?

The band of boys who had been taunting the Jewish child circled Esther as she lay on the ground. They'd have kicked her to death given half a chance. Philippe paid the boys no more attention than he would a pack of snarly dogs. He jumped up on a barrel, cupped his hand over his eyes and peered off into the distance.

"Philippe." Her voice was small, barely more than a stream of huffs and gasps. "Philippe!"

There it was again. Where was it coming from? He turned and watched as one of the ring of boys drew back his foot. Clearly, he meant to lodge it in the ribs of the boy who lay on the ground.

Philippe jumped off the barrel and lurched forward. It was no business of his if one street urchin wanted to kill another, but he was not about to stand by when the fight was so unevenly matched. He grabbed the neck of one boy, then another, sending one, two, three spinning off in different directions. The biggest boy regained his balance and took a swing at Philippe but was instantly outmatched. Philippe was stronger than any three of them put together. They scattered like mice.

Philippe reached down and yanked the injured boy to his feet. "Get away with you," he hollered. He was about to turn his back when he spotted first the delicate mole on the corner of the boy's mouth and then the tiger-brown eyes that glittered like gold. Philippe's mouth gaped open.

Panting, nearly overcome with exhaustion and dirty from head to toe, the boy nevertheless grinned.

"Esther?"

⁓

Esther's story came out in one long stream of words. At the end of it, Philippe looked sheepish and turned pink, an easy thing for a person of his fair complexion to do.

"I should not have taken you to Catherine's house. Forgive me, but I thought that you would be safe there."

He could hardly take his eyes off Esther. It was the oddest thing. As a woman, Esther attracted him like no other, but dressed as she was ... how could he explain? *She* was a handsome *he*, rather than *he* being a beautiful *she*. Already it was becoming confusing.

A sailor standing on board the ship hollered down to Philippe. "Hey, you down there! There's work to be done!"

"Stay here," said Philippe. "We're short-handed."

"I need work."

"You, work?" Dressing as a boy was one thing, but working like a boy was something else.

"I've been working for the past month!" Esther's eyes sparkled with pride.

Philippe looked at her in disbelief. She was small, even for a girl. What could she lift?

"Where is the first mate?" Esther looked up to the deck.

"He's sick. Most of the crew is sick."

"Then I'll have to talk to the captain." Esther took four broad steps and jumped up on the gangplank.

"Esther!" Philippe hissed.

"My name is Pierre," Esther hissed back as she scampered up and onto the ship, hitting the deck with the soft thud of a cat. Philippe raced behind her, white with dread. If she were found out …

Esther spoke plainly to a sailor. "I am here to see the captain."

"Below deck." He turned away.

"Est—Pierre!" Philippe lunged forward in a clumsy attempt to grab hold of Esther's arm. She dodged him with a small laugh and plunged through the hatch to the cabin below.

"What's this? Get a move on," the sailor snapped at Philippe.

With his eyes continually drifting back to the hatch Esther had disappeared into, Philippe put aside his seabag and hoisted a sack of grain onto his back.

The captain, lying in his bed below deck and still weak from food poisoning, considered himself a good judge of character. He looked Esther up and down. The boy seemed honest enough and said that he could read, write and count. The captain propped himself up on his elbow, flipped open the Bible and pointed to a passage. "Read anything," he commanded.

It was a different sort of Bible than the Bible at home. Yet the pages were still thick, the lettering still beautiful. Her eyes fell to the page and she read: "Then said Jesus to those Jews which believed on him, *If ye continue in my word, then ye are my disciples indeed.*"

The captain nodded his approval. She was hired. Eighteen barrels of wine and two hundred and twenty sacks of grain were to be delivered to the warehouse. Could she handle that? Yes, Esther said quietly as she closed the book. The words she'd read stayed with her. Was it that simple to become a Christian?

The captain groaned and turned over in his bed. Many's the time he'd come down with food sickness, but this time seemed worse than most. If he ever laid eyes on that cook again, he'd wring his bloody neck.

"Take that away." The captain motioned to a plate of spoiled food.

With a pewter plate in hand, Esther went off to find the ship's galley. She had never been below deck before. It was a mysterious place. The captain's quarters were elegant, with a finely carved wooden table, chair and bench, all fastened to the floor. Such elegance disappeared, though, as she approached the galley. Pigs would not have been happy in such filth. She covered her nose. Rats scattered as she ducked her head and entered. Grease and oil were spilled out on the floor. Maggots feasted off the entrails of carcasses that hung off the shelves. Even the vegetables were maggoty. Something caught her eye. The grain in an open sack moved. Such a thing was not possible. She looked more closely. It was riddled with worms. Only a crate of fruit seemed untainted. Esther picked up a pear and examined it cautiously. The skin was not broken. Quickly she plunged the fruit into water and bit into its sweet flesh. She gobbled it down, seeds and all.

Taking two steps at a time she raced back up the wooden steps, popping up on deck like a rabbit from a hole. A pale-faced sailor standing in for the first mate waved his hand toward a rough board propped on top of two half barrels. Ink and a logbook lay at the ready. "Captain says you are to be the counter. Sit here, then," said the sailor.

Esther grinned at the astonished Philippe, took up her post and, with quill in hand, counted off the sacks and barrels as they were removed from the ship.

At last the work was done. The sun had not yet set, and so the two friends plodded through the town in search of hot biscuits and cups of wine.

Philippe stopped in the street, glanced at Esther and laughed. She spun around and looked first at him, then down at her clothes. "What are you laughing at?" Her clothes fit. The little bosom she had was wrapped tightly in strips of cloth. Her breeches were tied at the waist with a rope, but many boys did the same.

"It's your walk."

"Walk? Of course I walk. Should I fly? Tell me, do you Gentiles think Jews can fly, too?" Esther planted her hands squarely on her hips and thrust out her lower lip. That did it. He laughed until he thought he'd choke.

"Oh, look at me!" He swaggered across the road. "I am a boy." With his hand poised in the air as if holding a teacup, he twirled.

Esther looked cautiously about. No one was paying them any mind. Her face flushed. Perhaps there was more to being a boy than dressing like one.

"Walk like this." Philippe planted two feet firmly on the ground and made strides from one side of the road to another. "And when you run, kick up your legs and move your arms like this." His arms sawed back and forth. "Now, I will show you how to catch." He picked up a stone and flung it at her. Esther ducked. "There's much work to be done." He laughed again. It seemed that there was little that didn't amuse him.

Before they reached the alehouse, Esther felt a sharp pain in her belly. She clutched her middle and gritted her teeth. The pain rolled in and out. Never had a soul needed a privy more than Esther did at that moment.

"You must have eaten something," said Philippe.

"No, all I had was a pear." How was she to know that she had washed the pear in tainted water? She had done herself enough harm to warrant a whacking good case of the trots.

Philippe looked around. There were two grog houses directly ahead. Likely there would be a privy behind one or the other. Men pissed against a wall, of course, but sometimes there was a two- or three-holer in a back lane.

"There!" Philippe pointed to a wooden door behind the second tavern. He ran ahead, opened it and peered inside. A three-holer all right, and empty, too.

Esther, still clutching her stomach, staggered forward and slammed the outhouse door behind her.

"What's that you're after?" The owner of the grog house opened the back door, tossed out a bucket of swill and jeered in Philippe's direction. Philippe dithered. He kept his eyes fixed on the man, not wanting to draw attention to the outhouse. "You'll find nothing to steal hereabouts. On your way," the man yelled again.

Philippe edged back. He'd pick a spot on the road and wait.

As for Esther, her relief was instantaneous. Sitting on one of the three holes, she let out a deep sigh. Then, with the deed done, she made to pull up her breeches. The stink of the place would make her spew if she stayed a moment longer.

"Make room."

Esther's head bobbed up. There, in the doorway of the outhouse, stood the most enormous man she had ever seen. He filled the doorway—he could have filled two doorways!

The giant undid his belt. "Nothing like a good shite to make a man happy, is there?" He roared with laughter, while his beard, belly and hair all wobbled in different directions. He turned around and dropped his pants. There, not an arm's length from Esther, were two enormous, pimply, hairy, warty buttocks. And he was backing up. The huge buttocks were closing in.

Esther put her hands in front of her face. Did he mean to sit on her? Should she scream for help? How would it be to die in a privy, squashed by an arse the size of a ship!

At the last possible second he shifted and thumped down onto the next hole. But the worst was yet to come. He farted. Esther's eyes and nose burned as the stench enveloped her like a cloud. What to do?

"You're a quiet one." The man spoke with great satisfaction. "Now, some like to talk while having a shite, and others, like yourself I expect, do not." His words were accompanied by a symphony of toots and grunts. Esther leaned forward. If she could just reach her breeches and pull them up without exposing herself.

"A good shite is one of the pleasures of life," the man confirmed, waxing philosophical.

"Esther?" Philippe stood on the other side of the door and hissed through the cracks.

"What's that?" hollered the giant. "Who are you after? Only men in here."

The door creaked open. Philippe's mouth gaped at the scene before him. Esther sat on one hole, the giant on the other. Their breeches were pooled around their respective ankles.

Chapter 19

—

"Not a word, Philippe." Esther marched down the road.

"I wasn't going to laugh." Philippe did his best to keep up with her.

"Laugh?" She spun around.

Philippe gulped. Then it happened. He had no control. It was a spasm. An attack. He folded his arms across his belly and bent so far forward he nearly fell over. He'd never laughed as hard in his life. And when at last he thought he had some control, he had only to look at Esther to start howling all over again.

Esther turned on her heels. Was there no end to the humiliation?

Philippe stumbled behind but it was a hard thing to walk and laugh at the same time.

As they approached Catherine's house Philippe's laughter was quelled.

"Take this." Esther reached into her pocket and pulled out six coins, each one hoarded for the express purpose of somehow, some way, getting them to her friend. "Take care that your aunt does not see you give these to Pearl. She may be kind to you, but she is cruel beyond description to that girl. She beats her without mercy. If you cannot find her, go to the back stairs off the kitchen. Pull back the rug on the third step from the top. There is a small hole and a cup behind it. Put the coins in there."

Philippe nodded. He pocketed the coins while Esther hid in a bush on the side of the road. Truth be told, he didn't much like his aunt, but he needed someone to care for his little brother Mathieu, at least until he could get him onto a ship as a cabin boy.

Esther waited, hardly daring to take her eyes off Catherine's house. The sun was setting. A long dusk came and went. Still, she waited as it grew dark.

Philippe finally emerged. He was pale beyond words.

"You must leave." He spoke in a low voice. "Catherine has accused you of theft."

"Theft? But I took nothing!"

"Do you have a gold miniature of the king?"

Esther nodded. "It was mine to keep. Catherine herself told me."

"Do you have it still?"

"It was lost, on the road perhaps, or on the beach. The last I saw of it was in Catherine's house." Was that cursed thing forever to plague her? "But never mind that. How fares Pearl? And how is your brother?"

"My brother is well. He has grown."

"What of Pearl? Did you give her the coins? Did you tell her to hide them well?"

His smile vanished.

"Philippe?" Esther's heart beat hard. "Is she ill?"

"I gave her the coins. She did not want them at first, but I pressed."

"Then what is wrong?"

"She is no longer called Pearl."

"What do you mean?"

"No, it is enough."

"It is not enough. What has happened? Is she by the fire? Is she again a kitchen slave? I must know." Esther pulled at his arm.

"Enough, she is alive. That is all." Grim and resolute, Philippe would say no more.

Later, they sat on the beach and watched the stars come out. As waves lapped softly against the shore Esther let the sand run through her fingers and considered. She must leave Pearl's fate in God's hands for a while longer. She had come to understand that fate opened the door to choice. This time, Esther knew exactly what her choice would be.

⌘

They were shipmates now, each bent to their task. Philippe tended to the ropes, the rigging and all matters concerning the sails aboard ship. Esther worked below deck.

"What's that smell?" A sailor sniffed while winding rope around his forearm. Philippe, too, took in a deep breath. Cake? No cake was ever made on a ship like this one, of that Philippe was dead sure. He followed the aroma to the galley only to find Esther on her hands and knees scrubbing. A cake shaped like a loaf of bread sat on a sideboard.

"I made it for the captain. It's called honey cake. My Maman makes it on Rosh Hashanah. Here, I made one for you." She handed him a smaller cake which he wolfed down in the blink of an eye.

Philippe had never, not in his entire life, tasted anything as wonderful. He marvelled at Esther's ability. She would do well on the ship, of this he had no doubt.

Sailing up and down the coast of France was uneventful, if happiness can be called uneventful. Over the next few months they travelled between the coastal towns of Bordeaux and Nantes.

As Esther slaved in the galley, never complaining, she adjusted to the close space. Work was the price of freedom. Except for the four hours after a Christian service on Sunday, spare time was a rarity. In those free hours Esther set to learning the workings of the ship. It was a hard lesson for any man, but for a girl born to a confined space, both mind and body needed training.

"That be the mainsail, main topsail, main topgallant sail." Philippe gave names to every part of the sails and the rigging. Together they sweated the lines, lay aloft and cast off gaskets. Philippe showed her how to sheet home a sail and stow it again, how to box a compass, tie a bowline and make knots: reef knots, sheet knots, bowline knots, clove hitch, rolling hitch. When the chance came, she took a trick at the helm, stood forward at the lookout and ran aloft to overhaul the rigging. Her fingers were nimble, her mind quick and her feet quicker still.

She did not shun heavy work—on the contrary. Arms that had once grown tired from sewing could now heave, belay and coil ropes. Legs that had found running unfamiliar now scampered up and down the rigging to the masts. Her body grew strong and lean. Her hands would no longer give her away. Once they had been wrapped in raw chicken skin to make them soft; now her palms were as hard as her feet. Esther laughed. What would Catherine have said?

By night, Esther and Philippe sat on the top deck and looked up at the stars.

"That cluster is the Archer, the Plough, the Bow. And that one there is the greatest of all, the North Star." Philippe spoke with pride, as if knowledge gave him some power over the stars.

It was on one such night, when the stars were pinpricks into an unseen world, that Esther, propped up on an elbow, asked Philippe about his family.

"Cook told me that of all your family only your brother Mathieu still lives."

He nodded. He had never told his story before. But then, there had been no one to tell.

"It was a three-day journey by foot from the ship to my village, but I hadn't been home for the longest time. How my mouth watered for my mother's stewed onion pie and a taste of her wine. I'd made it as far as the bend in the road, my own village not a stone's throw away, when I spotted a boy, the small brother of an old friend. He was well growed, so it took me time to recognize him. I was about to call out when he ran off. I walked on, only to see half the village gathered—why, I couldn't tell. They laid down their tools and stared at me—no word of greeting. One old man told me to go no farther. He said my family was dead." Philippe hung his head. It was a hard thing to say these words out loud.

"The men of the village, men I'd known all my life, tried to keep me from my cottage. They called out, 'Get away! Don't go near!' When I turned and looked at the cottage, there were boards over the door, over the window, and I understood. All those I held dear lay dead and unburied within. Then the air filled with woodsmoke. Lit torches surrounded me. They meant to burn the cottage to the ground! There was a clamour—

screams and yells, men, women, children, too, crying out. And through it, a miracle!"

Philippe turned and looked at Esther wide-eyed, as though the memory both frightened and amazed him. "It's God's truth—at that moment I heard a wailing from within the cottage. It was a child's cry! They meant to burn the child alive!"

"Why?" Esther sat up, astonished.

"They feared that whoever still lived within the cottage carried the disease," Philippe answered simply. The memory of the plague was never far away. "The strength of Samson came over me. I ripped the boards off the door with my bare hands." Philippe looked down at his hands as if seeing them for the first time. "And when I looked inside, I saw ..." His voice drifted and grew weak. He shook his head. "I pulled my brother Mathieu off our dead mother and then I left. I will never return. I will find us a new life, somehow."

Looking to the sky, then, he named his sisters, pointing to a star with each name: Brigitte, Antoinette, Marie, Thérèse. And his brothers: André, Émile, Henri. He tried to say the names of his parents but feared that he might sob.

"You are a good brother and a good friend," whispered Esther. They were on a ship with a full complement of sailors and there were eyes about, even in the dark. Esther could offer no more comfort than words, although she would have dearly loved to put her arms around him.

After a time, Esther fell asleep, feeling safe under a canopy of stars.

Philippe looked over at the sleeping girl. Why did she stir him so, and what should he do about his feelings? It wasn't that he didn't know what to do with a woman. But Esther wasn't like any female he'd ever known or was ever likely to know.

What could he do? It was Esther he loved, but it was Pierre
Mausiette who was lying beside him.

∽

If Esther appeared odd to the crew, if she had effeminate ways,
none on board let on, lest they lose the best cook most had ever
known. Of course, no one noticed that pork was no longer avail-
able, that meat and dairy were separated, that salt horse was no
longer offered. To the best of Esther's limited ability, Jewish
dietary laws were applied.

Toward the end of summer the ship had sailed farther down
the rocky coast toward the seaside town of La Rochelle. The wind
was soft, the sun high in a blue sky. The men languished here and
there, some below deck playing cards, others going about their
work slowly. The real labour would begin within the day when
they put in to port.

"Will you come up?" Philippe stood on deck with a foot on
the rigging and pointed aloft.

Esther, holding back hair that had escaped from a leather
thong, looked up to the crow's nest and beyond. *Yes, yes, more
than anything*.

"Follow me!" He laughed as he dangled off a line.

Esther hoisted herself up onto the mizzen shrouds, then
grasped the ratlines that formed a ladder up the mizzenmast.
Higher and higher they went, one after the other. Words were
swiped by the wind, and so it was his actions she copied. He
grabbed hold of the shrouds, not the ratlines, and Esther did
the same. He threaded his way around the running gear and
Esther followed, looking neither down nor sideways, only up.
The shrouds narrowed near the masthead. Phillip yelled out,

"Mizzen top," then scampered over the short shrouds.

And then they were there, at the very top of the ship and as close to God as man could come. As the ship rolled, the masts swayed, pitched and yawed with ease. Wind rushed past Esther's ears, bringing a sort of silence. Surely her heart would break over the sheer beauty that surrounded her. Could there be anything on earth or in heaven this wondrous? Her very soul soared. The sea rolled out before them, a scattering of diamonds tossed down from above. The ship below, past the arc of canvas, was a narrow line. Esther shouted into the wind, her hands extended as if to embrace the world, her world, the world she claimed. The tireless wind made her eyes water. A river of tears streamed down her face. If she had to return to the Jewish Quarter right now, if she had to disappear into housekeeping, giving birth and child-tending, this moment alone would be worth everything. *Thank you, thank you.* The words were whispered in her heart.

Esther spied in the far distance, not yet in view to those below, three large stone towers that guarded the entrance of the port city called La Rochelle. They climbed down, Esther as sure of her footing as a mountain goat.

It was a busy place. From this great commercial port ships set out for Cayenne, Madagascar, the West Indies, Mississippi, New France, Canada, too. It was all she could do not to cry out with laughter and excitement. Such sights, such colour, such commerce. As the ship docked against the wharf she could smell cocoa, vanilla and tobacco. Fish traders stood alongside ships bargaining for cod, salmon, conger eel and fish oil. Even now merchants were haggling over fur pelts, Canadian timber, spices from the Orient and exotic clothing. In the warehouses beyond, cotton, sugar and indigo awaited shipment to Paris.

The gangplank bounced and swayed under her feet. She went over the list of supplies to be purchased for the ship's kitchen: two sacks of beans, one sack of flour, four barrels of pickled meat, a jar of olives, dried fish, a dozen rounds of cheese, hardtack, fresh vegetables and fruits. And spices—how she would have liked to sample a few. All the treasures in the world were at her feet.

"Wait for me!" Philippe yelled out from the deck. But it was hard to keep from moving forward. She passed well-wishers on the wharf waving hello or goodbye, merchants, waifs, blind and one-legged beggars, dogs, cats, carts and wagons of every size and description. There were taverns aplenty. Beyond the heavy, iron-studded doors she could hear the roars of rowdy men and the high-pitched squeals of women. Occasionally a door would fly open and, as a dam might burst, a great swell of noise would flood the streets. The energy of the place swirled around her, intoxicating and wonderful.

Casks, sacks and kegs were ordered and sent back to the ship, and by the time Philippe was released from his duties, her work, too, was done. The two spent a happy afternoon together, the happiest she had ever known. They visited a tavern and hoisted a mug, and ate heartily. With full stomachs, Esther and Philippe carried on down the port.

Toward the end of the wharf came a smell so putrid, so loathsome, that Esther nearly keeled over with sick. She stumbled toward it, curious but with a sense of foreboding.

"It's best we go back," said Philippe.

"What is that foul smell?"

Philippe pointed toward a ship that sat high on the water. "It's a slave ship. Look."

There, on a beach at the far end of the wharf, away from the commerce of the day, sat strangely shaped bundles of wood. What's more, something inside the bundles moved!

"What is it?"

"They are cleaning the hold of the ship and have brought the slaves on shore. They are kept in a wooden jail."

Philippe stopped. Esther could not. She walked on, incapable of doing otherwise.

Thin stalks of wood, the likes of which she had never seen before, were formed into large circles. The bottoms were stuck deep into the sand while the tops were bent inward and tied together with rope. She drew closer, closer still and stopped in front of one such contraption. White, liquid eyes peered out from blackness. Dozens of eyes, terrified eyes. Transfixed, Esther approached the wooden bars. Women, men, even children, all naked, were packed together so tightly that none could move or sit. Who were these strange people—were they people at all?

Esther stopped, her feet rooted to the ground. She reached out to the bars. The whip came between her and the bars with such ferocity that a cloud of dust sprang up.

"Get aways from them. Does ya wants your hand bit off?"

Esther looked up into the ruined face of a slave driver. On a misshapen head hung malformed lips, blistered and diseased. His face was marked with the pox, each pit sprouting tufts of grey hair, and his bulging eyes were as red as raw meat.

"Away with you!" he hollered. They were *his* slaves, his to whip and starve and beat as the mood struck him. He snarled and turned his attention to the task at hand, reloading his cargo back onto the ship.

The slave driver opened the latch to one of the wooden jails. She heard a small, involuntary cry and then realized that it was she who was crying out. Each slave plodded forward. The males were attached to each other by means of ropes that circled their ankles. The females walked alongside. The small ones staggered beside their mothers. It was hell that was parading before her. Esther could hardly watch, and yet could not look away. Bile rose up in her throat.

"Where are they being taken?" she whispered.

"To the American Colonies, mostly. A few to New France. Come."

The joy of the day drained away.

❧

By late afternoon the supplies had been brought on board and the water casks scraped clean and refilled. Added to Esther's stores were boxes of turnips and maize. The galley was a pretty sight. Everything in order, scrubbed, cleaned to the bone. None aboard had ever seen anything like it.

They would sail within the hour. Esther stood on deck and breathed in the sea air. She felt a pull in her belly. How odd. Esther was not given to sickness, not usually. She gripped the ship's rail, and felt a warmth in her loins. What was it? There was no pain, yet her breeches felt damp. Could she have pissed and not known? She crept down to the galley and stood alone. Slowly, she tucked her hand into her pants then pulled them back. She stifled a scream. Her fingers were stained red. What kind of pox had been inflicted on her? She held her hands up under a swaying cistern and washed away the blood. Her mind reeled with fear. Was it the plague? It was known that many plague victims died when blood seeped out of their bodies. But such an affliction was accompanied by sickness. Esther felt well.

Her mother's words came back to her. Women bled once every new moon. Could this be the thing that happened to women? The blood was for a baby, but when there was no baby the blood fell out. How long did this bleeding go on? There was no one to ask! What should she do? What punishment would be meted out if it were known that she was a female? And what of Philippe? He would bear the brunt of her deception. She had to get off the ship without being seen. There were shouts from the first mate. It would not be long before they would set sail.

She crept back down the passage from the quarterdeck toward the forecastle. It was the captain himself who called out from his cabin.

"You there, boy, get out the logs."

Esther turned and stood on the threshold. The captain, a fair man by reputation, tossed a ring of keys across a square wooden table. She could not will herself to move.

"What ails you? I said fetch me the log books."

Esther snatched the keys off the table and bent down to unlock the strong box, all the while trying to stop the flow between her legs. Her hands shook. After everything, after all her efforts … It was a betrayal, her own body was betraying her in a way she had never imagined.

The books were heavy and lifting them seemed to increase her problem. She placed the books on the table. A trickle of red dripped down her pant leg. She had to get off the ship—now!

"Captain." Esther's voice was as strong as she could make it. "I am expecting a cask of wine to be brought on board. I beg to be excused." She bowed her head slightly.

"Wine? Is it not yet on board?"

"Sir, a cask was damaged. Replacement is at hand."

The captain loved his wine. No ship under his command would sail without all provisions. "See to it at once," he roared.

Esther bolted out of the cabin, stopping only to mop up her leg as best she could. The gangplank was still lowered.

Philippe, where was he? She must explain. Esther leapt onto the gangplank and then landed on the wharf with a thud. The plank was pulled up.

"Pierre!" She heard her name being called out. She turned back to see Philippe standing at the rail. Ropes were being cast off. "Why?" His question was taken away by the wind.

Esther raised her hand in farewell. Forgive me.

*C*hapter 20

*E*sther spent the night hidden in a fishing shack among nets, ropes and fish guts. How long did this bleeding last? A day? Two days? Ten? If only there had been a woman to ask, to seek advice from. She knew that a woman experiencing this affliction (how could she think of it as anything but?) would simply bleed into her clothes. But a woman wore layers and layers of under-skirts. A man's breeches would not conceal her secret. Esther needed an invention, how else to carry on her disguise?

It was on the second day in La Rochelle, while wading in and out of the water along the beach, that an idea struck. The answer was in the water itself. She climbed up onto the rocks, peering into small pools. Esther reached into the sea and pulled up a sponge. Once it was dry, she undid the pocket that dangled from her belt, wrapped the sponge in a rag and attached it to the belt. It was a crude invention, and the rough rag chafed at her tender thighs, but it worked. Her secret was once again hidden.

Days passed before Esther found work as a cook on a Spanish craft. It was a mean ship, captained by a miserable man who didn't much care what happened on board and so left the running of the vessel to his first mate. The crew was a collection of brutes. A cabin boy of perhaps eight years of age was often the target of their cruelty and recreation. He was a slave child sold to the captain for the price of a goat. The boy would eventually gain his freedom, if he lived long enough, though that hardly seemed likely.

While Esther laboured below deck, the crew amused themselves by jostling the boy about. Shoving became hitting, and when they grew weary of that a seaman dropped a cask of olives on the boy's foot. The boy collapsed in pain while the sailors laughed themselves sick. The whimpering boy dragged his bloody foot across the deck like a dog hauling a broken leg.

Esther watched it happen. Though she had secured her protection against thugs the first time she'd delivered a loaf of freshly baked bread to the captain's cabin, she was wary of drawing attention to herself. Yet she revolted at the sight of such cruelty. She caught the boy's eye, then turned and dropped down into the hold. In the galley and out of sight, she bandaged the boy's foot. The skin was broken, revealing tiny, smashed bones. The boy fought back tears, but it was no use.

"Listen to me," Esther muttered under her breath as she cleaned his foot with boiled water. "You must find a way to make your value known. Only then will you be left alone." Esther looked at the bandaged foot with satisfaction. With luck, there would be no infection, but he would be maimed for life, of that she was certain.

"It's no use. I have no value," the boy hissed through clenched teeth.

"If you have no value even to yourself, then surely you are lost."

The days and nights passed uneventfully. From a distance Esther watched the boy and saw that, while he fared no better, he fared no worse, either. His presence was a constant reminder of Pearl. It would be best to buy the girl's freedom, but what if the cost was too high? And how would she negotiate such a deal? What if she and Pearl just ran away? If they were caught, it would mean the stocks for Pearl, prison, and worse, for Esther.

The day the Spanish tub tacked into Biarritz was hazy. Storm clouds lay like an unfurled blanket on the horizon. All hands were on deck. From behind, Esther heard a terrific flapping of the canvas, then screeches as the sails slithered down the main mast. The anchor cable was released from the bow and the iron anchor plunged into the water. The ship tugged as the anchor bit into the rocky sea bottom. It made an attempt to break free before settling into a soft rocking motion. With her hand shading her eyes against the glaring haze, Esther again and again looked to the shore. There was a good chance that Philippe had received her messages, passed from one sailor to another, as was the fashion. If he knew the name of her ship, it would take only a small effort to discover the time of the ship's arrival. All ships registered their comings and goings. But what would she say when he asked her why she had jumped ship in La Rochelle? Did boys know about this bleeding?

A small skiff was lowered over the side. Only the cabin boy was given leave from ship's duties, to deliver a letter to the harbour quartermaster. It was Esther's duty, as cook, to acquire new provisions as soon as possible. The boy with the broken foot was on the oars ready to take Pierre Mausiette, cook, ashore.

With practised ease, Esther took hold of a lead line, swung it out over port side and slid down the rope to land in the rowboat. He was too small a boy to manage the boat on his own and so the two rowed together.

Let him be here, she prayed as the skiff made for shore. And then, there he was on the wharf. Bronze skin, yellow hair, white teeth, and a sack of grain over one shoulder.

"Philippe!" Esther called out, waving. He saw her and waved back. The boy gave her a strange look, for certainly when the cook's voice was raised she sounded like a girl! Esther caught the look on the boy's face, lowered her hand and said little else.

Something was amiss. As the boat drew closer, Esther could see that what she'd taken for a smile on Philippe's tanned face was really a grimace. The sack of grain slid from his shoulder as he stood beside a docked seafaring ship that lay deep in the water. Dozens of common seamen were running about the brig, two or more up the shrouds, others dangling from the rigging, each to their tasks, still more padding about on deck. Whatever ship Philippe was working on, it was one destined for a long journey, and soon.

The cabin boy manoeuvred the skiff toward a ladder attached to the wharf, dropped the oars and secured the boat to a post.

"Esther." Philippe whispered the name.

Esther looked up sharply. It was their agreement that he would never use her real name, ever. She looked at the boy on the oars— had he heard? The boy just looked down at his feet.

"What is it?" Esther scrambled up the ladder.

"Catherine ..." he began.

Esther's breath caught in her throat while her hand flew to her mouth. Catherine knew of her whereabouts. There was an arrest warrant out for her. That had to be it. She had to flee, she had to get back to the ship.

"No, no. It's Pearl." Philippe reached out for her. Dear God in heaven, how he wished to hold her, crush her to his side, comfort her as a man might a woman. Just as quickly his hand dropped to his side. He cast his eyes to the ground. He did not know how to say what must come next.

Esther turned back and stared. "What, then?"

"She is dead."

Dead? Pearl dead? No, not dead. Sick maybe, harmed perhaps, but not dead. "How?"

"Pearl was caught coming down the stairs. She was not allowed above stairs, not ever. They say that she would not tell where she had been. That she clamped her mouth shut. She attacked Cook, and Cook only defended herself."

Caught on the stairs? Might she have been going to their hiding place? Esther grabbed her middle and bent forward. Pearl—she couldn't take it in. As for Cook, the woman was so full of venom she could die from swallowing her own spit. Pearl, attack Cook? If there was madness about, it was that anyone could believe such a thing. Anger replaced horror. She turned on Philippe. "Why would Pearl attack that cow you call Aunt?"

"I do not know. As God is my witness, I was not there!" He hung his head. Neither gave any thought to the boy who sat wide eyed and wide eared in the skiff that bobbed on the water below the pier.

"Was it the coins? Might Cook have found the coins and accused Pearl of being a thief?"

"I think not." Philippe reached into his own pocket and pulled out a small leather purse. "I retrieved this for you. They were all under the stairs in that hiding spot." He placed the purse in Esther's hand.

"Oh," she moaned. The tears began to fall. "How, I must know how?"

"They say she fell against the grate … her head … I am sorry." Philippe looked the very picture of misery.

Esther could hear no more. Pearl, the child, the little bird who had harmed no one ... it was unjust. She turned away and began to walk toward town. Soon the walk became a run.

"Where are you going? Stop. Do not go near the house. You have no kidney for revenge. Stop!" Philippe ran up beside her.

Esther's feet carried her forward with the force of a gale. She stormed up the hill toward the market. A horse reared up and whinnied. Food vendors stood behind carts and hollered:

"Chestnuts, warm chestnuts."

"Pigeon pies, fresh pies."

"Water for sale, fresh from the spring."

Philippe chased after her, giving little thought to his berth on the seafaring ship. Abandoning a ship might well put him at the nasty end of a cat-o'-nine-tails, but no matter. "Wait," he cried. But there was no stopping Esther. Up she went, up and up into the town of Biarritz.

She passed the parish church, passed the large houses behind iron gates and tall trees, and then she stopped in front of the home of Catherine Churiau and Madame de La Grange.

It was there that Philippe caught up with her. "They are not here," he huffed. "It is what I have been trying to tell you. Catherine dismissed most of the staff and left. I know not where any of them have gone."

Esther's fingers wrapped around the black iron bars as if squeezing them with all her might would take away the anger. She pressed her face against the gate and looked into the empty garden. *Oh Pearl, I left you too long. Forgive me.* Philippe was right. She had no kidney for revenge. Although, if truth were told, Cook was a wicked old cow, and it would prove no hardship to any if she were dispatched to the other side.

"Your brother Mathieu—what of him?"

"He is well. I found him at the home where he once lodged."

"And Marie de La Grange?" Esther let go of the bars and drew in what little breath was left to her.

"Gone too, with her daughter."

Esther and Philippe made their way back to the wharf and sat on a stone wall looking out to sea. A wind was building. The sky had been threatening rain all day. Ships in the harbour were battening down the hatches.

"We sail to the New World on the next tide. Mathieu is cabin boy. A cook's been hired, but they are short a galley hand. Think of it, Esther—they say anything can happen in the New World."

Philippe's babble about this new, great adventure was unceasing. Try as she might, Esther could hardly take in more than a word or two. Why had she waited?

"Cook once said that it did no good to take people out of their place. Pearl's place was by the fire." Esther squeezed her eyes shut.

"Enough." Philippe tuned and faced her squarely. "You are not listening. It's a new life that awaits, Esther. Away from this old world and its old ways. They say there is land for the asking in the Carolinas." As Philippe spoke, a soft rain began to fall.

"Come with us, Esther. We could begin again, all three of us. We could be together. I don't mean … you wouldn't have to marry me … I would accept what you have to give—we are friends."

He would have taken her in his arms if such a thing had been possible, if she were not named Pierre, if she would have had him. Right from the beginning he'd known that this girl, this Esther, was different from anyone he had ever known. It was as if … as if … the world around her was not as important to Esther as the world she saw ahead of her. But he had hope—even now he had hope.

"I must go and fetch my brother. We're leaving on the next tide. Meet me at the ship … if you can."

He had tarried as long as he dared. If this was the end, so be it.

She watched him walk away, down the hill, out of view.

"Philippe? PHILIPPE!" Already he was too far to hear her call. She might have run after him. Instead, Esther rested her chin in the palms of her hands. What of this new life, this New World? She had heard the names, exotic names like Savannah, New York, Boston. Sometimes life took turns. Was this such a turn? What if there really was freedom in this New World? Might Jews, too, find an equal place? Might she find a home? Pearl was gone, and Philippe was leaving. What ties did she have to this land?

There was a clap of thunder. Esther looked up at the darkening sky. Black clouds were fast approaching and the wind had picked up. Was it a sign? Very well, she would make a choice. It would be the New World and a new life. Esther jumped down from the wall and made her way back to the wharf.

She recognized the limp. The cabin boy, surrounded by the Spanish crew, turned and gazed at her as she approached. From that distance it was hard to tell what their intentions were, but she had a sense of them. First they huddled around the boy, and then they turned toward her. They fanned out into a line. Their shoulders were hunched, their eyes narrowed—they had a menacing look about them, like a pack of dogs. She had seen this look in men's eyes before. They moved toward her. The boy shouted something. He pointed at her. What was he saying? *Girl.* He'd called her a girl. They knew. The boy had found a way to make himself indispensable. He had learned his lesson well.

The men started to lope toward her, but they were lumpish, a ragged bunch of sailors who hadn't yet found their land legs. What they lacked in speed, however, they made up for in fury. She had made fools of them, and they meant to teach her a lesson.

Esther pivoted on her toes. She was quick, light and frightened. Fear was a great fuel.

Biarritz was a town she knew well. Esther turned up a muddy path, more track than road, and raced ahead, past the lemon trees, past the orchards. Up and down, around one building and down another road. Around and around, until she was sure they had lost their direction. Twice they'd nearly overtaken her. Once they'd been close enough that, from behind a wall, she'd seen one of the sailors stop and snort like a horse. Sweat had collected on his moustache. His black eyes had searched the trees and shrubs. He'd started toward her, closer, closer, until a mate had called out to him. *"Si,"* he'd yelled back, then turned and was gone.

Cupping her arms across her belly, Esther staggered on until she came to a crossroad. It was there that she remembered. The boy had seen her with Philippe. She had endangered both Philippe and his brother, just as she had endangered Pearl. Philippe would be watched until his ship sailed, of that she was dead sure. Never, ever again would she bring harm to a friend. There was no question, she would not be joining him now. Esther put her back to the road post and slipped down until she sat on the ground, her legs sprawled out in front of her. The wind dried her tears before they had a chance to fall. Once again fate had won out over choice.

The next day brought more rain. On the second night she cried less and slept under stone cold steps. The following night she fell into a stupor behind a garden wall. Dogs chased her and people shooed her away, some with pitchforks, others with tongues that hurled abuse like rocks. Esther groped her way down roadways and lanes, not taking in her surroundings. Food was scarce. She plucked fruit from trees and bought bread when she could. The rain did not let up. It ran off roofs and down gutters, turning roads into simmering, bubbling streams of filth.

Twice she was bidden to come into a house and dry herself. But Esther just shook her head. The fear of removing her clothes and exposing her identity was too much.

Once she found refuge in a church. "Hear, O Israel: the Lord is our God, the Lord is One! Blessed is His glorious kingdom for ever and ever," she whispered as she crossed the threshold. She looked to the stone statues, searching out the kindest face. Mary. Esther stood in front of the statue until a priest came along and shooed her away. "Dirty boy," he muttered.

A tinker offered her a jacket and blanket for a good price. Reaching deep into her pocket she fingered the few coins that lay hidden in the folds of her body linens. She purchased the rough blanket but no amount of shaking would rid it of lice. Soon she, too, was covered in lice. Again and again she plunged into cold rivers, ponds, even ditches to rid herself of the vermin.

One day passed into the next, and the next. With each step she became more miserable, more disheartened. What did the road matter if there was no destination? At crossroads she simply went one way or other, without thought or care.

A week passed, perhaps more. She came upon a town and was soon lost among its back alleys. Roads twisted in odd directions with no rhyme or reason, so that a body heading west could soon be heading south, or north, or east. If she passed a fair, she took no notice. If soggy jugglers juggled and drenched puppets paraded or pranced, she did not care. And so it was that Esther, worn out, infested, hungry and broken, found herself standing at the gates of the Jewish Quarter of St. Esprit.

Chapter 21

❧

*E*sther stood quite still, so still that raindrops lay on her brow and lips. Her mouth gaped as her eyes tried to take in her surroundings. How could this be? What mighty hand had guided her here? She reached out to steady herself against the wall by the gate before pushing back her cap and raising her face to the sky. The rain that had abated for a time had returned.

Wagon wheels rattled on the cobblestones behind her. "Out of the way!" cried the driver. Esther flung herself against a wall. Hooves and wheels sent up a spray of mud.

She wiped her face with her hand. The wagon turned a corner and the streets became suddenly empty. Despite the scene around her, the wet brick at her back and the rain on her face, it all seemed unreal, dreamlike.

The sun was about to dip below the horizon. The toll collectors had left for the night, so she walked on, incapable of doing anything else. Tallow candles flickered from within each house. Soft prayers, sung and hummed, drifted and mingled with the rain. The sounds wafted toward her, greeting and caressing her. It was the Sabbath. She half expected a voice to call out to her, to chastise her for being late. Esther stumbled and again righted herself. She had been away for almost two years.

Esther passed the synagogue, the meeting house, the familiar buildings that had been her whole world when no other had existed. How small everything looked, how clean and contained. She stumbled over one bridge, then another. And there it was, Papa's shop. Tears mingled with her sweat.

"Stop. Who goes there?"

The voice was familiar. Although it was not yet dark, a lantern dangling at the tip of a long pole moved toward her. It was Abel, the watchman.

Esther ducked into the shadows as Abel passed by. Slowly, slowly, like a mouse from a hole, she poked her head around the wall. She had a good view of the steps that led down to Papa's shop. She waited until she was sure that Abel was a distance away and then, in a sudden burst of energy, she dashed out and hurled herself down the stairs. An empty trunk, the sort of large case Papa transported his bolts of cloth in, stood to one side of the shop door in the open stairwell. Again Abel called out, he was coming closer. Esther squeezed between the trunk and the wall. How she hated small spaces.

"What is it, Abel?" a second voice called out from the street above.

"I saw a boy, a Gentile, running this way," Abel called back.

Esther sucked in a breath. Now there were two hunting for her.

"Which way was he going?"

"Toward David Brandeau's shop, I think."

"Best tell him."

"Pity to interrupt *Shabbat*."

The watchman clomped down the stone steps. Esther, standing behind the trunk, slammed her back against the wall. He was a hair's breadth away. If she reached out, she could touch him. Footsteps echoed from within the house. The bolt slipped. Esther squeezed her eyes shut.

"Abel? What is wrong?" It was Papa's voice. *Oh, Papa.*

"Good *Shabbos,* David. A boy was seen coming in this direction."

"What boy?" asked Papa.

"A Gentile, I think."

"I'll look out for him," said Papa.

She heard footsteps scraping against the steps. "*Mazel tov* on your daughter's match, my friend. A rabbi's son for your daughter. To think—a rabbi for a son and a rabbi for a son-in-law—a double blessing." Abel chuckled as he walked back up the stone stairs.

"Yes, yes. Thank you. Good *Shabbos,*" said Papa as he closed the door.

"And to you." Abel's steps faded away and all was quiet.

Esther breathed deeply. Sarah was to be married to the rabbi's son. Was it Isaac? She crept out from her hiding place and stood in front of the door. With one hand she touched the *mezuzah* and with the other the window. What fun it had been to watch the bubbly glass being fitted into the door. Mama had clapped her hands and she and Sarah had danced in a circle. They had all been so proud. It was all so very long ago.

Esther pressed her face against the window and looked through the shop and down the little hall toward the glow of candles. The light was poor but she could see everyone seated at the table. A boy bobbed up and down. Was that Joseph? How he had grown. She could see only Maman's hands as they reached out toward the Sabbath candles.

"Come, my beloved, to meet the Bride. Let us welcome the presence of the Sabbath. Come in peace ... and come in joy ... Come, O Bride! Come, O Bride!" Maman's hands floated above the candles. Esther closed her eyes. *Come, O Bride!* She slipped back into the past. She was a little girl again, a small, friendless child in a grey world. *Never mind, my daughter, never mind.* Maman wrapped her arms around her. Oh, how good it felt to be warm. *Pay no attention to what others say, you are loved, you are loved.* She could feel her mother's arms around her. What did it matter that she was not born of this woman? She was loved. *Maman, I love you too.*

But Esther was too greedy to keep her eyes closed for long. There was more to see, and she hungered after every glimpse.

Papa's back was toward her. It would have been good to see his face, but there was no time for regrets. There was baby Samuel. Look, look at what a handsome little boy he was! And there was Sarah. Oh, how fat she had become. There was a tall man sitting beside her. Was that...?

Someone stood. It was Papa. He turned toward her. He could not see her, but she could make him out well enough. He looked so much older. *Papa, you have another daughter. I am here, Papa. You have another daughter still living!* Papa reached out. All went black. He had closed the door between the shop and the house.

No, no, no! She wanted to scream, to beat her hands against the door. All she asked for was a look. It wasn't fair.

Her legs buckled. Esther slid down into a damp, cold pool of water, knocked her head against her knees and cried.

VILLE DE QUEBEC, NEW FRANCE, SEPTEMBER 1738

"Are you telling me that you did not make your presence known?" Intendant Hocquart leaned forward in his chair.

Startled, Esther looked over at the intendant. Behind him, through tall windows, stars glittered. It had to be midnight or beyond. She shook her head and said simply, "No."

"You must have realized that by turning your back on your father, you would never know anything more about the woman who gave you life."

"To learn about her is to learn about myself." On this she was resolute, so much so that Hocquart glanced, however briefly, at an invincibility rarely seen in one so young. It unnerved him.

"But surely you wanted your family to know that you were alive?"

"Who of us wants to be forgotten? Who will remember us if not our family?"

"And yet?"

"And yet I did not go in."

Hocquart sat back and considered all that he had heard. This family, this *Jewish* family, was much the same as his own in its petty trials and tribulations. He himself was the third child in a family of fourteen. He had a brother he detested, sisters he adored and a fearsome grandmother. His mother, too, loved profoundly and worried continually, as if to do otherwise would invite catastrophe. And, as a boy, he had also wondered why his father demanded his sons follow in his footsteps when he himself seemed the unhappiest of men. Hocquart emptied his wine glass and peered into the dying fire. He had not anticipated finding similarities, much less an affinity, with this Jewish life.

Hocquart did not signal a servant to tend the fire but added a log himself. He then refilled the two glasses with a deep, earthy red wine—fruits from the rich soil of his beloved France. He sipped while he pondered. He was not yet so taken in by the tale that common sense did not prevail. The girl had found herself on her family's doorstep in the midst of her own very grave crisis. Why, then, had she not availed herself of their sanctuary?

"You had discovered that the life outside the Jewish Quarter was not all you had dreamed. It might even appear that the world from which you hail is—kinder. Tell me, then, why you did not return to your family when you had the chance?"

The frustration in Hocquart's voice was apparent.

"Hope," she said simply.

He could not have heard correctly. He asked her to repeat herself.

"I have learned that I can live without love and food and even shelter, but I cannot live without hope. In my father's house there was only *certainty*. This I knew in that instant when my hand was poised to rap at my father's door. I knew then that I could never, willingly, return."

Hocquart sank back in his chair. It was hope that had compelled him to board a ship and suffer the perils of a dangerous crossing to this New World. It was hope that kept him in this land. It was hope that propelled him forward with the sure knowledge that one day Quebec would provide France with boundless resources. Yes, he understood hope.

"Had I known what awaited me ..." Her voice became small.

"What was that?"

"Hell. It was hell that awaited."

"Go on."

And as the night wore on, so did the story of Esther Brandeau.

*C*hapter 22

❧

*T*he rain did not stop. The Jewish Quarter of St. Esprit, now well behind her, was a dream, an apparition of a past existence.

Day in and day out it poured. Esther walked on, too exhausted to understand that her situation was dire. Her direction was as unsure as her footing. She was running away from the past, and looking for nothing more than a place to rest. The roadways yielded to mud. She had stopped counting the sunsets and marked the time only by the feel of the weather. Again and again she slipped and fell into pools of muck. It was getting colder.

On this day, when the rain had mercifully relented and was little more than a spit, a thunder of hooves made her ears perk up and her head swivel. It was the sound of danger. The voice in her head that had often bidden her run now told her to leap—leap as high and as far as she could. She jumped into a hedge, then scratched and clawed her way through it until she lay flat out on the wet ground on the other side.

Dozens of horses, maybe more, came roaring down the road with such force that the very ground beneath her trembled. Gold-trimmed carriages stampeded past without thought or care for the surroundings. Ladies and gentlemen sitting in comfort behind pulled shades and drawn curtains poked their noses out then pulled back. There was only poverty to see, and so they did not look.

Drivers flicked their whips and urged their beasts on, faster, faster. Frenzied horses, their eyes wild, kicked up mud, leaving great grooves in the already rutted road. It was a royal procession. While the peasants of France starved, the royal court carried on with an opulence and splendour never before seen on earth. Perhaps fifty carriages raced by, maybe more. And then they were gone.

Esther flopped over onto her back and looked up at a sky that was as flat and grey as a pewter dish. Had she stayed with Catherine, might she have been in such an entourage? Might she, too, have been part of such a callous, unfeeling world that lived behind curtains?

The ground beneath her was cold and brittle. The stubble of cut hay was as sharp as needles and poked through her thin jacket. She was soaked through and covered now in cuts and scratches. She stood and walked on.

⁓

For the price of a coin, Esther climbed into a cart that was already packed with peasants travelling from one village to another. The direction of the cart was of no concern to her. And when the burden of the passengers proved too much for the mule, Esther and the peasants were left along the roadside.

Soon it was not the rain that drenched her but fever. The sticky sweat that covered her body now turned into a slimy coat. Her teeth bumped against each other. She shivered and yet felt hot, so hot that steam seemed to rise from her body. Esther stumbled in every direction looking for a place to curl up in and disappear.

A well-trodden path led to an ornate wooden door. Prickly bramble bushes crept up on either side, nearly disguising it.

With the little strength left to her, Esther pushed the door open. A lone candle burned brightly on a far stone altar. Stone pews lined each side of this tiny chapel. Esther stumbled across the threshold. *Hear, O Israel: the Lord is our God, the Lord is One! Blessed is His glorious kingdom for ever and ever.*

Grasping the ends of the stone pews Esther crept toward the altar. If only she could see properly, but the light shivered and bent. There was Jesus on the cross, and in an alcove to the side stood a small stone girl with stone wings. It was Mary. She could go no farther. Esther lay along the pew and fell into a deep, tormented sleep.

"Child?" A gentle and agreeable voice called to her across a vast space.

"Maman?" Esther opened her eyes, blinked and looked up toward a small, vaulted roof. Brilliant morning sunlight filtered in through stained-glass windows, burning crimson embers on the stone walls. The sun, oh, the glorious sun—it had stopped raining.

"Child, wake up."

Esther turned her head slowly and looked into sea-blue eyes half buried in a nest of wrinkles. The face smiled and more wrinkles appeared. The woman bent forward—only then could Esther see her attire. The woman was a nun.

The nun disappeared from view then returned with a cup of spring water. She held the cup up to Esther's lips. Water dribbled down Esther's chin. Her head was propped up and cupped in the palm of a large hand. Again she tried to open her eyes and again she beheld the face of a nun. The light had changed. It was darker now, midday, perhaps.

"What is your name?" the nun asked kindly.

Esther swallowed the water and tried to recall her name. Even now, in the fog of illness, she did not reveal herself. "Pierre Mausiette." Esther's voice wobbled.

"Well, Pierre, can you sit up?"

Esther nodded and made the effort.

The nun wore a dark, rough, woollen robe, rosary beads tied on a belt, and a large wooden cross around her neck. A band of white cloth stretched across her forehead was attached to a veil that hung down her back. Her eyes, nose and mouth—those parts needed to breathe, see and eat, were visible. She crossed herself, then leaned down to help Esther stand. It was no use. Esther managed only to sway in two directions before falling back down onto the stone pew. Undaunted, the nun circled her arm around Esther and, with a great grunt, pulled her up onto two shaky legs.

"Where are you taking me?" Esther whispered.

"To the convent."

The word *convent* hardly registered. "Wh-why are you doing this?" Esther stuttered. It was not only her legs that refused to cooperate but her tongue as well.

"'*Suffer the little children to come unto me,*' said our Lord Jesus. Come along now."

With the nun's arms supporting her, Esther got to her feet and made her way slowly out of the chapel. Though the sunlight smacked her like a blow to the face, she managed to cross a road and stumble down a grassy path. They stopped in front of a hedge. It took a moment before Esther realized that there was a door embedded in the shrubbery and that the hedge disguised a wall. As with the chapel door, brambles and vines nearly hid it completely.

The nun reached into the shrubbery and yanked a rope. Somewhere in the distance a bell rang.

A small peephole in the door opened. A tiny face peered through a wooden grille. The shadows of the bars fell upon her face.

"It is you, Sister Angeline. What have you brought us?" Satisfied that no harm would come her way, she threw open the wooden door. She wasn't a woman at all, or even a real nun. She was a young girl dressed in a simple brown robe with a small veil covering her hair.

Once again the nun thrust an arm around Esther's waist and helped her forward. The young girl leapt out of the way as Esther was nearly pitched into a large, enclosed compound.

"Just a boy, fresh faced, without a whisker on him. He was sleeping in the chapel. He's light enough, but help me just the same. We'll put him in the garden hut," said the older nun.

The young girl slipped her arm around Esther and they carried her to a thatched hut at the edge of a large garden. Once inside, they tumbled Esther onto a small mound of hay.

The older nun dusted herself off and surveyed Esther from above, rather in the way an old hunter might view his good catch.

"He has lice, that's for certain. I shall inform the Mother Superior. We are in need of a messenger. Perhaps God, in His infinite wisdom, has planted this creature in our path to provide for us." The nun turned her attention back to Esther. "Have you been baptized, Pierre Mausiette?" When Esther didn't answer, the nun leaned down and bellowed into her ear. "I ask you again. Are you a Catholic, and have you been baptized?"

The nun's voice echoed in Esther's aching head. "Yes, I have been baptized," she whispered. It wasn't Catherine's words that prompted the lie, it was desperation. Bells rang in the distance. A blanket was tossed over her. The girl and the nun hurried off, leaving Esther to fall again into an uneasy slumber.

Esther awoke to a new day, feeling, if not entirely well, not entirely ill, either. Sun seeped through the slats of the door and showered the earthen floor with pinpricks of light. She glanced toward a click-ing sound. There, atop a three-legged stool in the corner, perched the young girl. She looked up from her knitting and might have smiled, it was hard to tell in the dim light. Before either could say a word, the older nun filled the doorway like a large block of wood. She lumbered into the hut and, hands on hips, stood above Esther.

"You are awake, at last. Never did I see a boy sleep as you have. It has been three days. You may call me Sister Angeline. Do you know where you are?"

Esther shook her head.

"You are very near the village of Clisson, near Nantes. Ah, there you are, Claire." Sister Angeline turned to face the young girl. "Claire has worked for us most of her life."

The girl was plain with a broad face, a flat nose and small, dark eyes. Wisps of nut-brown hair lay plastered against her face, while the rest was hidden behind her veil. Her lips, full and ruby coloured, were her saving grace.

Claire did not look up, did not meet Esther's eyes. Instead she bent to collect a wooden bowl beside the straw pallet. There was a sound to her walk, a sort of *shush-shush*. The girl was lame, her left leg seemingly useless.

"Claire works in the gardens," said Sister Angeline. "She has brought you soup many times over the past few days."

Try as she might, Esther could not recall the past few days. *"Merci,"* she said while propping herself up on her elbows.

"We are a convent of some hundred souls. We are in need of a messenger boy. You must gain approval from the Mother Superior to stay. You do want to stay here, do you not?"

Yes, she wanted to stay, more than anything. Esther nodded, slowly, politely, with reverence. *"Merci,"* she whispered. Messenger boy? Her thoughts were still scattered, but perhaps ... "Might a messenger *girl* not also be suitable?" Esther asked.

"And what use would another girl be to us? Ha! No girl could go out on the road on her own. If you have a sister who needs employment, she will not find it within these walls. Now, you must bathe first and rid yourself of the lice." The nun rolled up her sleeves and motioned to a iron-braced wooden bucket.

Esther pulled her knees up to her chest. The nun stood above the bucket and swirled soap chips into the water. Slime coated the water's surface.

"Merci, I can take a bath on my own."

"What's this? I have ten brothers, so you needn't be modest. Up with you and remove those clothes. Claire, burn them. The last messenger, may he rest in peace, left behind trousers and a shirt. The Lord, in His infinite wisdom, has provided." The good nun's thoughts were as plain as day. The likes of such a common boy would scarcely take a bath of his own accord.

Esther did not budge. Had the light been better, the nun would have seen terror on Esther's face. As it was, she thought the boy stubborn and perhaps superstitious. There was no telling what these ignorant peasants thought of bathing.

"Truly, I can bathe myself," Esther repeated.

"Very well. But mark my word, I'll scrub you within an inch of your life if I come back and find the lice still on you."

Bells rang out. As if hearing a human voice summoning them, the nun and the girl left Esther on her own.

Her pocket! Had she lost it? Had it been stolen? She crawled up onto her knees and pulled at the belt that circled her waist. The pocket containing her last remaining coins was still there. She took a deep breath, and only then did she take in her surroundings. The floor was earthen. The far side of the hut was filled with hoes and shovels. Beside her stood a shaky table and a three-legged stool.

Esther pulled herself to her feet. Slowly, as if fully expecting to confront a monster of biblical proportions on the other side of the door, Esther opened it and peered out into the courtyard. A large, choppy garden plucked clean of its harvest rolled out in front of her. Several small buildings, surrounded by fruit trees, also picked clean, grew against the outer walls of the convent. She could not lay eyes on the chicken coop but she could hear the *cluck-cluck* of the chickens, and there were pigeons *coo-coo-cooing* in the distance. She walked out on shaky legs, turned and beheld a massive stone castle, complete with stone arches and turrets. It was dark, gloomy and, to Esther's eyes, forbidding. Between her and this castle was a brick wall with more arched gates.

This discovery was enough for one day. Esther closed the door, peeled off her filthy clothes and stepped into the bone-chilling water. When next Esther laid down her head, she was, at the very least, scrubbed clean.

She had hidden the long strip of cloth that she used to bind her breasts. The rest of her clothes were burned. The nun combed and cut Esther's hair and tied it back into a small bundle at the nape of her neck. She was given trousers and a smock—too large, but they sufficed. Once again, the cloth bound her breats.

Claire returned bearing soup and bread. Esther thanked the girl, who responded by turning first pink and then crimson. Esther hardly noticed. Barley soup spiked with herbs and root vegetables filled her mouth and swelled her belly. How good it felt.

"You're to come with me and meet the Mother Superior," said the girl in a brave and lofty voice. Clutching a rickety walking stick in her hand, she turned abruptly and beat a path toward the castle as fast as her lame leg would allow. Esther wolfed down the bread and stumbled after her down a sandy path to a cobbled one, through one gate and then another.

The castle reeked of mildew and the stone floors were icy cold. They passed through two empty kitchens and various storage rooms before coming upon a small, circular stone staircase. Up they went, up and up and around and around, as if climbing the inside of a snail's shell. Esther pressed her hands on either side, feeling her way. The stones were wet to her touch and the steps underfoot were uneven. The damp seeped into her poorly shod feet. Still they went on. Although it was midday, not a speck of sunlight penetrated the thick castle. Torches blazed from iron sconces in the walls, casting small pools of light.

They came upon a grand hallway. Great, colourful tapestries hung on the rafters. There was even a soft rug underfoot. It had been a long time since she had seen anything as lovely! A silent nun, wizened and grim faced, stood like a sentinel in front of a grand doorway. There were no niceties or inquiries, just a nod to the girl. Esther, in her boy's guise, did not receive so much as a sideways glance.

The doors to the Mother Superior's rooms, although a hand's width thick and stone heavy, were sprung open before them. Esther had expected a sparse room devoid of feminine attributes. What she beheld astonished her. The rooms—she could see two from where she stood—were well appointed and lush, and although it was a grey day, tall windows let in great washes of light. Chairs sat by every window, and a large white bird, the likes of which Esther had never seen before, squawked in a gilded cage.

The Mother Superior stood beside one of the windows. Her noble bearing bespoke her privileged background. She was tall, neither young nor old, regal in appearance and dressed in sober clothing befitting her station. Being the daughter of a cloth merchant, Esther could hardly fail to recognize the fabric. It was of the finest weave, spun from the fleece of the first lambs of spring. Only a dark silk veil pinned to her hair, a large, jewel-encrusted crucifix resting on her bosom and a rosary hanging from her belt suggested that she was the Mother Superior and not a royal lady in mourning for her lost prince.

Her eyes narrowed as she beheld Esther. Her thoughts were plain enough. The boy was flea-bitten and ill fed, but still, the convent needed a messenger boy.

"Are you a Catholic?"

"I am," Esther replied to the floor.

"Look up. Let me see your face."

Esther tilted her head up. The Mother Superior stood quite still. Her stance was neither aggressive nor hostile, but there was something in her manner that frightened Esther. Panic seized her.

Esther was ill and tired. If she were to set upon the open road with no chance to recover, she would soon perish.

A large desk squatted in the middle of the room. On top of the desk was a rosary, not as fine as the one that hung from the Mother Superior's belt, but it would do. With reverence and respect, Esther reached for the rosary and holding the chain repeated, "Glory be to the Father, to the Son, and to the Holy Spirit, as it was, is now and ever shall be, world without end. *Amen*." She did not move or even twitch.

The Mother Superior smiled. She crossed the floor and touched Esther's face.

"Very well, you may stay as long as whiskers do not grow on your chin."

Chapter 23

❧

Life behind the convent walls was full and peaceful. Prayers —
matins, prime, terce, sect, nones, vespers, compline and
vigils—were part of the convent's daily life. Esther was required
to attend church once a day, which proved no great hardship. In
her heart, it was to the father of Abraham that she prayed.

She tended the gardens under the supervision of a cranky old
man from the village, who saw no point in speaking unless there
was something necessary to say. He came and went with the
ringing of the bells, and never in winter.

On this day the gardener had Esther smashing and crushing
mussel shells into bits and scattering them between rows of
parsnips and leeks. Esther did as she was told willingly, even
happily. There was a kind of freedom in doing as one was
instructed—besides, she liked gardening. Esther surveyed the
garden. The rewards of her labours were all there for her to see.

Freedom to be herself and to be alone with her thoughts came
with the ringing of each bell. The nuns, dutiful and silent, would

leave their work to attend chapel eight times a day. Esther would carry on alone, digging deep into the earth.

Although lame, Claire worked the garden alongside Esther. She was a child of few words to begin with, and the imposed silence of the convent appeared to be no hardship for her. When the silence was lifted for a short period each day they talked about which plants might go where—onions, spinach, parsnips and leeks toward the back of the garden, cooking and healing herbs toward the front, flowers for the chapel under the protection of the wall.

It came as no surprise to Esther when, with their hands dug deep into the soil, Claire told Esther that she would soon take her vows. Not final vows, of course—she was only thirteen—but the vows that would set her on the path to becoming a bride of Christ.

"Is this what you want?" Esther asked.

"I have met my dear father only twice, and just once that I can recall. But I am blessed that he thinks so highly of me that he would provide the dowry that would allow me admittance. No man would marry me such as I am. What other life could there be for the likes of me?"

How like Pearl, Esther thought. Not in face, of course. Pearl was frail and bird-like, while Claire was broad faced and plain. But they were alike in their unquestioning acceptance of their fate.

⁓

Once a week Esther carried letters locked in a small iron box to the nearby village of Clisson. Rocky fields were dotted with new lambs, old sheep and goats; the roads were hedged with budding flowers and the sky was open and blue. It was glorious to tip her face to the sun, to know that she had the freedom to go or stay. There were moments of deep regret for the mistakes she had made, the people she had left behind, but regret gave way to hope. And in hope there was a tingling excitement that tickled her insides in a way that made her laugh out loud.

The closer she came to the coast, the stronger the smell of the sea. *Philippe, where are you now? What world have you met?*

In the village of Clisson, Esther would hand the box of letters to a driver, who would then take it to the port town of Nantes. Her job done, she would wander the village, buying spices, olives, cheese and sometimes cloth, thread and needles for the convent. Occasionally she watched puppets dance (how she loved puppets) and twice she saw a play performed on a hay wagon pulled by an old ox.

It was on one such day, when the frost was still on the ground and winter not yet a memory, that an old actor—arrogant, untalented and ill prepared—gave a lofty performance of the devil in a dog's disguise. How evil was the devil-dog, how fierce with his hooked nose, and how slimy his forked tongue.

Esther stood in the crowd booing and cheering along with the rest. How delightful when the ox, still hitched to the wagon, raised his tail and let go a torrent of dung. It fell onto the ground in a great steamy glob. The crowd roared and greatly applauded the ox's discerning judgment. "Even your ox knows you cannot act," shouted the crowd. The ox, of his own accord, lumbered off. Having nothing better to do, the old actor, still standing on the wagon, waved goodbye. Esther laughed until her belly ached.

It was then, with the ox and the actor fading in the distance, that Esther spotted a boy with two crutches. He moved with a sort of grace, and his speed left her astonished. She followed him home.

"A woodworker made them, the father of a boy I saw at the fair. They are for you." Esther, standing near Claire in the spring garden, held out two new crutches.

Claire propped herself up against her hoe and stumbled toward the crutches. Her face was creased not with happiness but with pain. "I had such a pair once before," she said fondly. "But I gave them away to someone who needed them more."

"No matter, now you have another pair. They are a gift." Esther smiled as she held out the crutches.

Claire patted them as one might a gentle puppy. "I cannot accept this gift, but I shall treasure the giving of it forever." Once again she steadied herself with the hoe.

"Why? There is no one who needs them more."

"No, no, you do not understand. Any easement of pain distances us from God. It is God's pleasure that I am made this way. I must endure the pain." Claire frantically crossed herself as tears filled her eyes. "And you are a boy. I am told that boys are not to be trusted." But when she looked up at Esther's dumbfounded face, she knew that she had misspoken. Truly she had meant no ill will to pass between them. "I do not mean that *you* cannot be trusted. Forgive me. I ... have failed."

Esther stared at the girl. Failed? How could she have failed? Failed at what?

"To be a good nun one must be, above all things, *obedient.*"

"How are you not ... obedient?" Esther was puzzled beyond words.

"I think of you often, at night. I think of your eyes, your mouth ..." Oh, she had said too much! Her arms thrashed against the air as she turned and hobbled away, distraught beyond measure.

A week passed, then two, and still Claire had not returned to attend to her duties in the garden. Esther looked over at the gardener. Soon he would prop his tools by the fence and leave through the *porte des morts,* the door used to remove the dead from the convent. On this day Esther, too, laid down her hoe. She would go to the convent and find Claire. If she was caught she would be dismissed, of that she was certain.

The first bells rang at four in the morning, calling the nuns to prayer. Although it was still dark, Esther crept through the arched gate and into the castle. She stood in the second, empty kitchen and listened. To find the inner chapel, all she had to do was follow the sounds of voices raised up in song.

A hallway led to an open cloister that was beautiful beyond measure. Carefully tended early-spring flowers had already sprouted. Statues graced every corner, and stone benches were strategically placed for contemplation. Esther cocked her head. The sounds of song came from beyond two massive, wooden doors on the other side of the garden.

She pressed a flat palm to the wooden door. It would not move unless she pressed her side into it. She would not get into the chapel that way without being noticed. There had to be a further entrance. Esther slipped down another hall and up a small stair-case, always mindful of the sounds of song.

There was a curtain hanging on a wall yet no window was near. With a swipe of her arm she pushed aside the thick, red velvet to reveal a tiny door. It was iron-braced yet the size of it was better suited to accommodate a child. Why, it was more hatch than door! Esther unlatched it, ducked her head and crept forward.

At the end of a short, dark tunnel were flickering tallow candles. The singing had stopped but she was sure, almost sure, the sounds had come from beyond. Esther plunged ahead, mindful of the jagged stones underfoot.

Oh! She nearly cried out in surprise! She found herself at the very front of the convent's chapel looking down upon the bowed heads of a hundred or more nuns. Esther dropped to her knees, ducked behind a statue of Mary and crawled into a far corner with the speed of a hunted animal. She had stumbled upon the Mother Superior's private entrance to the chapel.

It took a moment for her eyes to adjust to the light, and when they did what Esther saw left her breathless. There, in the middle of the chapel and on her knees, was Claire. Her skin, blue with cold, was plain to see through her thin shift. Her withered leg lay at an odd angle from her body. Her hands were clasped in front of her, her head bowed. Even from this distance she could see that the girl wavered with exhaustion. How long had she been like this? It was a penance for some sin, that much Esther knew.

The service seemed to go on forever. Esther's legs grew numb and the dampness stiffened every limb. She closed her eyes and waited, but she must have dozed off, for when she next looked up the chapel was empty, save for the girl still on her knees.

"Claire," Esther hissed as she crawled forward. The girl did not respond.

"Claire."

Only when she touched the girl's shoulder did Claire look up. She let out a small cry and sank back on her haunches, frantically crossing herself.

"Why have you come? You will be seen." Claire looked at Esther with hollow eyes, and yet she did not appear to be afraid, only weary.

"I did not know what had become of you … I …" Esther felt foolish. She felt her own cheeks redden.

Claire's eyes filled with tears. Slowly, like one caught in a trance, she reached up and touched Esther's face. Despite callused hands, her touch was feather soft. "I have tried, with God as my witness I have tried to banish you from my thoughts. I prayed for a sign, and here you are. Thank you, thank you." Claire looked up at the crucifix at the top of the chapel. It was to Him that Claire gave thanks.

Esther fell back. Her mouth gaped open. "No. No." She shook her head vehemently.

"Hush. You have no whiskers. You are not yet a man and I am not yet a nun. I will never know what it is to love and be loved by a man." Claire crawled forward so that she was a mere breath away. "Would it be such a sin if I were kissed, just once?"

Esther's shock must have been plain to read on her face, because Claire's eyes grew wide and she scuttled backwards. "Why do you look upon me with horror. Am I so ugly?" She covered her face with her hands and sobbed.

Esther gazed helplessly upon her misery. "You are beautiful to me. You are a friend, my third friend. I have had only two others in my life and, although I will never see either again, I treasure having known them every day." Esther peeled the girl's fingers away from her face.

"And so you cannot even spare a kiss for a friend?" The girl looked up with liquid eyes. Tears shimmered in the candlelight, turning her pale face into glass.

"No, do not cry. It's me, don't you see? I am not what I say I am. Oh please, oh please. I am not what you think," Esther whispered into Claire's ear.

"What do you mean?"

"I am …" Esther, writhing in anguish, blurted out, "I am not …" Could she say it? Could she tell her that she was a girl, too? What mighty hand of vengeance would descend upon her once the truth was spoken? What retribution would be demanded? But what choice did she have?

"I am ..." The words stuck in her throat. "I am not ... a Catholic!"

For a moment there was silence. Neither spoke. Then slowly the girl rose up on her knees. She cupped her hand around Esther's chin and lowered her lips onto Esther's. Neither noticed a dark form shift in the back of the chapel.

~

The dew was still fresh when Esther left the convent. It had been her sanctuary, her reprieve for almost a year.

Three sunsets and three sunrises had come and gone since the kiss in the chapel. She had not seen Claire since. In that time, Esther had thought not only of Claire but also of Philippe and Pearl. Pearl might still be alive had she not interfered. What havoc would she unleash on Claire's life if she stayed on?

And it was time. Her body—and spirits—had healed.

Standing still in the garden overlooking fledgling spears of iris leaves and budding crocuses, Esther said her silent farewell. A flicker of light caught her eye. Esther looked up to the castle. There, standing in a high, leaded widow, was the Mother Superior. How was it that Esther had never seen that window before, or noticed that it looked out over the garden? Their eyes locked.

She knows, thought Esther, *she knows.*

Take care of her, Esther whispered in her heart. Then she turned and opened the *porte de mort.* Within moments she was on the path that would lead her to the town of Nantes.

Chapter 24

❦

One village looked like the next—hundreds and hundreds of tumbledown cottages and half-starved children hanging out of doorways. France was bursting at the seams with hungry people. And still Esther walked on. The direction mattered little, although she hankered to be near the sea. It was work she needed. There was no work, or at least none for a stranger.

It was no great hardship to be on the road. Robbers would hardly bother with the likes of a destitute boy. Nor was it difficult to find a safe haven in which to sleep. As the light drained from the day, Esther would make herself known to a small troop of wanderers. Most often they would be gathered around a fire, pulling all that they owned—carts, wagons, pots, wives and children—in close. Onions and leeks would be frying on the fire. The smelling was free; the eating came with a cost.

"What is your name?" Esther would ask a child, and then she would scratch the name in the sand. The children would trace the letters with their fingers and howl with delight. It was then that the old ones would turn from the warmth of the fire. What was this—the boy could read? It was a highly prized trick. Letters carried around for months were pulled out of sacks and packs and spread before her. It was true that there were people in the marketplace who would read for money, but Esther would read for a half loaf of hard bread, a cup of wine, a helping of onion stew. Her meal thus earned, she would listen as tall tales were told and songs were sung.

Many times she would have liked to stay and travel with one group or another. But soon young girls would dance around, pursing their lips, thrusting their hips and teasing. Boys, too, would wonder why the stranger took such pains to piss alone. A very long time ago, Madame de La Grange had told her that there was safety in naïveté. Esther now learned there was also safety in solitude, and so she walked alone.

A fortnight had passed and spring had arrived in full force. Flowers were pushing through the earth, and toads and salamanders kept her company as she walked.

She paused atop a hill and looked down upon a village by the sea. By the look of it, the plague had come and gone and laid waste to the village. Not even a whiff of woodsmoke hung in the air. She'd walk on through it, for there was no way around it.

This village had nothing to recommend it save a few shops, a blacksmith, a tanner (even from a distance one could scarcely miss the stink of leather cures), a cobbler and scattered huts that made do as homes. Standing in a doorway under a rough carving of a loaf of bread, Esther peeked in through the shutters. There was no doubt that this was the baker's shop, but there was no smell of bread in the air. It was not the Christian Sabbath. What kind of a baker would let a day pass without supplying bread?

Then came happy sounds. She put her hand to her brow and stared into the setting sun. The sounds of voices, raised up in song, wafted down the road. A boy of eight or nine, skinny, dirty and with a crusty nose, came gallivanting toward her with the gay abandon of a pony.

"Did ya see it?" he cried.

Never was a boy more full of excitement. And as happiness is contagious, Esther, too, laughed and shook her head. She had seen nothing on the road save the usual beggars, carts, horses and tradesmen.

"The hanging. Did ya see him swing?" The boy cupped his hands to his throat, made a gurgling sound and laughed all the harder. The smile died on Esther's lips.

The townsfolk, with arms linked and feet set to dancing, came tumbling down the road. Every face was flushed with drink.

"No bread this day," shouted a merry, middle-aged woman.

If this was the baker, then she was well suited to her trade. She looked as if she herself were formed out of bread dough. The woman had a round head with fleshy pink cheeks hung so low that they enveloped her chin. Button eyes were embedded deep into her face and below them sat a tiny nose and bud-shaped mouth. A huge bosom started under her invisible chin and slid toward the good woman's knees with barely a pucker in between. And her colossal bottom could be seen from the front. To be hugged by this woman would be to fall into a vat of risen bread dough.

The full parade was now in view. The old trudged forward, the middle-aged were propelled by wine, and grubby, scabby children ran around every which way. The bread-dough woman gave one child a friendly smack on the back of the head. The child smiled broadly. As for the rest, the happy throng went this way and that, each to his bed.

"Be you the baker?" Esther called out.

"I am, but there's no bread today on account of the hanging." The woman made her way over to the bakery and thrust her hip into the door to edge it open. Despite unlit ovens, the smell of yeast wafted out, greeting them both. Two of the dirtiest children charged past the baker and disappeared into the cottage. The door creaked on its old leather hinge and slammed in Esther's face.

Esther paused, then thumped the door with a closed fist.

"No bread today," the woman called out in a singsong voice from the other side of the door.

Esther pressed her nose against the hinge and hollered right back, "It's not bread that I want."

The door swung open. The woman rammed her hands on her hips with such force that a cloud of dust swirled up. "What is it you want?"

"I am a baker," Esther replied.

"You?" The woman snorted. "A mere boy is a baker?"

"I will make you a batch of bread at no charge," said Esther.

The drink was wearing thin on the woman. She was sleepy-eyed and longed for her bed. She looked Esther up and down. "What is your name?"

"Pierre Mausiette."

"From where do you hail?"

"La Rochelle."

"How did you come to be a baker?" The woman pressed a hand against the doorpost, narrowed her already pea-sized eyes and peered suspiciously at the strange boy in front of her.

"My parents, both dead, God rest their souls, were bakers." Esther made the sign of the cross over her chest.

The baker gazed up at Esther in a sleepy haze before shrugging and turning back into her shop. She made a sweeping gesture with an arm that could have doubled as a sail. "There are my ovens and there are my pots of yeast and flour. When I rise, I shall taste your bread. But if you steal from me, mind my words, I'll see you hang. It was a thief that swung today, God rest his sorry soul." The baker crossed herself and snorted. If the bread was decent, and even if it was not, she would sell it on the morrow. Meanwhile, she would have a well-deserved sleep.

The woman turned her back on Esther and disappeared. Moments later a muffled thud told Esther that she had found her pallet.

⁓

A blood-curdling scream rang out from the baker's house later that night. The baker stood on the threshold that divided kitchen from sleeping quarters and pointed a long, dirty finger at Esther.

"Who be you, and what are you doing near my ovens?"

As she hollered, her entire body jiggled. She proceeded to plunder her own establishment, picking up pans and trays, her eyes darting from pillar to post taking in the floor, the trough and the ovens. The place was clean. What madness had taken place while she'd slept? Who had dared fire her ovens and make use of her yeast?

Thinking was a strain for the baker at the best of times, and trying to understand just what had gone on while she'd slept off the effects of too much wine was taking more effort than was at her disposal. Her bafflement exhausted, she turned and peered at the boy. A memory, vague though it was, of letting this boy into her shop was only now coming back to her.

"I cleaned, Madame. While the bread rose and then baked, I had little to do so I …"

"Ohhhhh!" the woman cried as she pointed to four perfectly shaped brown loaves of bread. Without taking her pebble-hard eyes off Esther, she picked up each loaf in turn. They were the correct weight, perhaps lighter than she would have liked, but it was something altogether different that rankled her. She held a loaf up to the candlelight. The bread was without dark seeds popping out of its crust! What magic was this that bread was not made with grain? If this boy had been a girl, she might have suspected witchcraft.

Esther dithered, not knowing what she had done to incite such a response from the baker.

"Where are the seeds?" The baker held the loaf up to her nose and sniffed.

"They were too rough and large. I used a mortar and pestle and—"

"You ground the grain yet again!" The woman tore off a hunk of bread and shoved it into her mouth. Ahhhhh! What heaven was this? What earthly delights had this stranger brought to her? She gobbled down the entire loaf, and not once did she stop to pick seeds out of her teeth. The woman began to pace in front of her two ovens. It was easy to tell her thoughts since she mumbled them out loud. *"It is the best bread I have ever tasted. But this boy … a stranger."* She stopped her mumbling and looked at the boy. *"He's beardless and puny. What harm could he do here?"* Out loud, the baker snapped, "Can you tend chickens?"

Esther nodded and added, "I can read and write."

The woman's mouth gaped open. Read?

Esther silently cursed herself. Why had she said such a foolish thing? She was being boastful, plain and simple.

"Can you teach those two to read?" The woman pointed to the two children who lay asleep on a blanket by the fire. Esther nodded. The woman pondered and pressed a dirty finger to her lip. She hummed and hawed and did her best to appear deep in thought. As if a decision had suddenly been made, she snapped, "My name is Madame Seruanne, but all call me Baker. I will hire you for two sous a day. My husband is dead, and all but these two young ones, plus two brave boys who are off fighting for the king, are what's left to me." The woman crossed herself. "When my sons return, you will leave."

Esther nodded. It was a fair arrangement.

And so Esther became a baker's assistant in the village of St. Malo on the English Channel.

Chapter 25

Madame Seruanne, baker, placed her hands on her ample hips and looked about her. She was well pleased. The ovens, the troughs, pots and jars all gleamed in the morning light. Once a week, the boy, Pierre, cleaned and scoured the pots and poured boiling water into them, too. Madame Seruanne shook her head. He was an odd boy, and those eyes of his took some getting used to, but who was she to complain? The chickens had never been fatter or the cottage cleaner. She gazed up—rosemary, parsley, sage hung in tidy bundles from the rafters, giving the place a pleasant sort of stink.

That thing he did with the bread dough—taking a bit off and casting it into the fire and mumbling some sort of incantation—well, that unnerved her some. The boy said he did it to hear the sizzle of the dough in the flames. That was how he knew if it was a good batch or not. She had tried to do it herself when he was not about the place. She had tossed turd-sized balls of dough into the fire and listened intently. Why, she'd near singed her ear off trying to tell the difference between sizzles!

He was good with her children, her runts. Pierre was teaching Agnes and Paul to read, although it was only Agnes who seemed to get any benefit. Pierre even made letters out of bread dough, baked them and topped them with honey. Who would have thought to do such a thing? He was an odd boy, but God had brought him into her life, and questioning God would never do.

Summer had come and gone, then winter, too. The woods were filled with primroses, sparkling water tumbled down streams, and once again the peasants had begun to till the soil.

This day, as in the days past, Esther rose in the dark and baked until dawn. A child from the village could have been hired to fire the ovens, but memories of Pearl prevented her from having any children working in what was now *her* kitchen.

When golden loaves filled the wooden shelves and pies lined the counter, Esther would often take her leave and walk down to the beach. It was there, with the water lapping against the shore, that she would say her prayers. What better place to worship God than in the circle of His own creation? When her prayers were done, Esther would sit and let her thoughts stray to Pearl and Philippe.

As the sun set, she read Perrault's fairy tales to Agnes, Paul and the baker from a book bought from a travelling tinker. And when they fell asleep, she sat alone with her own thoughts. Much to her surprise, she discovered that she was content. Somewhere deep within her Esther Brandeau still lived, but with each passing year the memory of the Jewish girl faded.

As Esther slid a tray of loaves out of the oven one morning and placed them on cooling racks, she spied a gentleman of some breeding dismounting from a fine steed. He tethered the horse to the rail just outside the kitchen window. A pronounced limp marred his walk but his erect stance declared his occupation. He was a soldier, although he wore no uniform. He might have stood at the window and asked for a loaf but instead he barged into the kitchen and, hands on hips, surveyed the surroundings. Small though he was, he had a commanding presence about him.

The stranger peered at Esther through blurry eyes embedded in sockets as red as fresh meat. His pallor matched his teeth—both were yellow.

"A loaf for my journey," he said as he tossed down a coin. He rocked on his heels, then caught himself before falling over.

Esther slid another six loaves into the oven and tried not to giggle. He was drunk.

The baker burst into the kitchen, bobbed and grovelled as she handed the gentleman his loaf. "Good Sir, be you from the house on the hill?" she asked, in a high-pitched voice that she assumed, wrongly, made her sound more genteel.

"I did come from there. I was a guest." He did not bow or nod his head.

"Where might you be headed?" It was impertinent of the baker to ask such a question, he being a gentleman and she a mere peasant. But the man did not appear perturbed by the baker's nosiness; on the contrary, he seemed well used to conversing with the lower class.

"To the town of Vitre. It is a long journey by road but a much shorter one by ferry boat," he replied.

The baker nodded knowingly, though she'd never heard of the

place, had never been more than a league or two away from her own house.

"Your bread was the talk of the house party, Madame. You are to be complimented." He gave a slight nod of his well-shaped yet wigless head.

As a cow might curtsy, so did the baker. As she had not been scolded for asking one nosy question, the baker ventured another.

"You are without a servant. Where might he be?"

"My boy ran off, it seems." He took hold of the doorframe to steady himself. "Might you have a son to spare? I pay well."

The baker laughed heartily while patting her well-padded sides. "The ones not in the graveyard are in the army. All except my two little ones, feeding the chickens, and I'll not part with them."

"What of your assistant there? Surely a baker as accomplished as yourself is not in need of an assistant?" The soldier pointed to Esther.

Esther looked up and noted that at the very least the baker had the grace to blush. She hadn't made a loaf herself in almost a year.

"That one is not mine by birth, but I am fond of him, nevertheless."

"Alas, then I take my leave. My good woman, should you ever come to Vitre, you would be welcome to join my poor establishment. With bread such as this I would be the toast of the town in no time. I am the seigneur de la Chapelle." He clicked his heels, bowed and wobbled out the door. On his second try he swung his leg over his horse and rode out of the village with his loaf tucked under his arm.

Esther shook her head. He was a pompous ass.

Later that morning, as the baker trudged up the hill with her loaves of gold, Esther stood in the open door and breathed in the cool spring air. The year was 1737. It was hard to think that a year had passed. She waved to a neighbour and smiled at a group of children who were playing in the road. It was not the life she had expected, and her wandering thoughts were beginning to consider possibilities that awaited her, but she was in excellent health and in command of her own destiny. With the sun on her face she thanked God for her blessings.

"Good morning, Pierre. Forget your bread and come and play." A cheerful boy with a boil on his cheek and a scar down his neck raced up to the window and tugged at Esther's arm.

"I am too old to play," laughed Esther.

"No, come," Agnes and Paul, too, called out.

How lovely were the faces of children, how pure and untroubled, despite the dirt, the crooked limbs and marks of disease.

The boy with the boil pulled and laughed, then pulled some more. Esther propped her broom up against the door jamb and went to join the children. One, then another grabbed Esther's hands. Around and around they danced in a wide circle, singing happily. Bare feet scuffed the ground and knees kicked up toward the sky. The tune was familiar but not the words. No matter, she laughed along with them, only occasionally catching the odd word.

It rained one day,
As hard as the rain could fall
And all the boys of our town
Were out playing ball.

They threw their ball so swift and high,
They threw their ball so low.
They threw their ball in a Jew's garden,
Where they dare not go.

The Jew's daughter came walking out
Dressed up in silk, so gay,
Saying, "Come in, come in, my pretty little boy,
And get your ball away."

She took him by the lily-white hand,
And led him across the hall
And with a broadsword cut off his head
And kicked it against the wall.

She threw him in a new-drawn well,
Just fifty-five feet deep
With a catechism at his head
And a Bible at his feet.

"What's wrong, Pierre, why have you stopped dancing?" Sweet-faced Agnes, with brown hair so matted it looked like fur, pulled at her hand.

Esther's feet took root in the sand. The spinning had left her dizzy and the words had left her cold. The children formed a circle around her—grinning, cheerful children. She looked from child to child. Their innocent faces were so terribly at odds with the horrific words they were spewing. Slowly she walked across the road toward the baker's house and closed the door behind her. Was there no place on earth where she would be free of this hatred?

"Where are you going, Pierre? We haven't finished playing," cried Agnes as she banged her small fist against the shutters. In the distance, the children had resumed their song and their dance.

"What is wrong, Pierre?" The baker, back from her errand, barged into the kitchen and tossed her shawl over a hook.

"The song, the one the children are singing ... does everyone know it?"

The baker cocked her head toward the open window and nodded. "They are missing a verse or two," she said with a smile.

"But Jews ..."

"Best the children learn early to stay away from them. Murderers, the lot, and they drink human blood." The baker nodded her head and added a scowl. "Why does the king allow Jews in our land? France for the French. They should charge them more tax, more and more. It was the Jews that caused the plague, as well, you know."

"How?" whispered Esther. "How did the Jews cause the great plague?"

"What do you mean, how? They poisoned the wells. Everyone knows that."

⁓

It did not take many inquiries to find the ferry boat that would take her down the coast to Vitre. The journey was uneventful. As she sat on the deck and watched the sky, Esther tried to imagine a place on earth where she would find acceptance. Had Philippe found such a place in the New World?

It took her the better part of another week to locate Seigneur de la Chapelle. In the end, it was chance that led Esther to him.

Like most ex-soldiers, Seigneur de la Chapelle frequented a *guingette,* a tavern. It was there that Esther found him, swigging ale, not like a gentleman but like a common soldier awaiting a call to battle.

Esther squared her shoulders and walked into the dim alehouse. She looked like any young boy in search of a mug. Months spent kneading bread dough had left her arms and shoulders strongly muscled. A steady diet of fresh food had made her healthy and solid. And now her boy's stance and demeanour were perfect. Her bound breasts often caused discomfort, yet all who laid eyes on her assumed that she was a boy. And though her face still possessed a startling beauty, few cared to look beyond the boy's attire.

The tavern was typical—low-beamed, dark, smelling of unwashed men, brew and greasy pies. She spied the man right off. He sat in a far corner, his only company a mug of ale.

"My name is Pierre. I am told that you are in need of a servant." Esther spoke with confidence.

It took a moment or two for Seigneur de la Chapelle to respond. With great difficulty he raised his head but did not seem to look anywhere in particular. It was clear that he spent a great deal of time in this tavern.

"Who are you?" he sputtered.

"I am told that you are looking for a boy of all work," Esther repeated.

He had no memory of meeting Esther in the bakery, but he did need help in his rooms. Blurry-eyed and puffy, with a stream of drool dribbling down to his chin, Seigneur de la Chapelle peered up at Esther. "You can run a house, can you not?"

Esther balked. What was being asked was unreasonable—such a position was better suited to a housekeeper than a boy of all work—however, the aging soldier seemed to have no notion of what was reasonable and what was not. Esther nodded. "I can run a house."

"Come," he commanded, then stood, after a fashion.

Esther dropped her bedroll and caught him as he was about to take a tumble. And so Esther staggered to her place of employment with her new employer slung across her back.

Seigneur de la Chapelle's apartment was on the second floor of a building on the Rue de Talon. It consisted of a few chairs, three beds, bedding, a desk, table, three large, poorly executed paintings and several clay pots. Esther did not venture as far as the kitchen.

While Seigneur de la Chapelle snored on one of his beds, Esther sat down and considered her situation. The look of him, his pasty skin and yellow eyes, proved that he was plainly ill and a drunk, besides. But it was her own situation she must consider. She could not continue to pay for a lice-infested pallet in a filthy inn. A clean bed would be most welcome. And here there was no one to watch her or catch her up. Yes, she would stay, if only for a little while.

❧

"More!" Esther's employer slammed down a pewter cup on the arm of his chair.

Esther, sitting on a stone hearth, could have happily boxed his ears. He was tolerable enough when sober, but insufferable when drunk, and he was always drunk. Still, he provided a roof over her head and had not the slightest inclination to pry into her past. In return, Esther provided plain food, good bread and, to his surprise, a clean home. In short, with the exception of many drunken incidents, it was an agreeable situation for both of them.

Esther put down the tin of blacking and Seigneur de la Chapelle's leather boot to pour wine into his cup.

He groaned as he lifted the cup to his lips. "Battle wounds," he muttered, "the price of a life in service to a great king. To a great king!" he hollered, holding his cup high and then swished the lot down his gullet.

It wasn't only wine he consumed. To quash the pain of old wounds he drank large amounts of quinine mixed with water. Frequents puffs of something like tobacco sucked from a large pipe seemed to bring relief. "Hard to come by," he claimed. Wine loosened his tongue, quinine relieved ailments of the body, and the smoke from the pipe seemed to settle his mind. In this state, he wove many a great yarn without truth ever rearing its tiresome head. But today, as wine dribbled from his lips, the pain seemed worse than before. He could not keep to his story and drifted in and out of sleep as easily as he mixed past and present.

Two months had come and gone since Esther had carried her master home. Now here he lay on the sofa, languishing in dreamland, rocking his head back and forth. His lips were but a slit across his face and the furrows in his brow were so deep they resembled scars. His pain was real.

"Attack at dawn, at dawn, I tell you!" His sudden scream made Esther jump. He drew an imagined sword from an imagined sheath and waved it above his head. "Death to the British! Cannons—CANNONS! A field cannon ahead—take cover! It's the grapeshot, oh, the grapeshot—how it tears into the skin, how it burns." The old soldier moaned while attempting to staunch imagined blood flowing from an imagined wound.

"It is over now," said Esther, gently wiping his brow and adjusting a pillow behind his head.

"*Qu'est-ce que c'est?* Retrieve your pistol. Unsling those carbines. Bayonets! Oh, the blood, the blood …" He fell into a slumber only to awake with a start. "Come here, boy." He grabbed Esther's hand and pulled her to him. Spittle flew from his mouth and his eyes bulged with fear. "Soldiers die not with honour. They die of festering wounds or bloody flux. Remember the wars, remember the battles. In time, someone will remember what peace was like and make it again. Will you do that, boy? Will you make peace with time?"

Esther shook herself loose. He was not a bad fellow, but this could not go on.

⤳⤳

"Come, boy, market day. Let us venture out!" It was midsummer and Seigneur de la Chapelle was in fine form. For today at least, his pain and ailments seemed to have fled. He had slept the whole night through and met the day with a spring in his step.

Esther fetched him his ebony walking stick. An outing would suit her, as well.

The retired soldier wore a purple powdered wig, yellow silk jacket and pink stockings. Alas, they would not commit to his spindly legs and seemed happiest pooling around his bony ankles. No matter, he thought he looked like a fine specimen, and that was what mattered.

Esther, wearing her homespun jacket, tattered trousers and shoes of no account, set out on the town walking a few steps behind her employer. The outing would give her an opportunity to consider. It was time to move on. She had an idea but it was a daring one, one that would forever change the course of her life. Maman had said: *You must think before you act, Esther. Promise me. Promise that you will always think about the outcome.* Esther smiled. Yes, she would think this idea through before embarking on it.

Market day still excited her. Despite her seventeen years, she still had a child's love of puppets, jugglers and stilt-walkers.

"We shall have some roasted chestnuts, I think," announced Seigneur de la Chapelle. He passed Esther his walking stick while he fished around in his pockets for a few coins.

Distracted by the sights and sounds, Esther did not see the gilded carriage stop near them. Nor did she see the curtain move aside and a bejewelled hand reach out.

"Gilles, Gilles de la Chapelle," called out the singsong voice from behind the coach's curtain.

Seigneur de la Chapelle turned. A broad smile crossed his face as he turned toward the carriage.

"Catherine," he cried. "My dear Catherine Churiau."

*C*hapter 26

❧

*I*t was the carriage, white-and-gold hand-carved roses curling around the window, that Esther saw first. She leapt backwards before casting her eyes to the ground.

Seigneur de la Chapelle stepped out into the roadway and, like a lover at a balcony's ledge, gently lifted Catherine's hand to his lips. "You are as beautiful as ever, *ma chérie*."

When a deep, throaty laugh rang out from inside the carriage a shiver went down Esther's spine. Slowly, making no abrupt moves, she ducked behind her employer. If she did not draw attention to herself, likely Catherine would not notice her. Servants were a necessity put on this earth by God to attend to the needs of their betters, and as such, they were invisible. With her eyes still riveted to the ground Esther took a step back, then another, then another. She began to slip away into the crowd. *Let her not see me.*

"Pierre. Pierre, pass me my walking stick." Seigneur de la Chapelle snapped his fingers in the air. He turned. "Where is that boy? PIERRE!" he hollered. Ten, maybe more, heads turned his way. Pierre was a common name.

He turned back to Catherine. "My apologies, dear lady. The boy is a baker's assistant and a terrible servant. PIERRE MAUSIETTE!" he yelled over the heads of the crowd.

Esther took a breath. Should she stay or run? Surely running would just bring more attention to herself. No, there was no reason to assume that Catherine would recognize her. Esther came up behind her employer and bowed deeply.

"What is wrong with you, boy?" He snatched his stick and turned back to Catherine. "Now, my dear Catherine, where were we?"

"I would be delighted if you could attend a small party at Madame Auberge's home. Rue de Montfort. Do come as my escort." Catherine's voice dripped with sticky charm. Esther kept her eyes lowered, doing her best to avoid Catherine's gaze.

"Madame Auberge, lovely creature. I knew her father well. So kind of you to invite me."

"This afternoon, then."

Seigneur de la Chapelle bowed as Catherine's carriage rolled down the road. He stepped lively as he and Esther made their way back to the apartment.

Thoughts raced through Esther's head. It had been years since Catherine had last laid eyes on her. There was no reason to bolt. She should think it through, decide carefully. She would leave, certainly, but not yet.

⤫

"Ah, Pierre, is life not a grand thing? Here I was just moments ago pondering my future, when what drops into my lap but opportunity. It is good to have connections, no?" The old soldier sipped his wine and then spread his arms to allow Esther to help him into a new—almost new—coat. "Fill my cup. Did you see the woman in the carriage?"

Esther shook her head, not knowing what the best answer might be. She took a brush to his jacket but each sweep seemed to unearth new dust from its seams.

Seigneur de la Chapelle lowered his voice as if to share a secret. "Her name is Catherine Churiau, a courtesan. Years ago, when Catherine was a child, I was in the happy position to give aid to her poor, beleaguered mother. Of course the woman was never truly destitute, but, as sometimes happens when one is between lovers, she was for a time short of funds. Those were the days, you must understand, when I myself was at the height of my power. Oh yes, Pierre, I was a fine figure of a man." He strutted about like a peacock, then hoisted his cup to his lips and drank heartily. "Her mother, Marie de La Grange, was herself a famous courtesan who commanded men to do her bidding as easily as a great general in time of war. Alas, the dear woman fell ill some months ago."

Madame de La Grange was ill? How ill? Had she fully recovered? Esther stepped backwards. Seigneur de la Chapelle took no notice of Esther's reaction but, by happenstance, addressed her concern. "I have heard that while the dear woman is much improved, she is quite frail and given to reflections that must bore poor Catherine." He laughed, then continued with his babble. "It was the ambitious Catherine's dearest wish to be called to court. Sadly, her chance was missed when she failed to deliver a promise to the king." He leaned forward. "It was said that Catherine had within her household a great beauty. I have heard several stories. Some say that the girl was a niece, others that she was a servant, and others—ha!" He gulped the contents of his cup. "Others say she was Catherine's own daughter. *C'est incroyable!*"

"What happened to the girl?" Esther asked while helping him on with his boots. She dared not look up.

"Ah, the great mystery. Perhaps she ran away. But why would any girl run from such a future? No. Some say that Catherine, in a jealous rage, murdered her. How is one to know? But the king was much displeased. Catherine is now a *cocodette,* she is déclassé, and alas no longer welcome in the better homes. Catherine Churiau shall forever remain part of the great *galanterie*—the grand life apart from court." He laughed as he emptied his glass yet again. "Dear Catherine's ruin, shall we say, is to my benefit, for look at me now! I am the happy beneficiary of the benevolence of both mother and daughter."

The walls of Esther's throat seemed to stick together so tightly she could scarcely breathe. She felt for the back of a chair and leaned heavily upon it. Esther had taken from Catherine that which she desired most, the chance to be part of the king's own court. Esther was now Catherine's great enemy, and her vengeance would know no bounds.

Dressed, wigged and buffed, Seigneur de la Chapelle left the apartment in fine form. Perhaps, had Esther been better attired, she would have accompanied him as his servant; as it was, she was grateful for de la Chapelle's negligence.

Esther closed the door behind him and leaned against it. He would not return this day, or possibly even the next. She must use the time to think and plan. There was a thump at the door. He was a forgetful man. Esther flung it open.

"Pierre Mausiette, by order of the king of France you are under arrest." In the blink of an eye two blue-coated soldiers pinned her hands behind her back. Their savageness was so sudden she did not truly comprehend what was happening.

Arrest? She was being arrested? "On what charge?" she cried as her hands were manacled. They laughed.

Esther was marched through the streets. People made way. Some booed and hissed for sport. She stumbled, fell and once on the ground was pelted with clods of dirt. She was living a nightmare, for certainly this could not be happening.

There was no telling how long it took to reach their destination, as time seemed to have lost its course. Then there it was, first the looming, grey Palais de Justice and beside it a grim, squat building—the prison.

The rough wooden door of the prison was studded with iron and streaked with rust. Two soldiers stood on guard. One undid the manacles that bound Esther's wrists. A small, grilled window embedded in the door opened. Words were exchanged, but what was said was lost to Esther. She was cold, so very cold. Her shoulders and arms were nearly wrenched out of their sockets.

The prison door opened. A surge of foul, sour air fanned over her. She felt vomit rise in her throat. A small man no bigger than a midget stepped out into the light and opened his toothless mouth to roar something incomprehensible. He gazed at Esther and seemed pleased. "A good catch," he declared. His grin revealed chipped, brown teeth and his filthy beard still harboured remnants of his last meal. Lice that infested his uncombed wig seemed to have migrated down his body and lodged deep within his buttocks for it was there he dug, mining his arse with relish.

A hand landed on Esther's back and pitched her into the gloom. Pine torches, hanging over a narrow, curling, stone stairway, billowed great tufts of black smoke. She squinted and strained to see in the dim light. *No, no,* she wanted to cry. Esther bit down hard on her lip. The rocky steps underfoot were uneven and coated with a wet scum. Down and down she went into what surely had to be the middle of the earth. The poor light from above grew weaker and the putrid air grew colder.

Behind iron doors men moaned, rats squealed and water dripped.

At last the midget stopped and unhooked the great iron key-ring from his belt. A large black key went into the lock and the mouth to hell opened. She was shoved from behind. Esther stumbled forward only to fall upon straw dampened with blood and excrement. Rats scurried about without fear.

"You will come before the judge in the morning." The midget chuckled as he turned the key in the lock.

"Wait, wait, please!" Esther cried out. "Am I to know nothing of the charges brought against me?"

There was no response. Eyes were upon her but whether they belonged to rat or man was hard to tell. Slowly her surroundings came into focus. The eyes were human. In the gloom it was hard to count how many men were in there. Ten, perhaps? Twenty?

Esther stumbled toward a far wall. A scabby hand attached to a man covered in oozing sores shot out. She moved down the line until at last she found a place to sit. She slid down a wall that sweated slime.

There were no tears. No one cries in hell.

⤚⤙

Every hour seemed a day long, and yet a night passed. Esther looked up from her stupor. She moved slightly and felt the pocket containing her few coins bounce against her inner thigh. What a joke that she had not been searched. But then a thought—could she bribe a guard? If they knew that she had coins, would they not simply rob her? And if they searched her, they would find out that she was a girl.

She looked to the forms that surrounded her. They were more dead than alive and no threat to her. It was the guards whom she feared.

"Pierre Mausiette," a voice called out through the grille in the door.

"Here. Here." Esther scrambled to her feet. It was time to go to court. Her mind raced. She would plead her case to the judge. She would reveal her true self—she was a girl, a young woman. Surely they would take pity on her. But all judges were male, and how would a man, any man, understand her predicament? Besides, it was against Jewish law for a woman to dress like a man—was it against French law, too? How was she to know such a thing? And since it *must* have been Catherine who had pressed these charges, why had she not revealed to the authorities that she was a girl? But Esther knew the answer: Catherine would play out the jest for her own amusement.

The iron-braced door creaked open. The sound was ominous and foreboding. The midget motioned with his head to follow him. Esther's legs could barely hold her, and yet somehow she moved forward.

A guard followed.

They reached the top of the stairs. Streams of light filtered in through the bars, leaving stripes on the stone floor. Esther lifted her head to the light. *Never appear desperate.*

The midget was in front of her and the guard behind. If anyone could be bribed it would be the midget, but her timing would have to be exact.

The door swung open. The midget stepped aside. As she stepped forward he stuck his foot out and Esther tumbled headlong out into the blinding light. She lay sprawled outside the prison door on the cobblestoned street. The shock of it made her cry out. Her hands went over her head. She waited for a blow, a kick to the face, a boot to her belly. The midget, whooping and howling with glee, slapped his fat, short leg, bobbed his head, then slammed the prison door shut.

What had happened? Was it a mistake? Would they return to capture her again? Esther crawled in all directions at once, frantic, going nowhere. No judge. No jail. A small boy walked past and jeered at her. A woman carrying a basket covered her nose with a cloth and ran in the opposite direction. What joke was this? She pulled herself up and stood like an animal discovering an upright world. She made to dart this way, then that, her eyes searching, searching, for a safe escape. Sunlight pricked her eyes like needles. She raised a hand over her brow and looked around.

Something glittered in the early-morning light. A hand reached out from a carriage. Dangling from the hand was the gold-framed portrait of the king.

Chapter 27

⟨⟩

*E*sther lurched forward, her arms extended. She reached the gilded coach then stopped, wavering back and forth as if drunk. The portrait, hanging on a golden chain, was laced loosely through slender, gloved fingers, and swung like a pendulum in the brilliance of the day. The curtain in the coach's window moved, revealing Marie de La Grange.

"I thought … I had heard that you were …" Esther paused, her eyes riveted to the portrait.

"I was ill, my dear, for a long time." Madame's laugh was low and raspy. "I believe this portrait belongs to you. It seemed that you were in a great hurry to leave my house."

"It fell out of my pocket. I did not mean to offend you. I valued your friendship, truly. I left …"

"All of this is history. It is of no consequence now. You had a friend, a servant in my house."

"Pearl?" whispered Esther.

Marie de La Grange, heavily veiled in black, moved forward.

"If that's the name of the small bird who worked in the kitchen, then yes. She was very brave to deliver this portrait to me. It seems she discovered it in the folds of a dress that had been hidden in the kitchen."

"What of Pearl? What of her death?"

"Ah, that is a tragedy. Cook did not take kindly to the girl leaving the kitchen and trailing up the stairs. I believe she paid for her disobedience with her life."

"Pearl died because of me." Esther winced. The pain of Pearl's death came back to her tenfold.

"She was a sapling planted in the wind. There was nothing you could do to save her, and you have no time for reflection or remorse. It's yourself you must now save. My daughter bears you ill will. As you grow old, you will discover that one first forgets, then forgives. I regret to say that my daughter Catherine is not yet old and has a long memory." Madame de La Grange stopped for a moment as a cough overtook her words. "You must leave France this day, never to return. I have arranged passage for you on the ship *Saint-Michel* bound for New France. It leaves on the afternoon tide. With luck, you will be long gone before my daughter discovers your disappearance. In New France you must convert to Catholicism, it is the law. You *must* convert." Marie de La Grange, so dignified, so regal and fine, spoke quickly, allowing no emotion to interfere with her message or her plan.

Of course Madame knew Esther was Jewish. No doubt she had known all along. "Why are you helping me?"

Marie de La Grange paused. "Illness gives one time to reflect. My dear girl, it is a brave thing to follow your heart. I, too, followed my heart but if I had it to do over again, I might …" She coughed into a lace handkerchief. "It does not matter why."

She handed Esther the portrait. "This rightly belongs to you. Sell it in the New World if you can."

Reluctantly Esther took it. To refuse it seemed churlish. But how could she explain that it was part of a world she wanted nothing of?

"Remember, the *Saint-Michel* leaves on the afternoon tide. And here, you will need to purchase new attire for your journey." A small velvet pouch filled with gold coins was dropped into Esther's hands. The astonished Esther could barely mouth a thank-you.

Madame thumped the roof of the carriage with the top of her cane. The carriage lurched forward.

"Wait," Esther called out. "Wait, please." She ran to the carriage's window and leapt like a street urchin onto the running board. "Cook, might she reside with you still?" Esther's hands grasped the window frame.

"Yes, although I am not proud to say so." As much as Marie de La Grange detested Cook's temper and was appalled by the woman's coarse behaviour, the two shared a long history and many secrets.

"Perhaps she has mentioned her nephew to you? His name is Philippe. Might she have received a letter, some word?"

"Yes, she is very proud of him. The boy Philippe and his brother live in the New World, on the coast, she said. But the name ..." She paused. "But, I am sorry, my dear, I have quite forgotten it."

All hope was lost. How might she find him in such a place?

"No, wait. I do recall it now," said Madame. "Louisiana, that's it. He is living in La Nouvelle Orleans in the territory of Louisiana."

"Merci," Esther cried. Her heart soared. He was safe and yet he was so far away, so very far away.

Marie de La Grange gave Esther one last look. Even through the dark veil her eyes seemed luminous. Her natural elegance, her beauty, was not marred by illness or age. She placed her hand over Esther's, which still gripped the window frame of the carriage.

"'If I take up the wings of the morning, and dwell on the ocean's farthest shore, even there Your hand will lead me. Your right hand will hold me.'"

Her words, spoken softly, carried the force of a fist. The carriage again lurched forward.

Thunderstruck, Esther jumped down onto the ground and stood as still as a pillar of salt. That was a Jewish blessing, the same Maman had used. Madame Marie de La Grange was Jewish.

The carriage kicked up dust as it rolled down the road.

❧

Esther stood on the wharf wearing new trousers, blouse, vest, jacket, warm cape and a hat with a modest feather. While a smooth, beardless face prevented her from looking like a young man, at the age of seventeen she was still able to pass for a thin yet well-proportioned boy of fourteen. She had no trunk but carried a seabag filled with warm clothes, boots, blankets and squares of cotton for the curse that now visited her with monthly regularity and caused her nothing but anguish.

Esther took in the ship that was tethered to the wharf. She had enough of a sailor's eye to know that the *Saint-Michel* was a sixty-eight-ton vessel. It was adequate for a voyage across the Atlantic Ocean and captained by Michel de Salaberry, a good man by reputation.

Captain de Salaberry stood midship greeting passengers while keeping an eye on the wares being stored in the hold. As she walked up the gangplank, Esther repeated her newly chosen name. *Jacques La Fargue, Jacques La Fargue*. Pierre Mausiette was no more.

With two feet planted firmly on the deck, Esther removed her hat and bowed to the captain. "My name is Jacques La Fargue. My benefactress, Marie de La Grange, has secured me a ticket." Squared shoulders and a direct gaze were the best way to deflect curiosity.

Captain de Salaberry presented the first mate, a Monsieur Jon Bussy. He was a thin, brutish man who asked Esther to declare her religion.

"Catholic," said Esther.

He duly recorded this information in a huge logbook. Formalities taken care of, Esther slung her seabag over her shoulder.

"You are a sailor," Captain de Salaberry called out after her.

Esther turned back. Too late, the captain's attention was now diverted. How had he known?

As the passengers clambered onto the ship and sorted themselves out, Esther stood near the bow and looked toward the port and the hills beyond. Could it be that she would never see this land again?

A symphony of the ship's whistles sang out. Ropes were cast off and reeled onto giant tumblers. Towboats rowed the ship out into the bay, and soon they too parted company. Sailors went aloft to harden the lifts and brails and release the gaskets. Sheets and tacks were secured and the buntlines overhauled. They were away. France receded on the horizon.

Esther's ticket gave her a shared cabin, midship. While the crew in the forecastle slept in hammocks, Esther and her cabin mate bedded down on hard wooden bunks, one upper and one lower. Only a thin curtain separated their sleeping quarters from the throughway.

Families took to their bunks or walked the decks when able. Young men lolled in the throughway or sat at a wooden table where they would eat their meals, drink their fill and play cards to pass the time. They bragged and boasted about the wealthy life ahead of them in the New World.

"And what of you? What name do you go by?" said one such fellow, who twirled his feathered hat about. His red lips and powdered wig seemed odd in these rough surroundings.

"My name is Jacques La Fargue. I am to carry on past New France to the American Colonies, Monsieur." Esther placed one foot in front of the other, removed her own hat and bowed deeply.

"I am André de Laurent, and these are my friends." Robert, Louis, Charles, Édouard—their names, like their faces, were instantly blurred and would have been just as quickly forgotten had not a voyage of some fifty days, more or less, not awaited them. They were five fops—not a danger to her, but Esther knew to keep up her guard.

"Perhaps you play cards?" André's face cracked into a lopsided smirk.

Esther considered. To live alongside these fine fellows she would have to play her cards very carefully indeed. She bowed. "I am an unworthy player, I can assure you. But perhaps we will play a hand or two." That answer seemed to satisfy them for the moment.

A spotty, middle-aged man with rheumy eyes and a boisterous disposition declared himself Esther's cabin mate. "My name is Pascal Prudhomme. Crossing the Atlantic! A great adventure we are on." His hearty laugh was accompanied by a slap on the back that sent Esther stumbling into a post. Esther looked up at him with amazement. How on earth would she avoid such a man in a cabin that could hardly fit two cats? The problem was soon dispensed with. Upon reaching the open sea, Monsieur Pascal Prudhomme immediately became seasick and plunged headlong into the lower bunk. His constant vomiting soon fouled air already polluted with heavy perfumes and unclean bodies.

Days turned into weeks. It was a calm crossing, the calmest the crew had ever experienced. "It is like being in a lady's bathtub," was what one old sailor said, although what he might have known of a lady's tub was anyone's guess.

The sun, the wind, the assuredness of the blue sky above and dark water below was calming. Esther did not feel overwhelmed by the expanse of the sky or ocean. On the contrary, in this open space she could breathe. She stood on deck from sunup to sundown and often, squirrelled up against the bulwark, through-out the night, too. The nights were the best. How could she not marvel at the beauty of the stars? A map from God. Esther breathed in all of God's gifts and never failed to say thank-you.

"Hear, O Israel: the Lord is our God, the Lord is One! Blessed is His glorious kingdom for ever and ever." See, Papa, I remember. I will always remember.

One bright day, as the ship ploughed through sparkling blue water sending up curls of white waves, Esther watched with envy as the crew scampered up and down the ratlines.

"Go ahead, then."

Startled, Esther turned to face Captain de Salaberry. He had not made himself familiar to the guests on board these past many weeks, preferring to keep his own counsel.

Esther bowed deeply. "My apologies, captain. I do not understand."

"I've been watching you. You want to go aloft. Go on, then."

"How did you...?"

The captain threw his head back and laughed. "How did I know that you are a sailor? You carry your seabag straight back so as not to bump into the walls of the narrow passages. And you know how to be on deck yet stay out of the way of working sailors."

Esther grinned as she kicked off her shoes, grabbed hold of the ratline, hoisted herself up and then swung over the side of the ship. She scurried up the lines as if born to it. She stopped on the first platform and breathed deeply. A swirling wind played with the ribbon that bound her hair, and now it framed her face like a dark crimson halo. She pressed her body into a gentle gust and let go of the lines. She was released from the bonds of earth and could surely soar with the birds.

"What do you make of the horizon?" Captain de Salaberry called from below.

Esther raised a hand to her brow and stared intently to the west. "They be storm clouds, captain," she shouted from on high.

Captain de Salaberry stood as still and as straight as a sentinel. His brow was furrowed and his expression grew troubled as he looked toward the gathering storm.

❧

"All hands, all hands!"

The call was barely heard above the din of waves pounding the hull and rain beating against the deck. Hour after hour the wind rose up in a furious pitch. Winches screeched and timbers creaked and groaned. Sails, freed from their riggings, snapped and cracked like gunshots. Half a day had passed since Esther had spotted the clouds on the horizon. There was no sign of the storm abating—on the contrary, it was getting worse. Great waves now washed up onto the decks. Darkness surrounded the ship, and yet it was still day.

For the safety of the passengers, the captain ordered that the hatches be secured. With growing helplessness, Esther lay trapped below deck listening to the sounds of a ship under siege. She was trapped, held down, suffocating. The forecastle, where the crew bedded down, was flooded. Water crashed against the main hatch like surf pounding a pier. More water leaked into the cabins from above, creating pools of water on the floor. Two lanterns, fore and aft, swung back and forth, casting mad shadows over the wretched passengers. Steaming bodies and overflowing night-jars created a stink so odious, so foul, no man, woman or child dared take a deep breath. Esther did her best to steady herself, repeating prayers and words that would calm her breathing. Still the walls pressed against her.

The hatch opened just once. Those who still had their wits about them gasped and looked up like gaping fish in a pond. Esther grabbed hold of a post lest she hurl herself against the hatch and plead for release: *Let me out! Let me out before I smother!* She said nothing but hunkered down, her fear now so real that it had become a piercing pain in her belly.

Without explanation, a sailor from above tossed a coil of rope and a knife down. Esther gathered up the rope and cut it into lengths. Wordlessly she set to work tying passengers into their bunks—mothers, children and men alike. Untethered, they would fly about as the journey got rougher still, breaking limbs and creating havoc. Her cabin mate, the obnoxious Monsieur

Pascal Prudhomme, could hardly be shifted. He moaned as Esther tied him to his berth.

The foppish young men whimpered as she lashed them to posts, poles or anything solid. Their wigs had slipped or been pulled off altogether. Their once-painted faces and ruby-coloured lips were shiny with sweat. But it was the obnoxious André de Laurent who became the most tiresome. Tears spilled down his sorry face as he apologized for past crimes Esther knew nothing about. Apparently he was a thief. One particular crime bothered him—something to do with a servant. Esther wasn't listening. He wanted absolution, yet even the priest was pleading with God for absolution.

No one questioned her as she secured the luggage, the drinking-water barrels and the night-jars, too. All were past mouthing any words but prayers. Her job done, Esther tucked the knife into her belt and made herself small, praying not for life but for air.

A second day passed. The fear of encroaching walls, of suffocation, had not abated, but now cold and hunger gnawed at her. There was no food to be had. The galley could not be reached without going up on deck; nor, thought Esther, could the stove be lit in any case. Sea biscuits were passed around, satisfying neither hunger nor appetite.

The hatch flew open and a wash of fresh air blew in. "Who claims to be a sailor?" A hollowed-eyed sailor stared down.

Esther looked up. "Me, I can sail," she yelled.

"Here." He threw down an oilskin and a rope with a hook attached. "Get ye topside as soon as you are able." The sailor closed the hatch but did not lock it down.

Silent passengers watched Esther slip into the clammy oilskin. It was too large, but she wound the rope around her middle and secured the knife to her rope-belt. She latched the hook to the belt, then climbed the ladder.

The wind took the hatch. Steady, steady—she climbed out, measuring her steps with the roll of the ship. Rain whipped her face, salt stung her eyes, and within the instant she was soaked through. A gust pushed her toward the edge of the deck. Like a bird flying into a window, Esther was flattened against the bulkhead.

"Up the ropes," commanded the captain from the foredeck.

Esther cupped one hand over her eyes, squinted and tried to make out the shapes that hung off the ratlines above her. Two sailors, black silhouettes against a dark sky, were heading toward the mainsail. Rope was wound about them and each carried a hatchet or knife. Esther put her foot to the ratlines and began the climb. She hooked herself on with each step, measuring the pitch and the roll. The fear she felt down below deck blew away.

Despite breath snatched away by the wind and vision hampered by the sea spray, Esther climbed steadily. She slackened her body to roll with the pitch. Ahead, sailors lay along the pole near the end of the mainsail. Hand over hand, steady, steady, she pulled herself forward. Together they pulled in the main shroud, tying it off with bits of rope. There was nothing to hook onto; her life was in God's hands. This was life, her life. The thrill of it. She would have none other.

Dawn was an orange ball that rose up on the horizon. Esther had sat for the last hour curled up by the bulkhead. Sea salt had hardened her eyelashes and stiffened her hair and clothes. The back of her neck was badly chafed and her hands were rubbed raw.

She smiled. How could she not?

*C*hapter 28

❦

André de Laurent and his band of witless young men had given Esther some peace over the last few days. They had not mentioned the storm, or their less than courageous behaviour. But now, spared by God's good grace, they were looking for amusement.

The irksome André thumped the table like a lord and looked about expectantly. "A game, then, boy."

All five sat at the long wooden table in the thoroughfare holding a deck of very fine hand-painted cards. Esther had played several card games with one or two, but not all the silly young men at once. The cards were shuffled and dealt.

They cheated, and badly. Esther was doing these young men no favour by not exposing them as scoundrels. From the tales passed about among the passengers, she knew that the New World dealt with cheaters swiftly and without mercy.

Esther played and lost. "You have taken all that I have, gentlemen. I bid you goodnight." She was not fool enough to reveal her second money pouch—the one in her trousers, which also held the king's portrait

"I think not." André de Laurent bounced up, bounded around the table and hovered above her like a gleeful, predatory beast. "By my calculations you owe me thirty livres. It would doubtless go hard on you should we report to the first mate that a passenger has reneged on a bet. After all, my father and the father of my dear friend Louis, here, are investors in this ship. Neither the captain nor the first mate would likely take your word against ours." André de Laurent's grin now spread from ear to ear.

A new game was at hand. Not content with cheating, these fops were now attempting to blackmail and steal. But there was more to it, she could feel it.

"That may be, gentlemen," Esther said, in a lighter tone of voice, "but the well is dry, for I am now financially embarrassed." Esther stood and gave them all a deep bow before retiring to her cabin.

With her heart thumping in her chest she stood in the small space between curtain and bunk and tried to think. She could afford to give them a few extra livres. Madame Marie de La Grange had been most generous. Even after paying for clothes and a blanket she had more than fifty livres hidden. But if she succumbed to blackmail, would these loathsome ruffians simply demand more? Besides, it seemed that there was more to it than a paltry amount of money. What to do? They would soon reach the mouth of the mighty St. Lawrence River. It was imperative that she not draw attention to herself, not now, not when freedom was so close.

Esther peered into Monsieur Prudhomme's empty bunk. She reached down into her trousers and pulled out her money pouch. What came up in her hand caused her to curse out loud—for, indeed, it was the monthly curse.

Her trousers, her stockings were saturated. What a fool she was. She had boarded the ship prepared with folded linens, ready to cast the bloody evidence over the side of the ship. All she had to do was pull her seabag out from under the bunk.

Esther placed her money purse containing coins, the knife she had acquired during the storm and the portrait on a three-legged stool that stood between the bunk and curtain. Quickly she removed her trousers. She squatted and reached under the bunk and pulled out a pair of breeches.

Her back was to the curtain when André de Laurent yanked it to one side. On the floor and in full view were the offensive and bloodied trousers. André de Laurent stepped over them without so much as casting a downward glance. Esther jumped up, crushing the clean breeches to her middle.

He pushed his face into hers. "You will find yourself discredited in this New France. You are accused of cheating. And who would believe anything you had to say?"

Ah, his confession during the storm. That was what he was worried about. But she had not taken in a word of his babble. He was a fool. Worse, he felt trapped. All trapped animals are dangerous. She should say something to reassure him.

"Monsieur de Laurent …"

"What's this?" He spied the pouch. As he reached for it, he turned his back on Esther. "Look what I have discovered!" He held the portrait of the king in his hands and laughed out loud. And as he cried out he looked down to the bloodied trousers on the floor. "What else have I come upon?"

Esther snatched up the knife, lifted it as high as she dared and then jammed it into flesh. Fresh, red blood oozed and dripped onto the floor.

"I have a cut, Monsieur." Esther held up her bloodied hand.

Captain de Salaberry examined the portrait. It was, in the captain's opinion, an extraordinarily good one. The frame alone was beautifully crafted and solid gold. While not an expert in such matters, he guessed its value to be a thousand livres or more.

Not for the first time, Captain de Salaberry wondered at this boy's origin. This Jacques La Fargue was exceedingly handsome, if that was the word for his uncommon look. He seemed a quick-witted, pleasant lad, though there was secretiveness about him. But he was not a malicious sort, of that de Salaberry was sure. What should he do? André de Laurent and his mealy-mouthed comrades stood before him demanding justice for a gambling debt of some thirty livres. They were soft young men, all typical offspring of the weaker branches of the French aristocracy. They were also in a position to cause him financial problems.

On the one hand, this Jaques La Fargue had proven himself an able seaman. The boy was worth ten of these coxcombs that stood before him. De Salaberry considered.

"Land ho!" came a cry from the deck.

Captain de Salaberry laughed. Newfoundland! They were on the coast of the New World. In another week or more, they would be in Quebec and this matter would be turned over to his dear friend Intendant Hocquart.

Part 3

*C*hapter 29

✑

*I*ntendant Gilles Hocquart sat quite still. He had risen from his chair several times during the night while listening intently to the girl's story. Now he stood, pensive and reflective, at his window overlooking the St. Lawrence River. The sky was lightening. Dawn was near.

He looked back at Esther. Her head lay against the chair. One could feast on the depth of her eyes and the beauty of her face.

Hocquart looked away quickly and cursed. He would not allow himself to be bewitched. He motioned to the secretary. The man, showing no signs of weariness, laid down his quill. The two stood by the window and spoke in voices so low that if Esther were listening, she would hear them only as distant rumbles. The secretary nodded to the intendant, stepped back, then stood in front of Esther.

"You will follow me."

The secretary's words roused her. Wordlessly she stood and curtsied to Intendant Hocquart, although he did not turn to face her or acknowledge her departure. Esther trailed the secretary out of the room and down a staircase. There was no mention of where she was being taken. Perhaps to prison, perhaps back to the ship. No guards stood at the ready, and in that she found some relief.

At the bottom of the stone steps the secretary motioned to an old servant woman who sat in the shadows. The woman emerged from the gloom and draped a thick, dark cloak, as long as a shroud, over Esther's shoulders. With the secretary in the lead, they left the grand building to walk the still dark streets of Quebec.

Esther looked upon the narrow streets and open gutters. The buildings were made of granite, the windows had shutters, and the slate roofs were steep. It was a little France, tiny in the extreme. Despite overwhelming fatigue she took note of each turn, each twist. Even in the open air, in a country as big as the sky, the walls were closing in on her. She could not give in to this lethargy. She was tired, yes. She was trapped, yes. But she was not beaten. If only this odd man in front of her would give some hint of what was to come.

They came upon a chapel. The spire was pressed tight against a brightening sky. She knew that while the outside was plain, the interior would be elaborate, a tribute to a Catholic God.

"What is this church called?" She spoke to the secretary, who until now had not said a word.

"Notre-Dame-des-Victoires. A testament to our survival in this land." He offered no more information than that. They carried on. The secretary stopped in front of a three-storey house. Lime wash coated the exterior, and the lower windows were trimmed with thick shutters. He raised his fist against the wooden door and hammered hard. Long moments passed. Again he thumped. Finally they heard the thud of a bolt slipping its casing. A stout woman opened the door. The flickering of candles behind revealed her to be a broadly built woman of a rare old age.

"What hour is this to arrive on my doorstep?" The woman meant to scold the secretary but curiosity overcame her. "So this be she. The soldiers came last night and brought me word. Do not stand there letting in the cold. Get in." The old woman spoke a common, guttural French.

Esther ducked under the door frame and gazed around a large room. A poor fire smouldered in the hearth, and yet it was not as chilly as it might have been. It appeared that the walls of the house were thickly built to stave off the cold and retain heat. To the far side stood a length of board as long as a tavern table and as thick as a butcher's block. A great joint of mutton and a rind of cheese sat upon it. A pewter knife and spoon, rather grand for the surroundings, lay at the ready. Even in this gloomy light Esther spied dirt banked against the walls. Black cones of smoke from pine torches marked the ceiling, and mice ran freely from corner to corner. The house reeked of mould and decay. Another familiar but odious smell emanated from a pail in the corner.

As Esther surveyed her new surroundings the secretary pulled the old woman aside. He hissed into her failing ear, "She is a Jew."

The old woman's mouth gaped open. A Jew, was it? In all her years she had never met such a one. Where were her horns? All Jews had horns, it was common knowledge. Would they be in her forehead or farther back? The old woman strained to see the girl's head in the poor light. Perhaps they were retracted, like a cat's claws? She could see nothing. She would look again, in better light.

"What am I to do with her? Who is to pay for her?" Spittle sprayed in all directions as the old woman spoke.

So that was it. She was to board with this woman. Esther turned to face the two. "If I am to stay here then I will work for my keep, Madame." Her words were bold, but she had learned that timidity seldom reaped any benefits. Had Esther been looking more intently at the secretary she would have seen a look of surprise, perhaps even amusement, on his face.

"Work? What kind of work can the likes of you offer?" the old woman snarled.

"I can clean," Esther said.

"Clean? What is there to clean? I have swept the room this very day!"

Esther paused and silently cursed herself for not minding her tongue. "My apologies, Madame. I meant that I could wash. All I require is vinegar, soap, resin and perhaps wax."

The old woman's mouth dropped. Vinegar perhaps, but precious soap? Who ever heard of such a thing? Resin? Wax? "You shall nay turn my house topsy-turvy." She plunked her great bulk down in a rocking chair and took up her pipe. The jingle of a ring of keys accompanied her as she rocked.

"I can cook, as well."

Now the old woman's eyes lit up. "Make my breakfast, then." She turned to the secretary. "Mind, I still expect coin for her rent. If she cooks well enough, I can feed her some. She doesn't look like she eats much." The old woman clucked, lit a long, white clay pipe and rocked with surprising vigour.

The old woman waved away the secretary then turned her attention back to Esther. "What name do you go by?"

"My name is Esther Brandeau." How easily the words tripped off her tongue. *Esther, Esther, Esther, my name is Esther.*

"You will call me Madame Bonviet." The old woman chuckled. It was about time she had a servant.

Chapter 30

⁓

$\mathcal{E}$ sther pushed back the sliding doors to the *cabane*. Given her dislike, even fear, of small spaces, sleeping in a cupboard was only possible if she kept the doors ajar. She had slept a great deal this past week. As long as she was up before the old woman, there were no complaints.

And yet though she had slept, she was not rested. Night after night, fear arrived with alarming familiarity. She could not return to prison, dear God, please. Her stomach coiled in knots. No word had come from the office of the intendant. Waiting was itself a torture. Escape was her only option. And while she might easily flee from the house of Madame Bonviet, where would she go? The country was large and unfamiliar and winter was on its way.

If there was one consolation it was that, without the cloth strips that had bound her breasts, she could breathe freely. But there was no freedom in being female. She sorely missed wearing trousers. Several times she had taken great strides only to find her legs caught in the trappings of her skirt.

Esther swung her legs out of the *cabane* and stepped onto the cold floor. *Hear, O Israel: the Lord is our God, the Lord is One! Blessed is His glorious kingdom for ever and ever.* It would be good to speak these words out loud but for the moment she spoke them only in her heart.

The days passed slowly. She washed filthy blankets, stuffed mattresses with fresh reeds and straw and hung sheets out to be bleached by the sun. The floors had been scrubbed with hard soap, shaved and softened in boiling water. With sand and twigs Esther scoured the copper kettles and pewter plates. The brick oven out back, recently home to several fat rats, had been cleaned and fired up for baking bread.

Esther's hands were now cracked and blistered and flamed red. Her back ached from the lifting. Burn marks, from tending the fire and doing the ironing, ran up and down her arms. Then, when she least expected it, she was rewarded for her industry. It was a like a sign or a gift. Esther came upon the clothes of Madame Bonviet's dead husband. She examined them carefully. It would take work, but they would do nicely.

A second week passed into a third. Still Intendant Hocquart had not sent for her. To keep the old woman at bay, Esther fed her morning, noon and night, and in between as well. A stew hung on the knob at the ready and stone-ground bread was baked every day.

"I will do the marketing," she offered. "I will fetch the water," she said. Esther took every excuse to go out of doors and look around.

The market in Place Royale offered impressive choices. There was salmon, cod, eel, sturgeon and vegetables—corn, squash, fat cabbages and beans, along with apples, plums and olives. On offer, too, were local delicacies such as beaver tail and moose.

Dried peas were much in demand, as were hare and bear. While she could not bring herself to eat the fatty bacon called *lard*, she soon learned to cook with it to make *tourtière*—a mix of passenger pigeon and pig fat. Maple sugar—could anything taste as good?—was served over wild berries for dinner at noon and supper again at night.

Small businesses—many tucked away down narrow streets, others under canvas—were everywhere. Women in France often toiled alongside their husbands and fathers. But here in New France women worked as bone-setters, laundresses, wool-fullers, wig-makers, gold-beaters, book-binders, doublet-makers and burnishers. Everywhere she looked women ran shops, owned buildings—it was wondrous to behold! Still, it was toward the harbour that her attention wandered.

In the distance she could see several ships' masts rocking in the wind. One of those belonged to the *Saint-Michel*. There was another seagoing ship in the harbour. The name on the bow said *Saint-Charles*. From where did it hail, and what was its destination? She stood on the wharf a long time before she noticed small boats ferrying water casks ashore. They would soon be filled with fresh water. It was a sure sign that the ship was being made ready to sail. Besides, snowflakes had begun to fall. The ships would have to leave before they found themselves locked in by ice.

On that morning, nearly a month after her arrival, Esther returned with the marketing to find Madame Bonviet standing in her stained, coarse petticoat and chemise. Without a corset to hem in the fat, her great bulk swayed freely. A soiled lace cap covered her balding head and in her hand she held an unbrushed wig. The old woman cast the wig onto the table and there it lay, motley and tattered, bearing a startling resemblance to a dead cat.

"Where have you been? Who have you been talking to? Men, is that it?"

Esther stood on the doorsill and bent to scrape the mud off her shoes on the scraper.

"I am speaking to you. How dare you turn away?" She did not see Madame Bonviet's arm rise up. As Esther turned, the old woman's hand fell across her cheek with a resounding smack. Oddly, Esther heard the sound before she felt the pain. Tears of fury filled her eyes. She burned with the shame and anger.

"Slut! I need my breakfast!" Madame Bonviet stomped her foot like a spoiled child.

Esther ducked past the old woman and flew to the small cauldron that hung over the fire. Rage could almost overtake her. She must push it down, down and down. She must not do anything to jeopardize her plan.

Madame Bonviet sat at the table and waited. Her foul mood seemed to lift once she was satisfied that food was on its way.

As Esther stirred the pot, the old woman cast her eyes about the place. Her house had never looked so good. Why, who would have thought to put it so? And the food—*yum, yum*. She smacked her lips, tucked a freshly laundered cloth under her third chin and clutched a knife in one hand and a spoon in the other. *Yum, yum*.

Esther flung off her cloak and, using a dark muslin apron as a potholder, ladled a large helping of stew into the old woman's wooden bowl. As she had many times before, Esther caught the old woman peering at her head like a dog down a rabbit hole. In the past, Esther had been relieved that the old woman had done nothing but sit like a great ox smoking a foul-smelling pipe, and so she'd thought it best to ignore this strange occupation. But ignoring Madame Bonviet's presence was a hard thing to do. A skunk would have run from the woman's smell.

"Madame, might I fill a tub with hot water and help you bathe?" Esther spoke softly and with respect.

"What? Wash away my protection? I'd get sick, I would." Madame Bonviet tore off her cap, reached for the ratty wig and plopped it on her head. There she sat, a pig-in-a-wig. She plunged her face into the bowl of stew and, using the spoon as a shovel, sucked up the food. Her wig kept slipping, the strands dipping in and out of the bowl leaving a brown trail of juice up and down her chemise. Not a trace of the stew was spared her greedy tongue, but to make certain she picked up a loaf of bread, ripped off a hunk and mopped the bowl clean. Once finished, the old woman attempted to rise but succeeded only in falling back and depositing yet another fart into her sorry chair. If farts had been fuel, the woman would have flown.

"I have worked my whole life through, and what have I to show for it?" Her belly full she sat back and lit her pipe, further fouling the air. "I birthed seventeen in all and buried twelve, and then I buried my good-for-nothing husband at the end of it. Twelve children dead, and the ones left to me all but useless. It's a touch of brandy that I want. Take these." She unhooked the key-ring from her belt and hurled it at Esther. "In there." She pointed a crooked finger toward a far cabinet.

The top of the cabinet was filled with chipped crockery. Beneath it was a locked cupboard. Esther tried one key, then the other, listened for the click and retrieved a brown, earthenware brandy jug. She poured a goodly amount into the old woman's mug.

Madame Bonviet sucked back the brandy through teeth ground down into brown stubs. Esther placed the jug back in the cupboard.

"Wait!" she hollered. "I might want more. Keep the jug out."

By late afternoon, the old woman had consumed a half jug of brandy plus untold mugs of ale. It was as if her throat were a funnel into a hole in the sand. She slumped in the chair like a great beached whale, neither asleep nor awake but wallowing in that hazy world of drink.

"It's the outhouse I need." Groggy and unsure of her footing, the old woman tossed aside her pipe, stood and stumbled about. Her hands, as big as bear paws, were held out to steady herself against any solid object. It was no use, the old woman thumped back down into her chair.

"Let me help you up." Esther lifted the old woman's arm and pulled it across her neck. She was nearly sick from the odour. "Up, then." She strained to help the woman rise.

Who would have known, or even suspected, what the old woman would do next? With no warning, she shook her arm loose, thrust her fat hand up Esther's skirt and made to catch the girl's bottom. Esther screamed and reeled backwards until she was pressed against the far wall. Gasping, she stared at the old woman with horror.

"Now, now, my girl, no fear." The old woman gave her a gummy, drunken grin as she tottered back and forth. "Just let me get a feel of it. Something to tell my grandchildren."

Esther, her mouth agape, could hardly speak. "What? What is it you want of me?"

"Your tail, girl. I wants to feel your tail! For it is certain that Jews have horns and tails. It is well known."

Chapter 31

❦

It was almost dark when Esther donned her long black cloak. The old lady sat slumped in her chair. Her mouth hung open while her many chins sagged over her ample chest. She had eaten enough for six, had swallowed several drafts of ale and as much brandy besides.

"Please, let her not wake," Esther whispered. In an attempt to look like a simple maid on an errand she clutched a straw basket, then slipped the bolt and stepped out into the evening air. Almost immediately a mist enveloped her, plastering fringes of hair to her face. The cloak flapped madly about and the hood all but disguised her as she walked steadily toward the wharf. She'd have run, but she feared drawing attention to herself.

Once on the wharf Esther stood among caskets and kegs, briny rope, piles of netting and baskets. The air smelled of salt, woodsmoke and fish guts. An alehouse was behind her, a customs house and a repair yard beside it. Cats crept about, and a three-legged dog with honey-coloured eyes gazed up at her expectantly. She had nothing to give it, and so the dog dropped its sad eyes and loped away.

The mist down by the water had thickened into a fog, revealing and disguising as if on a whim. She scanned the wharf. Two boys, one shorter than the other, were rolling barrels out of a far shed. She turned and looked out to the harbour. Brigantines were anchored offshore among bobbing fishing boats. She spied first the *Saint-Charles* and then the smaller *Saint-Michel*. The sight of the brigantine that had brought her to this unwelcoming shore made her catch her breath. She pushed back the fear. Fear paralyzed, and she needed her wits more than ever.

Esther forced herself to look back at the *Saint-Michel*. The fog prevented her from seeing it clearly but she knew that the brig would have a skeleton crew of no more than six. The rest would be gallivanting around the town. The crew had last seen her dressed as a boy; none would recognize her in a woman's garb.

Voices rose up behind her. Esther slipped between two barrels and pressed herself hard against a wall. Above her a window opened and a bucket of filth was tossed down onto the road. The muck splashed at her feet. Not two arm's lengths away, a door opened, followed by the roar of an unhappy man. A sodden body was hurled past her. The man landed on his belly in the ditch.

"Let me not see you in here again." The door slammed shut.

The drunk stood, after a fashion, shook his fist to the sky and hollered like the devil. There was nothing for it, and so he slumped against the wall, his legs splayed in front of him.

Two soldiers on patrol, both wearing tricorne hats and dressed in heavy white overcoats that protected their blue uniforms from the rain, sauntered toward the drunkard, laughing. Esther retreated farther into the shadows. The drunk stood and staggered away as the soldiers carried on with their customary patrol.

Only when they had gone a good distance did Esther re-emerge. It was getting harder and harder to see out onto the water.

Head held high, she walked down the wharf toward the two boys shifting kegs about. They were both about her age, perhaps seventeen years, perhaps a little older.

"What flag does that ship sail under?" Esther, speaking to the taller of the two, pointed to the *Saint-Charles*.

The sailor did little more than glance at the dark figure before him. "French. The *Saint-Charles* sails under Boucherville's command."

Again she peered into the dim. The *Saint-Charles* sat low in the water; its cargo was loaded. It would set sail within the day, of that Esther was sure.

"What sort of captain is he?" asked Esther.

"A good one, by all accounts. Fair to his men."

"And what is his destination?"

The young man grunted as he heaved a sack of grain over a shoulder. "I hear the ship is to put in at Louisiana and then sail down to the Caribbean."

Esther lowered her hood. Her hair, once free of the hood's trappings, swirled around her. "What tavern does the captain frequent?"

"He's a gentleman, that one!" The second boy laughed and winked at his partner. "When he is not with his good wife, you'll find him there." He pointed to an alehouse on the far side of the pier.

Esther bowed and held out a coin. "Thank you for your trouble."

The kind offer startled the young man, who only then took the time to look Esther up and down. His jaw dropped. It was all he could do to keep his eyes in his head. Attractive females were

uncommon enough, for it was said that a woman with the face
of a horse could marry in New France. But a beauty such as this,
with nary a father or benefactor in sight, and in a seaport town
full of ruffians—well, it was a rare sight indeed.

"No, no thank you." He waved away the money.

Esther nodded.

⌒

"I am looking for Captain Boucherville of the *Saint-Charles*."
Esther spoke to a barrel-shaped man who held four steins of beer
laced in his sausage-sized fingers. He motioned with a tilt of his
head at a far corner.

Esther squinted and peered over at a well-dressed man holding
court. He was wigless, his brown hair tied into a tidy knot at the
nape of his neck. A handsome man, he looked out of place
among the rogues and brutes that would find a home in any
bawdyhouse or tavern in the world.

Esther glided toward the captain. She kept her focus only on
him, looking neither right nor left. Moses walking into the Red
Sea could not have cleared a better path. Flapping mouths fell
silent on either side. Flush-faced drunks leered, their eyes trailing
up and down her body; others were simply curious.

Be brave, her heart whispered. *Be brave.*

Above her, lanterns dangled from rough-cut beams, casting
oddly shaped shadows over the wooden tables. New France was
a civil place, as far as she could tell, yet she was surrounded now
by cutthroats. Most wore battered jackets and wide-legged
trousers, or breeches stiff with salt or filth. Fine silk stockings,
drawn over well-curved legs, were worn by some, while rougher
fellows settled for thick wool socks shoved into square-toed

shoes. Beer and cheap rum washed down their gullets with the unstoppable speed of a waterfall.

Captain Boucherville looked up as Esther approached. "And what, pray, has fallen into my lap?" The men around him glanced up too and laughed heartily. A wave of Boucherville's hand brought their merriment to a halt.

Esther had fully intended to launch into a prepared speech. She stopped. André de Laurent and his compatriots—Robert, Louis, Charles, Édouard—surrounded the captain. Their faces were blank and stupid. She stepped back. Did they recognize her?

"I am here to speak on a matter of commerce, captain. I wish to arrange passage." Esther did not falter, although her knees quivered. How would they know her? She was disguised, the room was dim and the smoke thick. But then, Catherine had once seen through her deception. No, she must not give in to such fears.

The captain studied the girl. "Who is this passenger?"

"My younger brother." She kept her eyes forward. If anything revealed her true identity it would be the colour of her eyes and the cursed beauty mark. She clutched her hood and pulled it across her nose.

"Your brother?" Captain Boucherville's eyebrows shot up in surprise. There were wild rumours flying about the city of a boy, discovered to be a Jew, who had arrived on these Catholic shores. The captain had been warned that upon leaving he was to check his ship carefully, in case this wandering Jew had stowed away. But there was no mention of the boy having a sister or an accomplice of any kind.

"Our parents live in the Caribbean," Esther carried on. She tried not to rush her words, but it was difficult. "He is to join them there. You see, captain, I am to be married, and it would be best if my brother not live in my married home." Everything now depended on her ability to lie. This man had to believe her, yet the boys by his side must not recognize her.

"I have a berth for him," said the captain.

"I can pay in advance. What would be the passage rate?" She could feel André de Laurent lean across the table as if to get a better view of her.

The captain studied the beauty before him.

"Seventy livres."

"That is robbery!" Esther spouted. The loathsome boys beside him smirked. She knew the game at hand. If she agreed to such an inflated sum, she would be showing desperation. The captain would get suspicious and all would be lost. She had to hold her ground. She had to!

The captain laughed, as did his young guests. "Indeed. Then let's say forty livres."

Esther nodded. "When do you sail?"

"The last rowboat out to the ship is just after dawn tomorrow morning. It will wait for your brother. If he is not on the *Saint-Charles* by first tide on the morrow, we leave without him."

Esther nodded, then took out her leather pouch and counted out the coins.

"Will you not join us for a drink? We will feed you, too, if you like." As André de Laurent leered he wetted his painted lips. "It is not often that we have the company of a beautiful woman."

Esther did not lift her eyes but stared at the rough planks beneath her feet. The captain sat back amused: boys will be boys.

"*Merci*, Monsieur, but my business is done." Esther turned and left.

Esther spent the night tailoring and sewing the dead Monsieur Bonviet's clothes. The old woman stirred but did not wake. Esther had been unable to shift her into bed, and so Madame Bonviet snored in her chair with one leg pointing north, the other south. Her cap had slipped, revealing thin, greasy hair plastered against a scabby skull.

As dawn approached, Esther pulled on Monsieur Bonviet's trousers. She had done a fine job cutting the trousers, shirt and jacket to her size. Dressed again in familiar male attire, she rolled the black cloak around a loaf of bread, tied it with rope and slung it over her shoulder. She tucked another hunk of bread into her pocket, along with two hard apples. She was going to Louisiana, although all on board would think her destination was the Caribbean. A new life awaited, and for that she would need a new name. Perrot le Flamene perhaps. No, too old-fashioned. Claude Thibodeaux was better. Her fears gave way to excitement. How good it felt to be in boys' clothes again! Esther crept out of the house without so much as one look back.

The town of Quebec was just waking. She passed a child feeding her chickens and a Negro slave girl carrying laundry on her head. The girl stopped and stared at Esther. Her brown eyes were as wide as a night sky. Esther smiled at her and carried on. Her smile was not returned.

Carts and wagons rolled by. Somewhere goats bleated, demanding to be milked, a baby cried, doors banged open and the contents of piss-pots were flung out of windows onto the street. It took a nimble and a quick foot to dodge the dung, kitchen refuse and filth that littered the way. It was safest to walk in the middle of the road, but then, that's where she would be most exposed to curious looks.

The fog at the water's edge was still thick. Snowflakes whirled around her, melting as soon as they touched down. All looked quiet enough. The dreaded *Saint-Michel* bobbed at anchor. The *Saint-Charles* was anchored at the end of the harbour. The soldiers on patrol were a good bit away. They posed no threat.

Esther spotted the tip of a small skiff with the name *Saint-Charles* painted on the side. All she had to do was climb in and be rowed out to the ship. Once on board she would again be free. She took a deep breath. Soon, very soon, this colony of New France would be at her back.

Esther sauntered toward the skiff, swaggering like a boy.

The young sailor, the cabin boy perhaps, looked up and nodded. "You be the passenger, then?" he asked. Esther nodded.

A dog barked. Esther turned and spotted the three-legged dog she'd seen the night before. "Have you come to see me off?" She laughed and tossed it a small piece of bread. She turned and made to climb down the ladder to the skiff. Five young men looked up at her. André de Laurent and his friends sat in the small boat. Their eyes, like hers, were wide with shock. It was André who stood and yelled, "It is you. *Arrêtez!* Stop!" Esther spun around. The soldiers in the distance, too, stopped and turned.

André stood up and lunged toward the ladder. Their collective stupidity was their undoing as the rest stood too. There was a splash and a holler, "I cannot swim!"

"*Arrêtez!* Stop!" The soldiers were running—toward her or the drowning men, she could not tell. Esther did not look back.

The boards of the wharf turned to cobblestones and then to trodden earth. Once, twice she stumbled. Her breath was short and her side ached. She ducked mules pulling wagons, horses and carriages, servants and slaves. She had to hide.

Esther crouched low behind a horse trough. A dog barked. She looked up to see the three-legged dog sniffing at her heels. "Go, go away," she muttered. The dog's tongue hung out of its mouth as it panted. "Go!" She felt human eyes upon her. She looked up into the black face of the slave girl. There was no expression on her face, only recognition of one trapped girl looking at another.

The slave girl slapped her thigh and called the dog to her. She turned her back on Esther and by doing so blocked the view of the passing sailors. The slave girl waited a moment, then, with the dog by her side, carried on down the road without looking back.

Esther yanked the rope off her cloak and flung it over her shoulders. The loaf of bread rolled into the gutter. She pulled the hood over her head and stood on two quaking legs. Then, after a long, deep breath, she proceeded at a dignified pace suited to a young maid out on an errand. Twice she saw the soldiers running between the houses. They were looking for Jacques La Fargue, a boy, not a maid in a cloak. At least that was what she hoped. She had no way of knowing if André and his gang had put it all together and now knew that the boy they had travelled with was really a girl.

Esther turned a corner and spied the dreaded old woman's house. With luck, the despicable Madame Bonviet would still be asleep.

Luck was not with her. Esther opened the door.

Two young soldiers, different ones, stood in the middle of the room.

"That be her. Jewish slut!" the old woman shrieked. The two soldiers recoiled from the old woman and looked from the hag to the beauty. "Where have you been? With sailors, I'll warrant. And who drank all my brandy? Took it with you, did you? Shared it with all the men in the port?" the woman spewed. "Well, now you'll pay. They've come for you. The intendant himself wants to see you. Ha! You're in for it now."

"Intendant Hocquart wishes you to attend him directly." One soldier removed his hat and, out of instinct perhaps, addressed Esther as one might a lady.

Esther nodded. "Might I be excused for a moment?" She gave the soldier a pleasant smile. While she looked flushed, the soldiers had no reason to suspect that she might flee. Nor was she under arrest. Their orders were simply to escort her to the Upper Town and the office of the intendant.

The soldier nodded.

Esther had left her clothes hidden in the *cabane*. It was Madame's foul mouth that diverted the soldiers' attention long enough for her to slip her skirt under her arm and duck out the back door. There she pulled her skirt over the trousers. Although still breathing hard, she left the house within minutes in the company of the soldiers.

"When is she to return?" The old woman stood on the door sill and shouted out into the street. "I must have my supper. Who is to make my supper?"

Once out in the morning light, the soldiers took the measure of the young woman who walked ahead of them with the elegance of a queen. Of course they didn't believe the old woman's curses. The girl could not be Jewish, since none of that faith were allowed in New France. As to her being a slut— if it was so, then all the better!

They came upon the Church of Notre-Dame-des-Victoires in the market square. Esther stopped and looked up at its spire. "I should like to go in for a moment." She desperately needed to still her heart and quiet her mind. André and his gang were nowhere to be seen. Still, it was best if she stayed out of view for as long as possible.

The tallest soldier considered her request. What harm could a visit to a church do? Surely the intendant would not object.

Esther pushed open the tall door. The coolness of the place was calming and the familiar whiff of incense enveloping. As she crossed the threshold she murmured, "Hear, O Israel: the Lord is our God, the Lord is One! Blessed is His glorious kingdom for ever and ever."

Hats in hand, the two soldiers took up positions at the back of the church.

"What is she saying?" one whispered to the other.

The second soldier shrugged. He could not make out the words—a simple Catholic prayer, no doubt. Nor, from their position, could they see that Esther did not make the sign of the cross but proceeded into the church with simple reverence.

Esther looked up at the statues and found what she was looking for by the altar.

Mary.

Chapter 32

❧

"*T*he girl awaits outside." Intendant Hocquart looked up from his work and bade the secretary continue. "The soldiers who escorted the girl here report that, at her own request, she went into the church and prayed at the feet of Our Mother of God, the Virgin Mary." The secretary bowed.

Hocquart lurched forward. "Leave me a moment." He waved away his secretary.

A Jew in a church kneeling to the Mother of God! What could this mean? The more Hocquart had thought about it, the more he was convinced that the girl must be an embarrassment to the king, no matter what their past connection. Hocquart felt light-hearted. Perhaps all that was needed was a simple conversion. To have a Jew embrace the true Catholic faith and recognize the horror of the Judaic religion would be an achievement to celebrate. He smiled and dipped his quill in a pot of ink.

"Since her arrival in Quebec she has maintained a great reserve and seems to be desirous of being converted to Catholicism ..." wrote

Hocquart. Yes, he was quite elated! He finished the letter, blotted it, sealed it with wax and eased himself back into his chair. He summoned his secretary. "Have her come in."

"You have three appointments waiting," replied the secretary.

Hocquart nodded. The business of New France had to come first. The girl could wait. He handed his letter over to the secretary, who slipped it into a leather case and then locked it in a small strongbox. Intendant Hocquart's letter to King Louis XV regarding Esther Brandeau would leave for France on the next tide.

❦

Esther passed the day waiting in a damp corridor. She was fatigued. She had spent the previous night tailoring the clothes of Madame Bonviet's dead husband. They chafed under her skirt. But what use were they to her? There was no escape. With winter on its way, flight across land was impossible. Esther put her head in her hands and might have wept had the eyes of the guards not been upon her. Hours passed.

Finally the secretary, that long, thin reed of a man, motioned her into Intendant Hocquart's office. Esther stood before the great man.

"It is the law of the land that all who abide in this land either be a Catholic or willingly convert to the true faith of Catholicism. Do you, Esther Brandeau, willingly agree to make such a conversion?" Hocquart gazed up at Esther with a seemingly dispassionate eye. He spoke solemnly, more in the manner of a priest in his pulpit than a man at his desk. "Must I repeat myself?"

What was the question? Oh, yes, he wanted her to become a Catholic. As a Jew she was despised, but as a Catholic she would be accepted. Would she not be the same person? If only she could sleep. She was so tired. The ground under her feet seemed to sway.

"It can be arranged that you will be put this day on a ship bound for France. Consider carefully. I ask you again, do you willingly agree to make such a conversion?"

Not trusting her voice, she shook her head, although, truth be told, it might just as easily have been a nod.

"But what is the meaning of this? Were you not seen praying at the feet of Our Mother Mary?" Hocquart rose from his seat, pressed his knuckles hard into his rosewood desk and narrowed his eyes until they were slits.

A heavy silence settled over the room. Finally Hocquart spoke, in a voice so low Esther had to strain to hear. "Perhaps, with time and education, you will see the light. It seems that your current living arrangements have proven unsuitable. My secretary has found you another place to live. Go." He turned his back to her.

Not knowing what to do Esther followed the secretary out of the room.

"There is a woman in the Lower Town who is with child. Her husband and her oldest son are out cutting wood and will not return until early spring. There are six more children at home." The secretary spoke without looking at her, as if her glance held a spell. He turned. Esther followed. It appeared that she would remain in New France for the winter.

⌖

While Esther waited for an audience with the intendant, the Canadian winter came on with an unexpected fierceness. One day the ground was brown and hard and the next it was blanketed in snow. It was a wondrous sight to behold. The snow fell from the sky like bits of clouds, landing on Esther's upturned face and her wool-covered hands.

The snow on the path to the door of the stone house had been tromped down. They were hardly in front of it before a small girl swung it open.

"*Bonjour.*" The cheerful look of the child gave Esther hope.

The secretary offered no salutation and barged past the child to stand in the middle of the room. He banged his feet on the wooden floor and clapped his hands together in an attempt to warm them up. Esther stood silently by the door.

They were in a great room similar to that of Madame Bonviet. A fire burned in the hearth, unlit tallow candles stood in holders on the walls, a long wooden table ran the length of the room and a bear skin was laid over a rough wooden floor.

"*Bonjour,* Madame Caron." The secretary nodded his head toward a woman who was large with child. She was pale and faded with wide, vacant eyes. Her raven hair had turned grey and limp. Her body had been made graceless from bearing too many children in too few years. And, whether the cause was rot or a fist, the woman was without her front teeth, and so her mouth was crinkled like a wad of wet paper. There was no telling how old she was—likely in her thirtieth year, although she looked like an old, old woman. She hardly seemed like a living person at all, though not quite a ghost, either.

The woman scarcely gave the secretary a glance. Instead, she looked plainly at Esther. "She is skinny."

"I can assure you that she is a hard worker," replied the secretary rather curtly.

Esther looked up at the secretary with surprise. Was he paying her a compliment or merely stating her attributes, as one might mention a slave's broad back or a woman's ability to give birth to a brood? Esther searched his face, but nothing in his manner revealed his thoughts.

The woman scoffed, then puckered her mouth as tight as a drawstring purse.

"What is her name?"

Esther spoke up. "My name is Esther Brandeau."

"Well, she has a voice, that's something. Can you cook?"

"Yes, Madame."

"Good, then make the dinner."

Esther removed her cloak and hung it on a hook. A variety of root vegetables lay in the dry sink. Without saying another word, she rolled up her sleeves and began peeling.

More children seemed to appear out of cracks in the wall. Though she counted only five, the secretary had said there were six in the house. Including the older boy who was away chopping wood with their father, that would make seven living children. There was no telling, though, how many babes had been birthed and died.

His duty done, the secretary opened the door and strode out, leaving a blast of bitter wind where he'd last stood.

As Esther turned to find a pot for the peelings she heard a baby's cry. The sixth child lay swaddled in cloth in a pot by the fire.

"Bring her to me," snapped the woman.

Esther picked up the babe and cupped her in the crook of her arm. She had to be at least nine months old, given the woman's current state, and yet the babe was no bigger than a newborn. And she mewed like a kitten rather than crying like a babe. Esther rocked the child in her arms.

"You are a beauty, little one," Esther whispered into the babe's ears.

"What's this? What are you saying to that child? She's been baptized." The woman lurched forward in her chair.

Anger, raw and unexpected, came over Esther suddenly. Had the secretary told this woman that she was Jewish, or had the horrid Madame Bonviet spread the word? "If she has been baptized, then she has a name." Esther handed the babe to her mother.

"Madeleine."

"Is there not a wet nurse who might take her on?" Although it pained her, Esther kept her voice light and sweet.

"And why would I pay for a wet nurse when I have milk aplenty?" The woman took out a withered, blue-veined breast, then leaned her head back against the chair and breathed heavily. Too many babies and too much work had reduced her life to toil without end. Her body was plain worn out.

In the dead of winter, with the snow pounding against the door and wind howling down the chimney, a midwife attended Madame Caron. Esther and the children listened to her screams as she called upon her Saviour to take her to heaven. But it was the baby boy that God wanted. There was no priest to perform the baptism, and so the children explained to Esther that the baby would go to another place—purgatory.

Not long after, baby Madeleine was called to God too, but she had been baptized, and so it was all right, she was in heaven. And so the winter of 1739 passed.

Esther stood and mouthed her prayers, as she did every morning.

"Esther, what are you doing?" Little Henri, the youngest of Madame Caron's living children, pulled at Esther's skirt.

Esther turned and smiled down at the child. He had a round cherub face, and yet beneath it was a raw-boned body that needed nourishment. "Come." She bent down and scooped him up in her arms. He was light, too light. They were all hungry now.

It had been a hard winter for everyone. Their food supply was now down to their last meagre rations. All they had left to eat was porridge and root vegetables.

"Tell me what you were doing." The child rested his head on her shoulder.

"I wasn't doing anything. Come, help me. I need to air these blankets." She sat him down and picked up the edge of a worn blanket.

"I saw you. I saw you talking to somebody." Henri was a child not easily distracted.

"I was saying my prayers. I say my prayers every morning." Esther spoke while pulling the rough blanket off the pallet.

"But you were standing up. You have to kneel down to say your prayers. And besides, prayers have to be said out loud. You were mumbling."

Esther ruffled Henri's hair, laughed, then bent down close to him. "A prayer should be a whisper in God's ear." She stood up and thought of Papa. The last time he said that to her had been just before she'd boarded the boat for Amsterdam—a lifetime ago.

Gunshots rang out, sharp, fierce and loud. An invasion? Was it the British? An Indian attack, perhaps?

"Marie, Antoine," Esther cried and spun around. "Henri, find your brothers and sisters." Again, a loud shot ripped through the

Lower Town. What to do? Where was Madame? Still in bed? The woman was ill most of the time.

"Hurrah!" the children squealed. Esther's eyes darted from child to child as they jumped and clapped. Their pale faces lit up and their mouths curled into smiles and laughs. And for the first time since Esther's arrival in the house almost six months before, Madame Caron came out of the alcove that was her bedroom and smiled. She had not recovered after the most recent birth. Even she knew that she would die with the next baby.

"It is the ice!" cried Henri. "The ice is cracking. White thunder. *La débâcle.* Spring is coming. Spring is here!" All the children dashed for their coats and mitts, *souliers de boeuf* and wool hats.

Spring? Esther shoved her feet into her sabots, pulled on her cloak and wool hat and followed the children outside. Madame Caron waved them off, then settled back into her chair by the fire. Her husband and son would soon return from the bush. They would bring meat and furs and wood. The family had made it through the winter, and with only two deaths.

The sounds of the ice cracking had brought many pale children out of their homes to celebrate the first sign of spring. A small parade trudged down to the harbour. There was little to see, yet still, they all gaped out at the St. Lawrence. Esther's cloak flapped madly about her legs. Spring was here. Her reprieve was over. Unless she consented to be a Catholic, a ship would soon arrive to take her back to France.

≈⁂≈

As was the custom, Madame Caron and her children went to church every Sunday morning for high mass and late Sunday afternoon for vespers. It was Intendant Hocquart's *request* that Esther attend church in the morning with the family, and she did so without complaint. She did not explain why she preferred to sit near the statue of Mary, and no one questioned her. She rose with the others as Father Des Ruisseaux raised his hands and said in Latin, "We believe in one God, the father, the Almighty, maker of heaven and earth, of all that is seen and unseen."

The bread and wine were blessed, and Esther stood alone as each member of the church knelt and bowed to the Host and ate the body of Jesus and drank his blood. *This is the lamb of God who takes away the sins of the world...* There were times when she listened intently, trying with all her might to use the little Latin she had been taught by Madame de La Grange so very long ago and make sense of what she heard. There were other times when she would simply let the words wash over her.

Sunday afternoons were her own.

When the last child had turned the corner on the way to vespers, Esther added wood to the fire, pulled out a large pot and filled it with steaming water to wash.

The pot was not so large as to allow her to comfortably sit. Instead, Esther stood up to her knees in hot water. With a jug in her hand, Esther poured warm water down over herself. The shock of it made her gasp in delight. She closed her eyes, ran her fingers through her wet hair, rubbed herself with soap shavings and again poured hot water over her head, her face, her body. The feel of the warm water as it ran between her breasts, the warmth of the fire as the logs crackled in the hearth, made her feel wonderful.

The door swung open. With her naked body shimmering in the firelight, Esther turned and stared into the astonished eyes of Monsieur Caron and his almost-grown son.

"She's a witch, I tell you. She has entrapped my poor husband and my stupid son. A witch! I'll not have her in my house. All they do is stare at her and follow her wherever she goes." Madame Caron stared down at the secretary, who sat behind his desk, "She should be done away with, her and her kind."

Madame Caron glared at Esther like a demented black bird, her eyes wild with rage. "A pox on you. May gangrene eat your eyes and stiffen your tongue!" And with more indignation than she had managed to muster in her entire thirty years, Madame Caron turned and stomped out the door.

Chapter 33

❧

*I*ntendant Hocquart, in his customary manner, addressed the issue at hand. If he noticed Esther's dishevelled appearance, he said nothing.

"You will be taken to live with the Ursuline nuns. They are a teaching order tending to the local children and are known for their patience and kindness. With their guidance, and good Christian toil, you will doubtless see the light and convert to the one true religion." The words *last chance* were not spoken but heard, nevertheless.

Esther followed in the secretary's footsteps, never speaking, never questioning.

"Mademoiselle." The secretary stood back to allow a cart to pass on the road, then turned to Esther. "The intendant has received a letter from the minister of Colonies in Paris, who speaks for the king. All efforts are to be made to hasten your conversion. Should these efforts fail, you will be returned to France to suffer the consequences." The secretary's long face did not betray any emotion. Nine months had passed since she had arrived on these shores and not once had he engaged her in direct conversation, yet here he was, seemingly intent on warning her.

Esther nodded. *"Merci,"* she whispered. The secretary turned and walked on as if he had never spoken.

The main door to the convent was tall, broad and iron-belted, but it was to the side door that the secretary took Esther. He pulled a rope. Within a moment the door opened. Behind the nun was a bright courtyard. Snow was still banked along the walls, but the middle of the yard had been cleared.

"Welcome, Esther Brandeau. I am Mother Saint Ignace. Come, I shall take you to our Mother Superior."

Esther curtsied and turned to bid the secretary farewell. Too late, he had vanished, and the door had closed behind him. A jail was a jail no matter what the name, and Esther knew something about jails.

Children were everywhere in the enclosed courtyard. Esther kept pace with the nun as they walked through the courtyard and into the school.

"We must not keep Mother Superior waiting. Come." Mother Saint Ignace padded off down the hall, bobbing her head in greeting to each child as she went.

The Mother Superior, a gaunt woman with liquid eyes and skin as thin as parchment, sat behind her desk. Esther crossed the plain room and curtsied deeply and with all due reverence. The Mother Superior gave a regal nod as she took in Esther's grace and beauty. Whatever the girl's background, she behaved with a certain nobility.

"Thank you, Mother Saint Ignace. Please leave us." A moment passed as the Mother Superior waited for the door to close. "I have been waiting for you, Esther Brandeau. I have heard a great deal about you."

Esther drew in a sharp breath and braced for the worst, but neither the Mother Superior's voice, nor her manner, changed. Instead, she forged ahead, treating Esther as if she were a student newly admitted to her school.

"You are too old to be a pupil, and yet you will be expected to follow the students' schedule. The sisters rise at four for prayers, but you will rise at five-thirty. You may, if you wish, help the girls wash and dress before joining us in the chapel."

"I like children," Esther whispered. This nun was kind, gentle even. Kindness was the last thing she had expected.

"Esther, come and sit." The Mother Superior motioned to a chair by the fire, then rose from her desk and stood beside a small portrait. "This is Marie de l'Incarnation, is she not lovely?" The humble oil portrait hung over the fireplace. A sorrowful-faced woman dressed in a black habit clutched a red-painted cross to her breast. "Our first convent was founded in 1535 in Italy, and it was transformed into a religious order in 1612. But it was our own dear Marie de l'Incarnation who founded the first Ursuline monastery on this great continent." The Mother Superior spoke with reverence, but stopped suddenly. "I am told that you can read and write and speak several languages. French, of course, but what else?"

Esther nodded. "Dutch, Hebrew and Ladino. I should like to learn English."

Hebrew and Yiddish were certainly of no use, in the Mother Superior's view. As for English, it was the language of the British heathens. The less said about them, the better. "And what of Latin?"

"I know a little." Esther spoke to her hands, which lay folded in her lap, but in her head she heard the sounds of Madame

Marie de La Grange's voice repeating verbs, phrases and Catholic prayers in Latin.

"An educated Catholic must know Latin. I hear, too, that you can sew. Very good. As for your religious education, we will start at the beginning with Saint-Vallier's *Catechisme* and prepare for your conversion. Do you know the catechism?" The Mother Superior did not wait for an answer. Instead, in the gentlest of voices, she began: "'Who created us and brought us into this world?' You will say, 'God.' 'Why did He bring us into this world?' You will say, 'To know, love and serve Him, and in this way to acquire eternal life.' Can you say this, Esther? Can you embrace the true God?"

In the mind of the Mother Superior, her conversion was a foregone conclusion. Esther would become a Catholic.

"Come, I shall take you to the chapel."

Silently the two walked the hallowed halls of the convent. The floors underfoot were polished wood and might have creaked had the Mother Superior not been so light-footed. One could not look far without seeing a crucifix or a small statue of a Catholic saint.

The doors to the chapel, at the far end of a dim hall, stood open. The gilded statues and sunlight-filled room made Esther blink. The light fell onto her head and shoulders. A group of nuns—the choir, perhaps—sang softly. Their voices melted into each other with the ease of a river flowing into the ocean.

"You too will one day sing, Esther Brandeau. And when you sing, God will enter your heart and prayer will come into existence. I shall leave you to your prayers. *Nostre domini Patri,* in the name of the Father, the Son and the Holy Spirit ..." The Mother Superior withdrew as quietly, as silently, as if she had never been there.

There were nuns singing all around Esther, and yet she was alone. She stared up at the statue of Mary. The cool, white stone hand petted a stone lamb. What did it matter what faith she practised? Was there not one God? Was the God of Moses not the God of Jesus? Were not Jews, Christians and Muslims all the children of Abraham?

"Mary," Esther whispered as she reached out and touched the foot of the pristine statue. "Did anyone ask you to convert to Christianity?"

Chapter 34

❦

*H*ocquart rose from his chair and crossed the room to look out the window. He did not need his spyglass to see that the river below was alive with ships and boats.

The secretary entered the intendant's office and waited to be recognized.

"Send her in." Hocquart did not look around.

Esther walked into this now familiar room and waited to be addressed. The secretary disappeared behind his curtain.

"Are you happy with the Ursulines?"

"They are very kind, Monsieur."

"And are they teaching you?"

"They are excellent teachers. I like being with the children."

"As a Catholic, you will be free to marry and have children of your own. What of that boy—Philippe, you called him," Hocquart continued. "If you were to find him, would he marry you?"

Esther paused. "He is my friend. I believe that the hardest thing in the world to find is a true friend. But he is lost to me, nevertheless. I know only that he is in Louisiana."

"Ah, yes, this is what Madame de La Grange revealed to you."

Esther nodded. She was not surprised that Intendant Hocquart had such a good memory.

"Then it comes to this: will you consent to conversion?" He turned and faced her. The question hung in the air. The secretary moved from beyond the curtain. He stood silently.

Of course it would come to this, Esther thought, a question, an answer and her life would be forever altered. She did not know where to look. All winter she had heard the voices of those who loved her, others who meant her harm, still others whose intent it was to use her as a means to their own ends. Which were the ones that would help her find her way?

Maman, dear Maman. *Here am I, Maman, on the farthest shore, and I do not know if God's hand can reach me.* She remembered what Madame Marie de La Grange had told her: "My dear girl, it is a brave thing to follow your heart." Perhaps it was bravery, now, that was truly required of her.

"Remember that actions are more important than belief." Papa had said. He *did* love her. She could see that now.

"I ask you for the last time. Will you, Esther Brandeau, yield to the one, true faith and agree to become a Catholic?" The timbre of Hocquart's voice was low and raspy. His patience was spent.

Esther looked into the fire. When one was safe and warm, it was hard to remember what it was like to be unsafe and cold. Intendant Hocquart's size and shape almost overpowered her yet she turned and faced him.

"Monseigneur, I have learned that fate and choice are mocked by chance. I pray in my heart that God controls that which is out of our control. And when the next world comes I shall say that

I have lived my life as best I could, and I give to the Creator all that I have learned, and that I remain forever in my heart, if not always in deed, a Jew."

Not even Hocquart could have predicted what came next. As he slammed his fist against his desk, a blast of wrath issued forth from the very depths of his self.

"I offer you everything—a new life, a chance to be truly liberated. As a Catholic you may go where you please, travel as you desire, marry whomever you want. Do you not comprehend the consequence of this ludicrous refusal? You have become the talk of court. A charge of theft awaits you in France. Guilt or innocence is of no consequence. You have flouted French law. You are an embarrassment to the king. Do you not understand what will become of you? Prison! You will be entombed for the rest of your natural life. Left to rot. Buried alive. For what, I ask you? To be free? What freedom is there in running and hiding? And why, above all else, do you now cling to a religion that you yourself have fled from?" Hocquart's composure had left him entirely and there he stood, quaking with rage.

Esther, too shocked to move, stood before him, unsure of what to do next. But neither his tirade nor his anger was spent. He leaned across the desk and stared hard into her eyes.

"Tell me, why do *you Jews* cling so tightly to a faith that can only bring you scorn and sorrow?"

The question fell on Esther like a dead weight. She looked back into the indendant's eyes. And then it came to her quite suddenly. He was not an evil man—on the contrary. He *believed* that he was offering her salvation! Was that it? Was that why he had made such an effort to convert her?

"Good sir, I hardly know myself of what I speak. But this I do know: I am from a great and noble people whose history extends in all directions, throughout all ages. To be a Jew is to travel on a thread that stretches from the beginning of time to the end of time. How could I be the one to break this thread?"

Hocquart could only gaze at the girl with astonishment. Whether he understood her sentiment was unclear. He turned and motioned to the secretary. "Sit and write." The tall man did as he was bidden, took up the quill and dipped it into ink. "Send this to the French minister of Colonies. Date it the twenty-seventh day of September, 1739."

The letter began with the customary salutations and then it turned to the matter at hand:

> *Regarding Esther Brandeau, the Jewess that arrived on our shores these many months past. She is so fickle that she has not been able to adjust herself either to life at the convent or to the several private homes in which I have placed her. She did not actually manifest an unseemly conduct, but she is of such flightiness that at times she has been as submissive as she has been perverse to the instructions that the zealous ecclesiastics have been minded to give her. I have no alternative but to send her back to France.*

Hocquart held his spyglass in both hands and looked out toward the river—the blue vein of water that led into the heart of this great country. He replaced the spyglass in its holder and sipped his brandy, allowing it to settle his thoughts and calm his temper. He did not need to turn around to know that the secretary had entered the room and now stood at his elbow.

"Have the letters been delivered to the ship?"

"They have, Monseigneur. The king and the minister of Colonies will each receive your correspondence as soon as God allows. The ship sailed on the morning tide."

"When does the next ship leave for France?"

The secretary dithered. He was at a loss to understand why Intendant Hocquart had insisted that the letters to the king and the minister be sent to France on the fastest ship in port when the girl was to follow on a much slower vessel, taking a round-about route.

"I will escort the girl to the ship myself within the hour. It leaves at high tide. But Monseigneur, if I may be so bold ..." The secretary paused. He was neither a meek man nor a subservient one; he was, instead, a man who knew his place within the social order. But there was something that the intendant had perhaps forgotten. As a good servant, he would be remiss in not mentioning it.

"Monseigneur, perhaps you do not recollect—certain items of clothing belonging to Madame Bonviet's late husband were taken, presumably by Esther Brandeau. A shirt, breeches and a jacket, along with stockings, have never reappeared. These may still be in her possession."

"I have not forgotten." Intendant Hocquart took a long, slow sip of his brandy. "Indeed, I am counting on it."

The secretary stood still. Intendant Hocquart turned and looked into his eyes. A moment passed. The secretary bowed.

❧

At Esther's feet was a carpet bag containing warm clothes and all that she would need for the journey. The Mother Superior placed her hand on Esther's head and said, "'The Lord shall guard your coming and going from this time, now and forever.' May you find peace, Esther Brandeau."

"Merci." Esther bowed her head and left the convent to wait on the road outside the convent door. She would not run, not this time.

The secretary came down the cobblestoned road and acknowledged her with a slight bow. As was their custom, the secretary set off, with Esther walking a few paces behind. There were no soldiers to escort her, no grand parade to lead the condemned young woman to the ship of doom.

The road down to the wharf was familiar and, in that way, oddly comforting. Quebec, the oldest city on this great continent, was a beautiful place. Esther breathed in the air and smiled at the three-legged dog. "This time I am leaving for good," she whispered as she stooped to pat its old head.

The secretary and the girl stood at the bottom of the gangplank.

"You will stand trial in Paris."

Esther nodded. She expected nothing less. The sky was a light blue, a sky of hope, a sky of the New World. Esther put her foot on the gangplank and turned to say goodbye. While the secretary had never been kind, he had never been unkind. She made to bow to him and stopped. He was plainly perturbed.

"What is it?" she asked.

"I am to give you this." The secretary handed Esther a small velvet bag. "Intendant Hocquart had the portrait of the king appraised and has paid you its full worth. You can be assured that it is the correct amount."

She was bewildered, confused even. The weight of it told her that it was indeed filled with gold coins.

"There is more. This ship will not be sailing directly to Paris. It sails first down the coast to Louisiana." He said the words slowly.

❧

The official residence of Intendant Hocquart loomed large over the town of Quebec. There was no telling if the intendant stood at his window looking down over the river at that moment, or if he held his spyglass in his hands. Nevertheless, it was to that window that Esther Brandeau, citizen of the sea, looked to. She stepped away from the gangplank. With grace and dignity, Esther extended her arms and curtsied deeply. In its simple elegance and flawless execution, it might have been the curtsy of a princess to a king.

Dear Reader,

I write this in the year of our Lord 1800 in what is now called Lower Canada. With Godless arrogance, the British now rule this land. My name is Guy de Bougainville. I was secretary to Gilles Hocquart, intendant de la Nouvelle-France, from the time of his arrival in Quebec in 1729 to his departure in 1748.

When Intendant Hocquart was recalled to Paris, he married the widow Anne-Catherine de la Lande, in Brest, France, in 1750. Alas, they remained childless. Hocquart died in 1783, a poor, although not penniless, man. It may be said of Gilles Hocquart that, during his nineteen-year administration, New France experienced a golden age of commercial prosperity.

Constant war between England and France left beautiful Quebec in ruins. After two centuries of French settlement and the hard work of our people, all was lost to miserable England in a face-to-face battle that took mere minutes. On the thirteenth day of September, 1759, on the Plains of Abraham, our brave commander, the Marquis de Montcalm, stood his ground against the contemptible British commander, General James Wolfe. There Quebec was defeated, and there, too, Montcalm and Wolfe met their deaths.

But what of Esther? I too have spent much of my life pondering the question, "What became of Esther Brandeau?"

The captain of the ship that was charged with returning Esther to France in 1739 swore until his death that he deposited her on the shores of France, and there she vanished.

Others on board said that Esther disappeared when the ship put in for repairs in Charleston.

When the ship docked in La Nouvelle Orleans, a female passenger reported spotting a handsome, smooth-faced lad of about fifteen or sixteen standing on deck. In particular, she noted his striking eyes. The passenger attempted to address the lad but alas when she approached him, he scampered down the gangplank and vanished into the crowd.

I am too old for romantic notions, but still, I live in hope that Esther Brandeau, formerly of France, found the freedom she was seeking.

Forgive an old man his senseless pondering. I have done my best to keep my doubts at bay and simply record all that I have seen and heard. Even now the quill in my hand shakes and the parchment before me fades. It will not be long before I stand awaiting judgment before the Lord my God. Would that I had learned from Esther Brandeau that life is an endless list of possibilities. Would that I had known what this girl knew all along, that no matter how many times circumstances might change our direction, God's greatest gift is the freedom to choose.

I leave you this story, to make of it what you will. Be kind, if you can. The times were hard.

—Guy de Bougainville,
former secretary to Intendant Gilles Hocquart

Author's Note

You can find references to the story of Esther Brandeau in the Provincial Archives in Quebec City and the National Archives in Ottawa, but the original record of her adventures is officially kept in the Archives Nationales in Paris. In a few handwritten paragraphs, it says that Esther embarked on a journey to New France on the ship *Saint-Michel*. She wore boy's clothing and went by the name of Jacques La Fargue.

Upon arrival in Quebec in September 1738, her true sex and religion were revealed. It was also disclosed that she was the (perhaps illegitimate) daughter of David Brandeau, a Jewish merchant who lived and did business in St. Esprit, near Bayonne, in the southwest corner of France.

As the story was told to Quebec authorities, Esther left her home in France in 1733. She set sail on a Dutch vessel under the command of Captain Geoffrey. The ship ran aground past Bayonne in the month of April or May. Esther was rescued by a seaman and taken to the home of Catherine Churiau, widow, of Biarritz.

Esther later left Catherine's home, donned male disguise, assumed the name Pierre Mausiette and, over the next three years, became a ship's cook, a shop-boy, a tailor, an errand boy for a convent, a baker and footman to a soldier. Before boarding a ship for New France, she also had the unhappy experience of being arrested in Noisel, France.

The tale within is one of *historical imagining;* it is a fictional account. Esther existed, and yet while Esther Brandeau has found a place in the footnotes of history, she has not found a place in history itself. Too much of what she did is unsubstantiated. She is shadow, presumption, hope and dream.

Perhaps Esther's story belongs more properly to the realm of myth, and one might *imagine* that Esther would delight in such a place.

Sharon E. McKay
Kilbride, March 2004

Glossary

birkhat ha-mazon — a prayer in Hebrew to end the Sabbath meal

cabane — a bed stored in a cupboard

cheder — school for Jewish children in which Hebrew and religious knowledge are taught

Caribbean — by the end of the 1600s, the French empire had established colonies in the Caribbean or Spice Islands, as they were often called.

circumcision — a surgical procedure in which the foreskin of the penis is removed; in Jewish tradition, the ceremony of circumcision, or *bris,* is performed eight days after a boy's birth

forecastle — the forward part of a ship, where the crew has quarters

futtocks — the middle timbers of a ship's frame

halyards — rope or tackle for raising or lowering a sail

ha-motzi — a blessing in Hebrew said over bread

hekdesh — a workhouse, sometimes an inn for travellers

incense — the burning of incense (often with charcoal, thereby creating smoke) is meant to create a path to heaven on which prayers might travel; in the past, churches were filled with stinky, unwashed bodies, making incense the room deodorant of yesteryear

keriah — in Jewish culture, the traditional act of grief performed by close relatives of the dead is to tear their clothes; this reminds us that the body is the garment of the soul, and while clothes (i.e., the body) can be torn, the soul is forever whole

kiddush — a prayer in Hebrew over wine, said by the head of the household at the meal ushering in the Sabbath

kosher — it is believed that food must be good for the body and the soul; the kosher laws are guides to those foods that affect the soul; meat and fowl must be humanely slaughtered; meat and milk must not be eaten together; it is forbidden to eat scavengers, predatory beasts (like lions) and fish (sharks), pork, or shellfish (such as oysters)

main topgallant sail — the sail immediately above the topmast and topsail of a sailing ship

mainsail — the lowest sail on the mainmast of a sailing ship

matzo — unleavened bread

mazel tov — a Hebrew expression meaning "good luck," or "congratulations"

mezuzah — a parchment inscribed with religious texts and attached in a case to the doorpost of a Jewish house as a sign of faith

mikveh — women's bath house

mitzvah — religious duty or obligation; the term has come to mean good deed; also applies to the biblical commandments that make up the Torah and form the basis of Jewish law and behaviour; the number of biblical *mitzvot* is 613

mizzen-mast — the mast next in line behind the main mast on a sailing ship

mizzen shrouds — the rigging supporting the mizzen-mast

petit bijou — French for a "little jewel"

ratlines — the small lines fastened across a sailing ship's rigging, like ladder rungs

rosary — a set of beads anchored by a cross; in the thirteenth century, Mary, the Mother of God, appeared to Saint Dominic with a gift of beads and said that the faithful would henceforth pray *Hail Mary, Our Father* and *Glory Be* while holding the beads

sabots (pronounced *sah-BOH*) — French word for the wooden clogs worn by the peasant and working classes; the middle class might wear them out of doors with stockings

shabbos-goya — a Gentile woman employed in a Jewish household to work on the Sabbath

shamash (pronounced *SHAH-mes* to rhyme with *promise*) — among his other duties, the *shamash* called the Jewish men in the town to morning prayers, which were usually said in the synagogue

shiva — Jewish ritual of a seven-day mourning period in which friends and relatives visit the family of the deceased

shul — school

souliers de boeuf — French term for shoes resembling moccasins, made from thick, coarse oxhide

spar — a stout wooden pole used to secure a ship's rigging

tallit — Jewish prayer shawl

tefillin (or *phylacteries*) — small leather boxes containing biblical texts in Hebrew, worn by Jewish men during morning prayers

topsail — square sail, next above the lowest on a sailing ship

tzedaka pushka — Hebrew term for a charity box

ziziyyot (or *tzitzit*) — fringes attached to the four corners of a garment worn by Jewish males that remind the wearer to acknowledge God at every turn

Acknowledgments

Canada Council for the Arts, my sincere thanks.

Barbara Berson, editor, thank you. Catherine Marjoribanks, a goddess who entered laughing and laboured over this book well past the call of duty. Sandra Tooze who made *Esther* pretty. And Julia Bell, brilliant illustrator, and Kate McDonald, cover model, who *is* pretty!

Anne Dublin, teacher and librarian, Holy Blossom Temple, Toronto, Ontario.

Lilianne Plamondon, historian, Quebec City.

Isabel Gil, director, Magalie Boutin, Tourisme Quebec, Deven Ghodiwala, computer guy who saved *Esther* many a time.

Burlington Library, Andrea Gordon and Marnie Griffin.

Christian/Jewish Dialogue Committee of Toronto, Holocaust Remembrance Committee, of which I have been a member these past ten years.

Dorothy and Angus MacLeod, travelling companions on *Esther*'s trail.

Support Crew: Plum Johnson, Elizabeth Grandbois, Barbara Haworth-Attard, Ylva Van Buuren, Judy Cohen.

A Coat of Many Colours: Two Centuries of Jewish Life in Canada by Irving Abella (Toronto: Key Porter Books, 1990). A great and inspirational book. "Esther Brandeau," an essay published in the *Histadrut Observer* by Dr. Isidor Goldstick.

Tina Horwitz, Vanguarde Artists Management Ltd., Toronto, Canada, intrepid film agent.

And David MacLeod, husband.